FACING THE DRAGON

A VIETNAM WAR
MYSTERY THRILLER

PHILIP DERRICK

SUNNYSLOPE PRESS - SEATTLE, WA

Sunnyslope Press
Seattle, WA 98116
www.philipderrick.com

Publisher's Note: This is a work of fiction. Names, characters, places, and incidents are a product of the author's imagination. Locales and public names are sometimes used for atmospheric purposes. Any resemblance to actual people, living or dead, or to businesses, companies, events, institutions, or locales is completely coincidental.

Facing the Dragon / Philip Derrick — 1st ed.

ISBN-13: 978-0999120200 Ebook
ISBN-13: 978-0999120217 Print

This book would not have been possible without Linda,
Matt, Travis, Ian, Michele, and Mary Thornberry.
Thank you all.

PREFACE

Vietnam was seen differently by every veteran who was there between 1964 and 1973. Each has their own story depending on the year and unit with which they served. Events contained in this book occur primarily in 1970. While effort has been made toward historical accuracy, this is a book of fiction, not a historical tract or memoir. The Second Battalion, 506th Infantry Regiment consisted of companies A through E and a Headquarters and Headquarters Company (HHC) at that time. There was no F (Foxtrot) company as depicted.

1

December 24, 1969
Albuquerque, New Mexico

Dad had an ironclad rule of never picking up any hitchhikers. He violated it only one time. Maybe because it was Christmas Eve or because the hitchhiker wore an Army uniform. Or maybe it was the pistol stored under the driver seat as part of our family vacation ritual, along with Mom making sure he put a spare key under the bumper.

Then again, it might have been because I asked Dad to stop. It was the first time I'd spoken to him since all the trouble at school. We both probably thought of the request, and the granting of it, as a kind of peace offering to each other.

We saw him on the morning of the trip's fourth day. If we'd sailed on by, we'd have totally forgotten him a few miles later. But we didn't. Instead, Dad eased our red Rambler station wagon into the wash by the highway where the soldier sat on his duffel bag, almost as if the meeting was pre-arranged. The hitchhiker looked at us, unsure if we had stopped for him. A nod from Dad confirmed it, and our new passenger was quick to put his bag in the back of the car while removing a large manila envelope. He took off his garrison cap, got in the rear seat with sis and me, and deposited the envelope in the side door pocket.

Settling in, he looked us over just like we did him. He thanked each of us individually for the ride, as if it had been a family decision.

"Hi. My name is Travis Nickels. Actually, make that PFC Nickels."

I shook his hand and said, "I'm Jim Peterson."

My little sister piped up with, "Hi, I'm Susan, but everyone calls me Susie. What's a PFC?"

Little sis was twelve and newly interested in boys, especially a classmate of hers named Joey Walton. That's why she took up the fire baton. It allowed her to perform at the junior high football games when he played. She really was spectacular, but I never told her so.

"Private first class, dummy," I said. I'd learned all the Army ranks from *Sgt. Fury and his Howling Commandos*, courtesy of Marvel Comics.

She ignored me entirely and asked our newcomer, somewhat dubiously, "Is there a second class?"

He smiled and nodded his head. "Actually there is," he said. "I was just that, a PV2 or an E-2, until three months ago. Now I'm an E-3."

Sis wasn't paying attention to his words as much as staring at him. He was a good-looking guy, about my size, and seemed to be about nineteen, with blue eyes and black hair like me. It was clear by the way she tilted her head that she liked what she saw.

"Is that good?" she asked.

"It means more money," Dad said from the front seat.

"Have you been to Vietnam?" she said, looking at the

red and gold ribbon on his uniform. Above it was a silver badge with a parachute imposed on a set of spread wings.

"Nope, but that hole in my military career is about to be filled. I report to Oakland, California, in four days to catch a plane to that jungle paradise." He threw in the last sentence as a flip remark, turning and looking out the window as he spoke.

Silence followed.

"How long have you been in the service?" I said.

"Seven months. Enlisted ten days after graduating from high school. Thought I might as well volunteer and get it over with rather than drag it out and get drafted later."

"Dad was in the war with the 45th Infantry Division in Germany." I turned my head in the direction of the driver, as if Nickels might be confused about who I was referring to.

"Sir." Nickels nodded respectfully in his direction.

Dad grunted without taking his eyes off the road.

Back when I was little I'd asked the usual, "What did you do in the war, Daddy?" But I never got much of an answer. The last time I asked was several months ago while we were watching a rerun of *Combat*, a TV series on ABC. Vic Morrow led his squad in taking out a tank and wiping out a bunch of German soldiers. Getting the usual nonresponsive grunt, I dropped it. A few minutes later Mom asked me to help her in the kitchen. Instead, she took me to their bedroom and quietly closed the door. Putting a finger to her lips, she led me by hand over to the closet and opened the door. Standing on her toes, she reached up to the top shelf and pulled down a shoe-sized red cedar box. She placed it on the bed and motioned me to sit down next to it.

"Put it back when you're done," was all she said as she left the room.

Looking back on it, I'm not sure what I expected to find. I knew somehow, without being told, that it contained answers to my question. Given Dad's silences, I didn't expect much.

Inside was a jumbled array of ribbons, medals, a 45th Infantry Division Thunderbird shoulder sleeve patch, various badges, National Guard paper citations, and several news articles from countries in Europe, along with some old black and white box-camera pictures from the war.

One photo showed him cradling an M-1 rifle in a jeep with a driver. Others showed Army buddies standing next to each other. Another had him standing in front of a crowd of miserable looking, newly freed prisoners in striped pajama uniforms. His gun was in one hand, and his other arm was around the shoulder of some kid with a shaved head. The kid appeared to be about twelve years old—small, thin, and not very healthy. Dad looked grim, and the kid had a shy, frightened smile, as if afraid to look directly into the camera. They were both standing close to what appeared to be a pile of bodies stacked outside a train boxcar.

On the back of the picture there was a date, April 29, 1945, written in Dad's handwriting. One thing was clear. The old man didn't sit out the war in an office filling out supply forms.

I was disappointed not to find more pictures of the war. The rest were touristy shots of the aftermath. Bombed churches, Nazi monuments, women in streets standing in lines and removing bricks from destroyed houses. That type of thing. Based on the handwriting on the back, most seemed to be from Munich, Germany.

Tucked under the newspaper clippings was a dark blue oblong box. Inside, lying on a velvet cloth background, was a five-pointed star with a laurel wreath.

Underneath the box was an Army citation dated October 28, 1944. It stated that 1st Lieutenant Tom Peterson was awarded the Silver Star for "gallantry in action against a superior force" and saving a platoon in his company. Now that was pretty cool. The problem was he never wanted to talk about the war. I didn't understand that. I mean, he was famous.

When I came out of the bedroom, Mom was sitting at the kitchen table holding a cup of coffee to her mouth with both hands.

"Well?" She peered over the cup rim and looked at me as if expecting me to say something. Instead I asked if I could go over to Steve Gorwood's. He'd bought a new Rolling Stones album he wanted me to hear.

Mom stared at me for a few moments before finally nodding. She sighed and said, "Maybe that's a conversation for another time. When you're older."

I left the room sensing her disapproval. Time moved on and I forgot all about it.

2

We stopped to eat at a Stuckey's on the highway. The blue-roofed restaurant chain was a family favorite, with the same layout and food at each location. Dad told our passenger lunch was on us. The folks ordered the French dip and lemonade; the rest of us got cheeseburgers and cherry cokes. Mom put a coin in the jukebox, and we ate listening to Elvis warning about "Suspicious Minds."

Travis went into the restroom and changed into civilian clothes from his duffle bag. It occurred to me he'd worn his uniform on the side of the road for a reason. What better way to snag a ride? Hey, it worked.

While eating, we learned more about PFC Nickels. He was a loner in the world, raised in a series of foster homes. He never knew his parents, since they were declared unfit due to drugs and alcohol when he was an infant.

I turned and nodded to my father. "Just like you, right, Dad?"

"No, not just like me," he said. "I was raised in an orphanage."

"Well, Mom can relate to you both," I said to Nickels. "Her relatives were killed in the bombing of Germany during the war. She married Dad when they met in the American Zone after the war."

Mom dabbed au jus sauce with a napkin at the corner

of her mouth and glared at me. She didn't mind the info coming out as much as me, a child, doing it. In the old country, kids kept their mouths shut unless spoken to. I didn't know a lot about her past, but that one thing was drilled into me. She spent years getting rid of her Germanic accent and preferred to release personal info on herself, by herself. I'd gone too far, sharing with our Army guest.

"Well, what I meant was we all seem to be alone in the world at this table," I muttered.

Susie played peacemaker, telling Nickels about all the difficulties involved in twirling a fire baton without being burnt in the process. He seemed suitably impressed.

After eating we checked out the concessions area. Band Aids? Check. Candy cigarettes in a fake Lucky Strike pack? Check. Postcards to mail home with pictures showing various tourist sites you saw during your travels? Check.

Stuckey's had just about anything a traveler could want. Susie got their famous pecan log roll. Dad and Mom each got a pack of Juicy Fruit gum. Nickels didn't buy anything but skimmed a few magazines.

While everyone else was looking around, I joined Nickels at the magazine counter where he was thumbing through an issue of *Hot Rod Magazine*. I picked up a newspaper. I read the morning and afternoon editions at home, along with our subscriptions to both *Time* and *Newsweek*. According to my school, I have an IQ of 130. But that's not something you brag about unless you want to get labeled a stuck-up egghead.

Here at Stuckey's the reading pickings were pretty slim. Eventually, I selected an old 1969 *Fantastic Four Summer*

Annual featured on a nearby comic book rack. Seventy-two pages of reading for a quarter. That was a bargain. I figured it would last longer than a pecan roll. It wasn't my first choice, but new editions of *Spiderman*, *The Doom Patrol*, and *X-Men* weren't available. Dad called all comics "funny books." He swore that was the original name for them when he was a kid, which only showed how dumb adults can be.

Back on the road we got into the usual swing of things. Dad was the driver. Mom rode up front and was responsible for finding the right stations on the AM dial. She was fair in parceling out country music (Dad, with Hank Williams or Johnny Cash), classical (Mom liked Bach and anything from the Big Band Era with Benny Goodman), and rock and roll (me, the Rolling Stones, and little sis, the Beatles). I was the navigator with a tattered old road atlas purchased at an Esso station in Asa, Oregon, two years earlier. Susie was responsible for the car trash being emptied at each stop.

"Might as well get ready for your life as a housewife," I said. That remark earned me a quick slug on the arm.

We'd had good weather traveling from the Seattle area through Oregon, Idaho, Nevada, Arizona, and New Mexico. Despite being late December, the forecasted sixty degrees held steady, making for a safe and easy trip. There was little to see most of the way except prairie, sagebrush, and an occasional animal as we sped along at eighty miles an hour. Mom, who disliked going over sixty miles per hour on the highway, kept silent because Dad said going sixty in such country was like being on the slow road to

Hell. We were set on seeing two things in the southwest before veering over to California and Disneyland: Carlsbad Caverns and the Grand Canyon.

The folks always wanted to go to the caverns. That was all right with me and Susie. We'd never been in a cave before, and the spooky aspect was appealing after the flat landscape of the southwest. Dad took us to task for calling it a cave, though.

"Look, it's not a cave. Caverns are given that name because they have lots of individual caves inside them. It's what makes them special. You'll see."

We stopped to refuel at a Conoco. While out of the car and walking the kinks out of our bones, Nickels announced he couldn't go any further with us. He didn't have any cash on him, which was why he was hitchhiking. Carlsbad was out.

"Where did your money go?" asked Dad.

"Lost in a craps game at the Greyhound station back in Dallas, sir." It was clear he was embarrassed. A flush rose to his cheeks, and for a moment I imagined him as a classmate of mine in Mrs. Carpenter's freshman English class.

Maybe Dad saw the same thing. "Well, Private Nickels, it's Christmas Eve, and in that spirit we're going to think of you as our guest on this trip. We'll get you to Oakland, then make our way south to Disneyland. Don't worry about the money. Things always have a way of working out."

"Things always have a way of working out" was one of Dad's favorite sayings. He really believed it. I didn't think of my father as a classy guy, but that was a classy thing to do.

"Hey, does that mean I can buy extra souvenirs at the next Stuckey's, Pop?" Susie asked.

"You should be so lucky," said Dad. He grinned. "But good try."

She shrugged and winked at Nickels and me, while whispering, "It never hurts to try."

Mom told Dad he'd better "put the pedal to the old metal" if we wanted to get to Carlsbad park before it closed. She liked using American phrases when possible. It made America seem more like home.

We were in Carlsbad an hour later.

The park was easy enough to find. Plenty of signs advertised Carlsbad Caverns National Park along the highway, and the exit was clearly marked. A small place called Whites City popped up just before the park. A sign by the side of the road announced a population of seven.

"Seven!" hooted little sis. "Since when is that a city?"

A winding ascent through a series of arid canyons led to the top of a mountain. We pulled into the visitor parking lot just before two o'clock. A large visitor center with huge windows was on our left.

A sign listed the visiting times and tours. The park closed at six o'clock during winter season, and the last self-guided tour was at three o'clock and would take about two hours. It listed prices for admission, and an arrow pointed the way to the entry gate. Mom had me and Susie put on light jackets, as the warm weather was cooling down. I'd been reading my comic and stuffed it in my jacket pocket to read later. It fit loosely.

We congratulated ourselves on making the last tour as the attendant took our ticket money. He motioned to his right, indicating the path to the amphitheater where a short presentation kicked off the actual tour. That route led us to a seating area of carved stone bleachers forming a semicircle with a small stage in front. I took a detour to use the restroom. Returning, I saw they'd already seated themselves at the bottom left with Nickels on the far right of the family, next to Mom. He saved me an empty aisle seat next to him.

The amphitheater held mostly families, some college kids, and a smattering of military in uniform. You could see the cavern entrance several hundred feet from where we sat. The amphitheater was built at the entrance to the caverns to allow people to see the millions of Mexican free-tailed bats fly out at dusk. It was supposed to be quite a sight. Unfortunately, they migrated south prior to each winter season, so we were out of luck.

A pretty female park ranger in one of the front seats stood and turned toward us. After welcoming everyone, she took a pointer and used it on a large info board set on the stage explaining the geological history of Carlsbad.

Despite her good looks and calm voice, my mind wandered. I didn't care about geology. I mean, rocks are rocks. Science was never an interest of mine. I found myself scanning the crowd, looking for something to occupy my attention.

Several girls in the crowd were definite lookers. One was a redhead on the far left. I found myself staring at her a lot. She didn't notice me, so I watched and drank her in.

I prefer redheads. It's a thing.

After a while I felt someone staring at *me*. It was so strong I gave up looking at the redhead and scanned the crowd left to right, section by section. I could feel the hairs rising off the back of my neck.

By now the ranger on stage had progressed to how the caverns were discovered by a local teen, decades earlier, but no one believed the kid.

That's when I saw him. Blonde crew cut. Big guy, well over six feet. The type you didn't cross.

He was on the other side of the U-shaped bowl of seats, wearing an Army green uniform and staring directly at us. I didn't doubt it for a moment. There are times when someone is caught looking at you and you know.

I *knew*.

An icy finger of unease slithered up my spine.

3

He spotted them as they entered the seating area. He was in his seat enjoying the fading sun, although the stone was losing some of its warmth. Leaning forward and staring, not daring to breathe, he thought it was as if Providence had sent them here at this moment.

Intellectually, he knew that was foolish. After all, he'd spent a long time, a very long time, tracking them down. The past two days he'd posed as a casual tourist visiting the caverns. In reality he was waiting and planning for their arrival. He knew they'd come, but not the exact day or time. All he'd been given was an approximation. It was enough.

With plenty of people around, he wasn't conspicuous. True, there was the uniform. It made him stand out more than someone in civilian clothes. But the uniform was non-negotiable. When the time came, it had to be visible. It was important they see it.

He'd learned long ago that the best way to hide was in plain sight. Luckily, there were many tours available here. A person could blend in as someone taking in more than one. Staying for more than a day didn't create suspicion.

He believed in Fate. It saved him in enough situations

that he didn't doubt its power. The badges and ribbons on his uniform testified to that. He had experienced the world and survived, while others who were smarter, stronger, richer, and more powerful had died. He'd learned to trust Fate—and his instincts.

The air was beginning to turn chilly. His dress greens provided little protection but he didn't mind. He had survived worse cold. Much, much worse. This was nothing.

He was chatting with the woman on his left when they entered. She was a pretty thing. Blonde with blue eyes. About thirty would be his guess. Light blue jacket, bell bottoms, and a colorful golden scarf around her neck. All topped off with some designer sunglasses. Probably divorced since there was no ring. What was her name? Lauren? Lori? Laura? Laura. That was it.

He knew she was drawn by the figure he cut in his uniform. Even at forty-four he looked impressive and knew it. Attracting women wasn't a problem. He enjoyed Laura's company and planned to ask her to dinner after the last tour if they hadn't shown up today. Her warm eyes told him she would have said yes. That wasn't going to happen now. Instead it was time to wrap up some long delayed business.

He smiled. He was going to be busy. Very busy.

4

I acted like I didn't see the man staring at us. No one else in the family was paying him any attention at all. Watching him out of the corner of my eye, I talked with Nickels as the ranger droned on.

"What will you be doing over there in Vietnam?" I said.

"Mostly trying not to get shot. I expect to be pretty busy since my MOS is 11B."

"What's an MOS?"

"A Military Occupational Specialty. Means your job. I'm an infantryman, 11B. If I were, say, a 95B, I'd be a military policeman. A supply clerk would be a 76Y. Works like that."

I asked him about his jump wings.

"Yeah, they require you to volunteer and do five jumps at Fort Benning to qualify. It's a three-week course and includes a night jump. I could say I did it as a challenge and to get the monthly jump pay bonus, but the truth is it was to impress all the girls." He grinned sheepishly.

"Does it work?"

"Hell, yes." He laughed.

"So you're going to jump out of planes over there?"

"Nah, there's only been one traditional mass combat

parachute drop in Vietnam—the kind you see in the movies. That was almost three years ago. Just too much jungle around. Easier to get where you need to go by chopper. That's why you see Army helicopters on TV news all the time."

The lady ranger was going over the various sites inside the caverns. In the Big Room you would see the Hall of Giants, Temple of the Sun, and the Bottomless Pit. She said you could toss an object in and you would never hear it hit bottom, hence the name.

"Don't worry, folks. We won't let you get too close." The audience tittered and she continued, describing the Rock of Ages among other attractions, but I wasn't really listening. The staring man was still staring.

Finishing her cavern talk, the ranger told us we had a choice. We could proceed to our left down the natural entrance of the caverns or go to our right and ride the elevator down.

Moving toward the amphitheater exit, I felt the man's gaze on my back. I casually turned my head and read the letters on his name plate. Ross. A few moments later when I turned around again, he was lost in the crowd. In a green uniform he should have stood out like a beacon.

I knew something about this guy, though, courtesy of watching TV and movies, plus reading comics and newspapers. With those stripes I knew he was a sergeant first class, a career man. The eight golden cuff bars on his lower right arm indicated he'd had four combat tours overseas somewhere. The Combat Infantryman Badge on his chest was identical to the one I found in Dad's shoebox.

It appeared that this Ross guy was as tough as he looked.

"Travis, why is there a red, white, and blue cloth background for jump wings? Where's yours?" I'd seen it on Ross, but they were missing on Nickels.

"Oh, that means you're in an active paratrooper unit on actual jump status. There are different trimmings for different units. The red, white, and blue one is for the 506th Battalion stationed in Vietnam as part of the 101st Airborne Division. We had to memorize all the active unit histories in jump school."

"If you noticed," he said with a hint of defensiveness, "my wings don't have an oval background. Means I'm jump qualified but not currently with a paratrooper outfit. When I get there I'll have one, and when I leave I'll keep the jump badge but have to ditch the trim when I arrive at my new unit."

"What's the shoulder patch with the black shield and an eagle head?"

"The 101st Division. Screaming Eagles. Paratrooper outfit. That's why there's a small tab saying 'Airborne' on top of the shield. I might be assigned to their 3rd Brigade when I report overseas and end up in the 506th.Who knows?"

I started to ask him about the other shoulder patch I'd seen, but it was clear he wanted to have some fun, so I dropped it. Everyone in line was smiling, laughing, or talking excitedly. Several downed a quick snack or drink at a concession stand to the side, while people held their places in line. The stand had a picture painted on it that said OLLIE's and featured a smiling boy and pigtailed girl chomping on hot dogs and downing a Pepsi.

The cavern opening itself was on the side of a rocky bluff topped with grass and looked like a giant yawning maw from some monster's mouth, waiting for the chance to engulf you. The tourist path was smooth with small gravel and lined with foot-high concrete sides winding downward into the mouth of the cave.

To get into the actual caverns you had a choice. It took a good sixty minutes to walk to the Big Room through the natural entrance. The alternative was to take one of the elevators in the visitors center. Considering the time constraints we were under in order to see the Big Room before closing, it was a no-brainer. Elevator it was.

Once in line, Nickels got an admiring glance from a cute high school girl who was there with her parents. She had long brown hair. A real Marcia Brady type. He smiled back but her mom frowned, took her by the arm, and whispered in her ear. She pulled her daughter away from our elevator line and moved over to the next available one. Nickels had a military haircut and even in civvies there was little doubt about his status. It was a reminder that soldiers were not popular in this particular war.

"Sorry," I said.

"Not your fault." His jaw tightened as he said it.

We were at the tail end of the line for the elevator. The man who stared at us earlier was nowhere to be seen.

I relaxed.

The elevators were futuristic ones with red digital readouts showing the levels as you moved down. On one side was a glass wall allowing you to see the rock shaft as your car plunged seventy-five stories down into the deep bowels of the earth in under a minute.

Coming to a halt, the elevator opened, and we spilled out into a short corridor, turned left, and stopped. Ahead was a large cavern, all dark and mysterious except for the adjacent aid station and small gift shop, reassurance you were not in some underground hell but in a civilized area. Tables and chairs from a tourist cafeteria were scattered throughout the main floor of the cavern.

The Big Room had a posted sign at the entryway stating there would be a five-minute delay before we could enter. I found an unoccupied bench and took my copy of *The Fantastic Four Summer Annual* from my jacket pocket and started to read. The Thing was about to hit Dr. Doom after announcing "It's clobbering time!" when a tall ranger in a Smokey the Bear hat appeared in the cavern entry and began to speak.

"Ladies and gentlemen, welcome to the Big Room. This tour is self-guided. That means what it sounds like. No one's here to hold your hand or urge you to stay or move. It's entirely up to you. Typically, there are four roaming rangers in the area. Today, because of sickness and the holidays, there's only one ranger available. He'll walk along the trail and stop at various points to discuss sites wherever clumps of tourists are bunched up. His job is to be an interpreter, lecturer, and traffic cop of sorts."

"Folks, you are about to enter one of the most famous parts of the caverns. The Big Room tour consists of just that—a Big Room. I mean a *really* Big Room. Imagine a room that holds six football fields and is one hundred feet high. That's the equivalent of a ten-story building. It's so large that the length of the figure eight shaped trail you'll be on is one and a half miles long."

"What also makes this cavern different, besides its size, are the unique sites along the way. These are well marked with lighted signs sharing important details."

He paused, scanned us, and nodded to a woman who had raised her hand. "Isn't it dangerous for us to wander alone in the dark?"

The ranger smiled reassuringly. "Don't worry, miss. Even though the pathways are dark, they're fairly level and easy to traverse. You're almost always near a lighted area highlighting one of the upcoming exhibits to help you find your way. While there are totally dark spots, most of your walk is similar to being in a dimly lit movie theater. If you get lost, our roaming ranger will find you. He has a flashlight and is trained in first aid. I should note I've been here seventeen years, and we've never lost anyone in the Big Room yet. Don't become the first by straying off the marked paths."

He stopped speaking and looked sternly at several in our group. "If you do stray, you may find yourself in a limestone water pool, fall into a gap where you will never be found, or put your hand out and accidently break off a thousand-year-old stalagmite. That there is a felony, even if you don't intend to do so. Don't put yourself in a bad situation and end up in jail. Be a tourist who obeys the rules and have some fun. You'll really enjoy this."

He paused for a moment and then continued with a smile. "Don't forget the temperature here is always a natural fifty-six degrees. If you brought a light jacket or sweater with you, that's probably a wise decision."

Scanning the group, I counted about thirty people. Most everyone had a light jacket with the exception of a few macho types. And Travis. He said earlier he had an Army overcoat in his duffel bag but would look like a schmuck if he wore it over civilian clothes. Still, I would have done so in his place. I'm not a fan of the cold.

The ranger looked at his watch. "All right folks. Our man on the scene should be in place now. Remember, his job is to answer any questions you have and then move on to help others. He'll make a last sweep at five thirty to ensure that everyone is out, and we'll lock up the elevator for the night."

With that said, and a sweep of his arm, he released us into the Big Room.

5

Traveling from light to dark, he entered the natural cave entrance where he'd timed his descent on the path two days earlier, in case the family used the elevator route. It was over a mile on the switchbacks and normally took an hour. That assumed taking in the various sights along the way and walking, not jogging. He'd completed a quick recon, walking fast when in view of any group and going into full sprint mode when out of sight. Two days of practice knocked the hour-long time span down to twelve minutes.

It helped that he was in excellent shape and the path was downhill. The trail descended through a tall and wide passage called the Main Corridor, and passed the Bat Cave, Devil's Spring, Green Lake Overlook, Boneyard, and Iceberg Rock. He paid no notice.

What mattered was that this path ended in the underground rest area near the elevators. Darting through this separate entryway from the natural route, he'd have a quarter-mile head start into the Big Room versus those taking the elevator. With people stopping to admire the sites in the Big Room, he was able to get to the pit area well before the tour group with the family arrived.

The question was where to best ambush his targets. The daughter would be easy enough. The father and the boy would put up resistance to his knife. The mother would be dealt with last.

Looking around on the pathway, he slid behind a rock enclosure jutting out from the wall. Five feet high, it lay in the shadows away from the pit, and was slightly to the left of the middle viewing bench. He had a good view, and the rock outcropping would prevent anyone from seeing him until it was too late. The pit was perfect, an ideal disposal point and relatively isolated.

He waited an hour as different groups walked through. They each had the same reaction, a kind of awe. The pit was actually a rift in the limestone floor but its mouth was gigantic. It looked like you were constantly in danger of falling in, despite the park fence. Inevitably a tourist would reach between the metal railings, pick a loose stone from the sharp incline leading down to the mouth, and toss the rock in while standing stock-still and listening for an echo. There never was any sound. "How far do you think it goes?" was the common question.

As each group trickled in, the old group would move on down the path to the left. It was an unstated but observed agreement. No one returned once they moved on. He only needed to keep a sharp eye on the path coming from Mirror Lake to be in complete control.

6

Some people aren't fans of caves. They don't like small, pitch-dark passageways with confined spaces. I'm probably one of those people. But that didn't apply to the Big Room.

After being in the dark for a minute, your eyes adjust and focus on a faraway light. You're in the upper portion of the cavern and you immediately see the reason for the name. It's huge. I mean really, really huge. Like medieval cathedral huge. You're lost in a vastness so overwhelming that each visitor murmurs quietly. Regular speech seems too loud and vulgar.

"This is so cool," Susie whispered.

Pathways were paved and mostly level, but dark. Everyone was careful not to touch anything or wander off the walkway. Dimly lit Park Service signs described what you were seeing.

The first exhibit was the Giant Dome in the Hall of the Giants. Measuring over sixty feet, it was—according to the sign—considered a column, since it actually met up with a part of the ceiling. Small pools of crystal clear water here and there cast reflections of giant stalactites hanging from the ceiling and stalagmites rising from the floor.

Further on, a gigantic chandelier made up of long ribbon stalactites hung from the ceiling like a gob of sugar frosting surrounded by huge columns. The ceiling itself looked like it was made of popcorn. A sign said moths lived close to the ceiling stalactites, but we didn't see any.

Strategic lighting gave a luminous beauty to the shapes and patterns formed by nature. The bright colors made them breathtaking. This part of the trail made me feel very, very small. A midget in the Hall of the Giants. It was humbling.

Approaching the Temple of the Sun exhibit, I realized my right jacket pocket was empty. My comic book wasn't there. I'd lost it somewhere between the entrance and where I stood. I was miffed. What would I read on the road after the caverns? I told Nickels what happened and went back to find it. I didn't tell the folks. They wouldn't have let me go, insisting we all stick together. Telling Nickels meant the folks would know where I was if they asked but wouldn't be able to do anything about it. Besides, I'd catch up with them as soon as I found it. No harm, no foul.

Actually, that's not the whole truth. Dad had been so mad at me for the past few days I knew he didn't trust himself to look me in the eye. We hadn't been close for a few years. He used to attend all my football games and even bought me a shotgun for my tenth birthday and a rifle two years later for us to go hunting together. Now we rarely talked. Our last sustained interaction was last month, with him teaching me to drive so I'd pass my learner's permit.

Some of it was because he'd become more involved at the factory. Strikes, foreign competition, shortage of supplies, all combined to make things difficult. I heard him and Mom argue about it. Liquidate and he'd come out handsomely, she said. Dad refused. He felt he owed an obligation as the largest employer in town to keep it afloat. As he worked harder at keeping the business going, we lost touch.

Then there was my school suspension last week. What a mess that was.

Moving backward on the trail meant moving away from the lighted exhibits, with plenty of dark spots on the path to be searched. I was almost all the way back to the entryway before I found my comic, none the worse for wear.

Walking back and passing the Temple of the Sun area, I saw a sign map showing a shortcut on the left. I'd save time and meet everyone quicker at the top of the trail loop.

I turned left.

The path shortcut wasn't level. Instead, it was a steep rise. My calves burned after a few minutes. Maybe going the normal route would have been smarter.

Moving along I saw people from our group coming down the path. Passing them I walked over a chasm with a metal bridge. No one in any of the groups I passed seemed to wonder or care why I was going "backward." As I realized the family would be bringing up the rear of the tour, I relaxed a bit. We'd meet up soon and share some of the upcoming sights.

A few minutes went by with no one passing me, when I heard a shout of some kind. It sounded urgent but unintelligible. The folks were probably telling Susie or

Nickels to stay on the trail. Or maybe they were listening for an echo. In any case, I didn't hear anything else. As I approached the top of the loop, a sign said the Bottomless Pit and Mirror Lake were around the bend.

Coming up to the curve, I heard another noise. A human voice. A hurt sound. Then a soft thump as if something heavy hit the floor. An eerie hush told me to approach with caution, although I had no idea why. Slowing my pace, I moved instinctively to the darker side of the path—away from the dim lights on the walkway—and peered around a jagged rock outcropping.

A gigantic hole, the famous Bottomless Pit, lay at the edge of a downward slope of smooth rock beyond the tourist path. It was bathed in park lights of red, green, and blue, resulting in a gothic scene of the damned straight out of Edgar Allan Poe. In front of the pit was the man I'd seen staring at us earlier. He was holding Mom by the throat in a tight one-handed grip—three feet off the ground. There was a smile of triumph on his face as if he had some long sought prize. She was beating her fists on his shoulders and kicking her legs against his thighs in an attempt to break free.

"Frank, don't," she gasped.

He kept his hand on her throat and bent down slightly, using his free arm to encircle her legs. Then he walked several steps over to the fence and threw her over the rail. It was as casual as tossing a wadded gum wrapper off a bridge and happened in the space of a few seconds.

A low wail of despair echoed as she slid down the fifty feet of smooth limestone on the lip of the pit. She tried desperately to grab hold of something, anything, to stop her descent into Hell. There were rock outcroppings and jutting boulders, and for several seconds her frantic attempts to gain a handhold looked possible. It was no use. She went over the edge into a black hole of nothingness. If there was a final scream, the pit smothered it.

I could only stare. This couldn't be happening. Did I really see my mother murdered in front of me? I wanted it to be a dream. Yet I knew it was true. And I knew I would remember every detail of the moment. The chill of the cave. The silent scream in my head. Somehow I knew this wasn't random. Death had followed us into the cavern. I leaned backward into the darkness of the pathway, paralyzed by fear.

The man didn't notice my arrival and walked over to one of the two viewing benches on his right by the pit railing. I dimly saw three shapes lying on the ground. He picked one up, threw it over his shoulder, walked to the railing, and tossed it over. He dragged the next bundle to the lip of the pit. A vicious kick sent it over the edge. The third bundle was smaller than the other two. He didn't bother to put it over his shoulder, drag it, or kick it over the edge. Instead he cradled it as he walked back to the railing. There he held it out with both arms and let it go. As it slid down into the pit's waiting mouth I knew whose body it was.

And if he turned around, I'd be next.

Holding my breath, my heart hammered so loud I was sure he'd hear. Outside my body, it was as silent as the moon. After swallowing my family into its dark fold, it almost seemed the cave felt it needed to pay a silent homage.

I'd heard no shots. Did he have a silencer? Was there even a gun at all? I didn't see one. Was there a knife? Even with the element of surprise, he must have a weapon of some kind.

At my feet were several loose rocks. I bent down and grabbed one, gauging the distance to him at twenty yards. The rock would not be of any use unless I could creep up on him and crush his head with the first swipe. One attempt was all I'd get. But the distance was too far to achieve any surprise. To try was crazy. Or so I told myself.

I was scared. This maniac had just killed four people. I needed to do something. Even as I told myself to act, my legs went weak. If he saw me, he'd do to me what he'd done to them. Afraid he'd smell my fear, I dropped the rock.

He cocked his head as if he heard something. I ducked behind a small outcropping before he turned around.

Get up! Run! I told myself. But I couldn't move. Instead I curled up in a ball. Paralyzed with fear, I shook uncontrollably and fought the urge to vomit. This man was Evil in the flesh. I shut my eyes tight and asked God for invisibility.

Crunching gravel on the pathway indicated he was coming toward me swiftly and with assurance.

Pass me by. Pass me by. Please, please, pass me by. Please, please, pass me by, I prayed. His footsteps receded as he went by unseen. Even with my eyes tightly shut, I sensed he was cool and calm. He was leaving the scene of the crime as if it were an everyday occurrence.

As he left, he began to whistle. The sound hung in the air long after he passed down the pathway.

***

How much time I spent crouched in the dark with my eyes shut, I don't know. I only knew if I opened them he'd be standing there. Watching me. It was a dumb fear. A stupid fear. A real fear.

At some point I opened my eyes but didn't move. I sat there not wanting to take a chance on meeting him as I left. When I summoned the courage to look at the luminous green glow dial on my watch, it read 7:02. The park officially closed an hour earlier. There'd be no rangers around or civilians. Just me and hopefully not him.

I walked cautiously back toward the entrance, and realized I hadn't considered the possibility of the park turning off the lights in the cave after closing. Apparently they kept them on, because I wasn't in total darkness, thank the Lord. I couldn't have handled that.

Water dripped from the ceiling into small ponds as I passed. Except for those occasional splashes of water and the muffled sound of my footsteps, it was as silent as a tomb. A crypt for my family.

I was still in denial about what I'd witnessed. Surely it was a mistake somehow. Death was an abstract notion you discussed in class or watched on TV while safely sitting in your living room drinking a soda or munching popcorn. It happened only to family pets or old people. Very old people. Mom and Dad were old, but not that old.

Somewhere in their forties or so. I'd never thought to ask. And now I never would.

The further along I moved, the more I felt the hairs rising on my arms. It wasn't from the constant cool temperature of the cavern. Before, the darkness wasn't a threat, but now it pressed around me like a living thing. I flinched at each curve in the pathway and tried to search every dark corner before walking forward, always looking to be taken by surprise. Was he lurking just ahead, ready to pounce?

There was no sign of the man named Ross.

At the iron-gated entrance where the elevators and cafeteria were, it was clear the cave was closed. No one was in sight and everything was locked away. The only way to get to above ground was to take the Natural Entrance route. Its path was too large for any type of gate.

It took over an hour to get to the surface.

Outside the caverns, I breathed the crisp night air. It seemed different. Intellectually I knew that was ridiculous. Yet deep down, I didn't doubt my feeling that it was different.

A deserted entry, boarded up concession stand, and drooping awning banners were the only things greeting me. A few hours before, they were all bright and cheery. Now everything was dismal black and hidden in the winter twilight. A sense of total abandonment threatened to pin me to my spot. Only the thought of Ross lurking nearby got me moving quickly toward the parking lot.

There was no sign of him or any park personnel. It was Christmas Eve, and everyone bugged out as soon as possible. The parking lot was empty except for our station wagon. The overhead lights made the car's red paint seem like blood in the dark.

"Get yourself together. You have a car. Get the spare key," I whispered to myself. Kneeling by the driver's side of the bumper, I felt for it. It was there all right. I opened the door, slid in, and locked it immediately.

Even with locked doors, I was shaking badly. Anger and grief surged through me. It was hard to think. I knew I needed to calm down.

Take deep breaths, I told myself. That seemed to help as I fought to bring myself under control over the next several minutes.

First things first. I needed to find the cops. Head to Carlsbad—the city. Get the word out to the highway patrol. Fear had made a coward of me and I let him get away. Now I needed to stop him. Quick.

I drove rapidly down the hills on NM 7 West. I didn't consider stopping in Whites City, population seven, and headed to US 62. Carlsbad itself was the only real option. It was a twenty-minute drive from the caverns according to the highway signs. A population of 22,000 meant it probably had a decent police department.

The city lights beckoned and an exit sign pointed me into town. Neither told me how to find the police station. A Texaco gas station attendant said it was on Second Avenue by the Tastee Freeze. Three blocks east.

I probably looked a bit crazy, because he asked if I was all right. Despite the poster behind him advertising You can trust your car to the man who wears the

STAR, I brushed him off. What could I say? Where to start? He couldn't help anyway. I was anxious, irritated, and waved him away.

Three minutes later I was walking hurriedly toward the glass front doors of the Carlsbad Police Station.

Then I stopped.

I stopped because—and I know this sounds freaky—I'm a *Twilight Zone* fan. I've seen every episode. At least five times. It's a heck of a show.

There's this episode where a woman finds herself dreaming she's in a hospital elevator in the dead of night, heading down to the basement. It opens up to a dark, deserted hall. At the end of the corridor is a pair of double doors—the type that swing open to accept a body table being pushed inside, because this is a morgue. The doors open and a nurse in uniform smiles while saying, "Room for one more, sweetie." The woman runs away shrieking. The next day she's late catching her plane for a trip and is coming up the ramp when the same morgue woman appears at the top but in a stewardess uniform. She smiles and says, "You just made it. Room for one more, sweetie." Our heroine runs back to the terminal and collapses. When she awakens everyone is abuzz about how the plane crashed at the end of the runway during takeoff.

The message I got out of that was to trust your gut.

As I approached the double doors at the police station, one of them was held open for me by a man, not a woman. And he was in a cop uniform, not a nurse. But what he said stopped me cold.

"Room for one more, fella." He smiled and kept the

door open.

I didn't shriek and run away. I didn't go through the door either. Instead, I walked rapidly back to the car, thinking furiously. *What the hell was I doing here?*

As I sat in the car thinking, I realized something. It was gnawing at me as I drove to the station, and now it was in front of me full force. I had no proof against this Ross guy. What was there to stop the cops from claiming that I killed my family and Nickels?

What I had done a week earlier at school would make me suspect number one.

7

One Week Earlier
December 17, 1969
Munson Lake, Washington

It happened at about quarter to three on Friday, in Mrs. Dixon's Biology class. It was the final class of the day before Christmas break, one of those classes prior to a vacation when the teacher pretends to teach and the students pretend to learn. Each side tries to stay out of the other's way until the three o'clock dismissal bell. We were waiting for that bell as the signal to "get the hell out of Dodge."

Me, I was sitting in the back where the glass jars of various fetuses were lined up on the shelf behind an array of microscopes. I was playing paper football across the table with Steve Gorwood. Gorwood was a good guy but a lousy player. I could flick that folded up paper triangle through the raised thumbs of an opponent pretty good, if I do say so myself. Steve...not so much. I was beating him pretty bad when he nodded for me to look over my left shoulder. I didn't really want to. I knew who was over there wanting my attention.

Her name was Rita Human. She was pretty, smart, and

a cheerleader. But I wasn't sure if I wanted to really get involved. Still, Steve kept glancing over at her, no doubt encouraged by her pretty face silently asking him to do so. I gave up and turned around.

Rita smiled and, without a word, bent forward and passed me a note. Then she opened her textbook and pretended to read.

Steve crooked a questioning eyebrow at me, but I didn't know if I wanted to read the note or not.

Let me make one thing clear. Rita is hot. I know she likes me. The question was, should I do anything about it. I decided not to read it in class and put the note in my wallet. I didn't know what was in it but now was not the time.

Meanwhile, Steve's transistor pocket radio was pumping out the usual: bulletins about the war (the total dead for the entire year had hit 11,600 and 45,000 overall since it started five years earlier), some ads (Harrison's Men's Store was running a big sale of 40% off for the holidays), and some bubblegum music ("Sugar, Sugar" by the Archies). We could get away with this because of Mrs. Dixon's policy of "See No Evil, Hear No Evil, Speak No Evil" on days like this. As long as you had your experiments done, no homework missing, and were quiet—which meant she couldn't hear anything—she tended to look the other way. Hence our game and the radio set on low.

That's when Cleveland Tanner kicked in our third floor classroom door and stood in the doorframe with a silly grin and a gun. After a delay of several seconds, while everyone stared at him with open mouths, Tanner raised his gun to the roof and let loose a round, yelling, "Jim Peterson, your ass is mine."

When the gun discharged, Mrs. Dixon screamed and ran past Cleveland and out the door. We could hear her wail of terror as she dashed down the stairwell. Cleveland took no notice of her except for a disdainful glance as she sped by. He merely replanted his body in the doorway again with his feet apart to prevent further escapes.

Looking over at me, he turned the gun in my direction, yelling, "You got this coming, Peterson!" and fired.

The loud crack had the guys in the class reflexively diving for the floor. The girls held their hands to their faces and screamed. I fell down and clutched my abdomen with both hands as a red stain spread on the front of my shirt.

Cleveland sauntered over, looked down at me, and laughed. This was followed by a walk to Mrs. Dixon's desk where he proceeded to put the gun on the table. He pulled up her chair, plopped his butt down in it, and put his feet up on the desk next to the revolver. Interlacing his fingers behind his head, Cleveland looked pleased with himself. Meanwhile, the class dissolved into a replica of an overturned ant hill, with everyone fleeing as fast as possible.

I was groaning on the floor in a fetal position when the principal showed up. I didn't think much of Mr. Alt, and he didn't think much of me. Alt was about five feet four inches and weighed around 300 pounds. He was a bespectacled fireplug of a man. But I admit he showed some nerve that day. He came into the classroom, taking in the situation with Cleveland, who was leaning back in Dixon's chair—gun and feet on the desk, showing a shit-eating grin curled from ear to ear. But, lo and behold, if fat little bastard Alt didn't come over and lift all five feet ten inches and 165 pounds of me gently into his arms and carry me down the three flights of stairs to the main office.

He paused only once, at the classroom door, to tell Cleveland, "Stay right where you are and don't move."

Cleveland smiled back, but he didn't move.

The hallway was empty except for a straggler who backed up against the wall to clear a path as we went by. I had my arms wrapped around my gut and was moaning softly. When we arrived at the main office, Alt took me past the secretary's desk and laid me down on the couch in his office. It was just long enough for me to be stretched out on its leather cushions.

Alt tried to see if he could do anything for my wound by pulling my hands away from the red mess of my stomach. Moaning, I begged him to stop. He did so a bit reluctantly yet secretly relieved, I think. He assured me an ambulance from Memorial Hospital was on its way. Memorial was three blocks away, and we could expect a quick response time.

Behind him I could see Mrs. Dixon. She looked pale, with tears running down her cheeks. She had olive skin, brown hair, green eyes, and was a definite looker. A real Sophia Loren type, if you know what I mean. I felt a little sorry she was having to suffer through all this.

The ambulance siren announced its arrival. The principal went to get the medic while Mrs. Dixon sat shivering in a corner chair, clutching her hands in her lap.

Alt burst back through the office door with the medic,

who knelt by the couch.

"It's okay," said the medic. "You're going to be okay."

He began to gently pry my hands away from my gut as I continued to moan. Alt asked him if I was going to be all right. As soon as the question was asked, the long-awaited three o'clock dismissal bell rang throughout the building.

"Is he going to be all right?" asked Alt again.

Before the medic could reply, I did.

"Hell, yes," I said. I sat up, wiped my ketchup-packet stained hands on the couch, and walked calmly out of the office.

All three adults there—the principal, Mrs. Dixon, and the medic—stared at me in disbelief.

At the front door, I turned around and waved. Alt's face grew purple as he realized what happened.

As I said earlier, he and I didn't get along. This sort of thing was one reason why.

Yeah, the whole thing was a put up job, a joke.

Cleveland was a buddy of mine. We'd been friends since the third grade. At sixteen, he was a year older than me and best known around town for his motorcycle and related escapades. The latest was this past spring when a German Shepherd chased him as he rode by on his bike. The two got entangled, causing his bike to flip. Cleveland was thrown ten feet, spread-eagled with his body eating pavement all the way. He was a bloody mess.

Being in the hospital without skin on large parts of his body and pins put in his leg gave Cleveland plenty of time to think. When I visited him there, he told me he'd he didn't need school anymore. He was sixteen and could get a car and a job. What was the point of staying in school? And if you are going to leave, why not do so in a memorable way? I thought his idea was pretty cool. Consequently, our little play with the pistol shooting blanks was born.

But actions have consequences. Cleveland got expelled. I got a week's suspension—not that the school's punishment got me off the hook with my folks.

Dad was especially pissed.

"For a kid with an alleged IQ of a hundred and thirty, you can be quite the idiot," he said. "When the hell are you going to grow up?"

Despite my escapade, Mom and Dad decided to go through with our holiday trip. The hotel reservations were already made. We were committed. They took me along with the understanding that my family punishment would be decided upon our return.

8

December 24, 1969
Carlsbad, New Mexico

Parked outside the Carlsbad Police Station, I now realized what an idiot I'd been for faking a gun shooting in my own school. What would I think if I were a cop and found out about that after hearing my story about Ross? I'd toss Jim Peterson in a cell and throw away the key. At the very least, I'd be suspect number one and not free to go or search anywhere.

There was one thing in my favor as it stood now. No one knew a crime had been committed. They wouldn't suspect anything was wrong until my family failed to return home in a week. Then it'd get messy.

If I didn't want to be running away from the law myself, I needed to track down Ross fast and make him talk—if I didn't kill the bastard first. I'd always known about the gun Dad kept under the car seat on long trips. I knew, without having to check, it was still there.

I drove around for a while and then parked the car behind a dumpster on the far side of a nearby cafe called the Bluebird. To track Ross, I needed money and a plan.

A check of my wallet revealed two dollars, which wasn't

going to get me far. A look in the glove compartment and the car side pockets coughed up loose change totaling a grand total of twenty-seven cents. A search of the suitcases in the car resulted in no money, but as I was going through them I wondered if I could sell them. When this occurred, I started to cry. For the first time I let it all out in huge gulping sobs and hot tears. Once it began I couldn't stop. And the questions came rushing in.

What kind of monster was I? What type of person coldly tries to get money from the belongings of the dead? How did my mother know Ross? Had Dad or Nickels been the target or innocent victims? And Susie, what the hell did she do? Nothing, except get in the way. Worst of all, I turned out to be a coward when needed.

I sat in the driver's seat pounding the steering wheel, kicking the door, and cursing myself. At first it seemed to never end, scaring me even more. But eventually, like all things, it ceased. When that happened, I found myself brooding.

Mom called him Frank. I'd seen his nametag with the letters spelled out in white on the black background. So the name of the guy was Frank Ross. He was an E-7 sergeant first class, heading to the 101st Airborne Division in Vietnam. Same as Nickels. Where was his departure point? Somewhere in California, but the name escaped me.

In the rearview mirror I saw the large manila envelope Nickels had stuffed inside the side pocket of the back door. I retrieved it and opened it with the dim hope there might be some cash. Then I remembered he'd lost all his money playing craps at the bus stop. I tossed it aside in disgust and sat there feeling hopeless.

The cafe was closing. The last worker bundled up against the night chill got in her car. Probably hurrying home for Christmas Eve with a family around a warm fire.

My vision blurred as I looked out at the sky. I'd never felt so alone. I rubbed my eyes with the heels of my hands to wipe away the tears. The stars were clear and sharp in the desert night air. Somewhere up there was God. Down here the Devil was loose.

I wanted to crush Ross's head with that rock so bad it hurt. A real man wouldn't have let this happen. He would have stopped it somehow. So what kind of guy was I? Was I really a child? Maybe I'd been fooling myself, thinking I was a man. I'd made the high school varsity football team as a freshman, smoked a few cigs, and browsed *Playboy* magazines. I was supposed to be a hard-ass, but when push came to shove, I'd blinked and hid like a chickenshit.

With that debate raging over and over in my head, I fell asleep.

I awoke at dawn, shivering. The air in the car was freezing, and the weather was in full winter mode. I needed something for the cold. A real coat of some kind, anything to replace the flimsy fall jacket I'd been wearing. I rummaged through Travis's duffle bag and found his long grey Army overcoat complete with waist belt. It fit perfectly and was warm.

Sleep had crystallized things. Blaming myself was of no real use. The only way to make it right was to get Ross. I'd do whatever I had to do. With that resolved, I drove around to the back of the cafe.

There was no finesse involved in my illegal entry, just a rock from the parking lot thrown at the rear door window. Inside I found a cardboard box and tossed in bread, condiments, prepared foods from the fridge, silverware, chips, and canned drinks. Even though I didn't think I could eat a bite, I knew I needed to keep my strength up.

The cash register took some time and a strong kitchen knife. There wasn't much, $67.54 to be exact, but it was a start. I left Dad's camera on the top of the cash register along with a note that said I was sorry.

The two bucks and change in my pocket would give me a full gas tank. I had almost seventy dollars and a box full of food to last for several days. Ross was somewhere down the highway on his way to Vietnam via California. It was my job to find him before he left.

After filling up at the Texaco, I brushed up against the manila envelope I'd tossed on the front seat the night before. I knew it didn't contain money, but now that I looked at it, it was full of...something. Reaching inside, I pulled out a sheaf of papers and a brown file.

As I went through the papers, I realized I was holding orders for Nickels to report to Vietnam and debark from Oakland, California. This had to be where Ross was going as well. I'd find him there! I had a destination.

Over the next two days I drove for twelve hours straight each day, stopping only to eat from my cardboard box at a rest stop or park. The atlas map in the glove compartment was my trip navigator. I marked places to park and eat, along with rest areas for the night. I also made sure to stay at least five miles under the speed limit. The last thing I needed was to be pulled over by a cop and have to explain driving the family car by myself, without a license and with out-of-state tags.

That last thing happened near midnight three days later.

I was twelve miles outside Bakersfield, California, when the siren sounded. The curse from my lips was directed more at myself than the cop. A check of my speedometer showed ten miles over the speed limit, not my usual five miles under. I'd gotten complacent listening to the car radio blaring Creedence Clearwater Revival singing "Fortunate Son" instead of paying attention to the white glow from my speedometer. That slipup resulted in coming down a hill and gathering up speed when the cop spotted me.

I faced a choice. Pull over and hope for the best...or run. The problem with the second option was the lack of anywhere to hide on the highway. There were no turnoffs or trees in sight in the dark. If I tried to run, he'd call in more cops with his radio. As much as I dreaded the idea, I pulled over.

When he parked behind me, there was a long pause. I'd seen enough TV to know he was probably running my plates. That would come back clean. But I was starting to sweat, because I knew what was coming next. My license—or rather my lack of one.

The patrol car door opened and a dark figure slowly approached the car. His flashlight methodically searched the inside of the vehicle. He walked up to my window and tapped it lightly with his knuckles.

"Driver's license, please."

What could I say? I struggled to come up with something, anything, as I slowly lowered my window. His flashlight beam again roamed the car interior.

"Hey, kid. Are you in the service?" He cocked his head back toward the rear seat where I had placed Nickels's duffle bag after taking out his army-issued overcoat two days before.

"Uh, sure, Officer. 101st Airborne Division." I smiled up at him. Maybe I could get out of this after all.

"Hmmmm. I was in the regular infantry myself. Korea. Second Infantry Division. Not a fancy outfit like yours."

Oh, hell. This asshole thought I was some kind of prima donna. Now I was in worse trouble than before.

"Get out of the vehicle, son. Let's see that license."

I got out of the car slowly. Very slowly. My mind was racing. If ever there was a good time to come up with something, the time was now.

I had nothing.

"License, soldier." When he said that, I thought maybe his mistake in taking me for a soldier might work in my favor. I decided to try a long shot. I had nothing to lose.

"Actually, Officer, it's Private First Class Nickels." I slowly reached back into the car and took the manila envelope from the front seat. Pulling out a copy of Nickels's orders to Oakland with transit to Vietnam, I gave it to him.

"I'm on my way to report for a flight to Vietnam out of Oakland. Coming up on my report date. I got a little over anxious driving. Sorry."

He took the paper and examined it with the flashlight

while I stood there in Nickels's coat. Then he shined the light in my face.

"Son," he said, "do you have any idea what you're getting into?"

Any thought about lying to him flew out of my head when he asked me that. Of course he was asking about going to Vietnam. Well, that wasn't going to happen. But I found myself thinking of everything that had occurred over the past three days and what was still to come if I was to catch Ross in Oakland.

I looked at him and said, "Yeah, I have, Officer. But it's necessary." And I meant every word.

The flashlight didn't waver from my face for what seemed an eternity.

"Okay, kid." He gave the orders back while looking me up and down in my Army overcoat before snapping off the light. "Good luck, Airborne."

With that he wheeled around, got in his car, and drove off as I stood watching.

It was a close call, but I still had a chance to make things right.

9

I arrived at Oakland on December 28, feeling better about everything. I had a few dollars left and could only hope I'd arrived before Ross. By how much didn't matter. As long as I could get my hands on the bastard, I'd work it out with the authorities one way or another.

Directions from a cashier at a 7-11 got me to the Oakland Army Terminal where the entry gate boasted a large sign stating THIS WE WILL DEFEND. Now all I had to do was identify Ross when he showed up.

I parked the car close to the gate by the side of the road and sat there nervously clutching Dad's pistol in my lap while watching as men arrived for shipment. Well over a hundred appeared every sixty minutes. Some as singles, some with girlfriends crying, others with families waving from departing cars. Across the road, a small group of anti-war protestors waved Viet Cong and North Vietnam flags while chanting slogans. "Hell no, we won't go!" and "Ho, Ho, Ho Chi Minh is gonna win!" seemed to be favorites.

The whole disorderly mess made finding Ross at the gate impossible. There were too many distractions with the arrival of so many people. He might have gone through in the hours I sat there. I'd no way of being sure he hadn't.

Meanwhile, I was bushed and smelled bad. I went looking for a local motel but they were packed with incoming soldiers, families, and girlfriends. Besides, with less than twenty dollars left on me, I was too low on cash to afford a room. A motel clerk took pity on me.

"Go to Daly City down the road. It's run down, but you'll find something you can afford. Don't leave your room at night unless you want trouble."

Eventually I found a place, but like he said, it was run down. Peeling paint with trash in the hall. People yelling in the street at each other at two in the morning. It had hot water in the shower, though. For the first night in days I slept in a bed. It had broken springs and some strange stains I didn't want to know about, but it beat the car.

The next morning I took stock of the situation. I had enough money to eat breakfast and lunch, and then I'd be broke—out on the street with nothing and no way to find Ross. If I went to the cops now, they'd think I had been fleeing from my murders and making this all up. Sleep had once again clarified things. I knew what had to be done.

It was the only shot I had left.

I got the manila envelope with Nickels's records. I'd read them before, but what I was considering now warranted a closer examination.

Inside was a stiff 9x12 brown file folder with bold black lettering: *201 File Personnel Records Jacket, United States Army*. Apparently you took this from your old duty station to your new assignment. It had to be important because on the bottom of the folder were the words: Department of Defense, Alexandria, VA 22332. If found, take to nearest U.S. Post Office or mailbox, return postage guaranteed.

Included were Nickels's fingerprint cards, an initial

security check by the F.B.I., orders to Oakland/ Vietnam, promotion orders to PFC, an order authorizing wearing of jump wings, something called a Form 20, an enlistment contract, a G.I. Life Insurance form with the Sisters of Charity in Pennsylvania as the beneficiary, a physical questionnaire signed by a doctor, and a immunization record.

I ditched the fingerprint cards. We matched up almost perfectly on the physical. I was about an inch taller than Nickels, but that could be explained. I was ten pounds lighter and that also could be considered normal. No suspicious stuff there. My blood type was A Positive, just like his. The immunization record had to go. I didn't know all my past shots, so I figured that was my best option.

The Form 20 seemed to be a recap of everything in the file on one form. It had duty stations, dates of promotion, MOS and where trained, ribbons and medals, aptitude scores, Army schools, etc. Lots of stuff on the form was in pencil, which made sense since things change. I erased several entries and put in my own info, including a small identifying scar on the back of my head that I got when I was three and fell off my tricycle.

When I finished giving the records a makeover, I went downstairs and asked the clerk where I could find a cheap barber shop. My hair wasn't really long, but it would help to have it army-short when in full uniform. An hour later I was newly clipped and in G.I. mode.

Inside his duffel bag was the uniform Nickels had been wearing when we first picked him up, along with a pair of boots, socks, tie, belt, and cap. His dog tags, name plate, and jump wings were all in a separate loose leather-like case, plus a tin of Kiwi black shoe polish and a stiff plastic case for toiletry items. It took an hour to shine up his jump boots and work out the folds in his uniform. It fit pretty well when I put it on.

One big problem was I had no ID card. Based on what I'd seen at the front gate, I thought I might have a solution. But first I needed to get rid of the car and its contents.

After removing the plates from the Rambler, I walked a block and found an empty dumpster. I didn't throw them inside but pushed them under the bottom. The family luggage and the contents of my wallet minus Rita's note were left under some scrap boards in a pile of high weeds in a nearby field surrounded by a fence with a KEEP OUT sign. I found myself breathing heavily when I left them there. Would I ever see, or touch them again? I felt like a criminal and the guilt came up my throat like bile.

My plan was to catch Ross at the Oakland Army Terminal, then retrieve the car, plates, and luggage later. If that didn't work out, it would be better if they were found separately, when I was well away from here. I didn't think the cops would put two and two together, but there was no sense in taking chances.

I drove the car through an automated car wash and parked a mile away from the Army terminal, behind a large professional building. A clean looking car is less suspicious. The cops probably wouldn't get a complaint about it remaining in the same spot for a while, given the number of people going in and out of the building.

I kept one family memento. Under the driver's seat I

found Dad's pistol where I knew it would be. I wrapped the standard snub-nosed .38 in a hand towel and stuffed it down to the bottom of the duffel bag.

That done, I locked up the car one last time, secured my file in one hand, hoisted my duffle bag on my right shoulder, and began to hike toward my do-or-die moment.

At the main-gate sentry shack a military policeman (MP) was checking a steady line of people going in and out of the post. Each man was flashing his military ID—the very item I didn't have.

Pretending to tie my boots allowed me to scope things out while waiting for a break in the line. I saw my chance and started toward him. If this didn't work, I would be in jail real fast.

"Hi. Uh, I've got a problem. Here are my orders to report, but I've lost my ID card."

He gave the orders a quick scan, glanced at my uniform and the file in my hand, and jerked his thumb toward a wooden building just outside the gate. "That's the ID building, bub. You'll find what you need in there."

When I entered I saw ten other soldiers lined up in front of two harried civilian clerks. I breathed a sigh of relief. I wasn't alone in being without my card. Silently I thanked the Good Lord for all the draftees who didn't see losing an ID card as that big a deal. Looking behind me, I saw another five soldiers ready to replace me. Some lost their cards but others said they were there to renew. No wonder the clerks were having a hard day.

"I lost my ID card."

"Do you have any other form of identification?" The

clerk couldn't have acted more bored if I were reciting the first fifty names from page one of a phone book.

"No. Everything was in my wallet, but I do have my orders, and my 201 file," I added helpfully.

She looked me up and down as if sure I was one of the dumbest individuals on the face of the earth, then placed a form in front of me. "Check the last box. Sign your name here. Staple a copy of your orders to Vietnam to the form. Put both in the outbox on the table by the camera, and stand on the X taped to the floor."

Five minutes later I had a brand new card with my picture and signature on the front along with the fingerprints of my two index fingers on the back, all courtesy of Uncle Sam. I was now, to all intents and purposes, Travis Nickels. At least the gate guard thought so as he passed me through.

A sign directed me across the tarmac to an old airplane hangar serving as the processing facility for those bound for Vietnam. Inside the door was a uniformed front desk clerk, one of seven available to process people. The loud hum of hundreds of men waiting to be processed, playing pool and ping pong games, or chatting—along with blaring TVs—greeted me. Many men already had on newly issued olive green baseball caps and jungle fatigues. MPs with nightsticks strolled around the swirling mass, looking to break up fights or anything else that might cause a problem. The place had all the charm of an old bus station.

I signed in with the clerk, and my orders were checked. I was given a voucher for meals and directed to the medical line, where we were given missing shots prior to departure.

I told them I lost my shot record and they administered the full list by air gun. The result was a painful throb in my right arm as I was directed to the uniform station.

We were sized up by sight and tossed five sets of olive drab jungle fatigues. Hats and jungle boots followed.

"Sign this form. It states you were given your clothing issue and are responsible for same. Move along, move along, ya think we got all damn day?"

It happened so fast I didn't know what I got. Sign now and check later seemed to be their motto.

The new clothes fit like crap, but that didn't matter. My mind was focused on finding Ross. I walked the halls for the next six hours, looking for him. No such luck. By then all I wanted was a place to stow my duffel bag and get some shut-eye.

Easier said than done. The hangar was huge, converted into a maze of 20x20 cubicles of plywood with twelve bunks per cubicle. People tended to take refuge in the nearest cubicle so I had to walk quite a way before finding a bed of my own. Sitting on the cot, I told myself not to worry. I'd made good time getting there. The gun was hidden in the bottom of my duffel bag, and Ross had nowhere to go before tomorrow. I'd track him down here and end this.

Above my bunk was a sign: Do Not Lie on Bed with Foot Gear on. On the other wall a sign warned: No Smoking in Bed. I stowed my gear in a footlocker at the foot of the bed, secured it with the lock, and lay down on the cot in my clothes. Too tired to take my boots off, I found myself saying, "Fuck the Army" as I dozed off.

10

December 29, 1969

"Rise and shine, gentlemen. Breakfast at 0530. If you expect to eat, you need to do so now. No cubicles to be occupied as of 0530 anyway, so it's your choice to eat the fine chow supplied by Uncle Sam or not. Don't be found on your bunk past that time or expect to be on a work detail immediately thereafter." This announcement was followed by the sound of boots treading down to the next cubicle and the speech repeated all over again.

Blinking, I turned over to see another guy staring at me from the bed across the way. He looked at me and laughed.

"Man, you look like something the cat dragged in, for sure."

I was too busy rubbing the crust from my eyelids to reply but swung my feet on the floor and sat up. After a quick stretch I stood. "Is there any place to get some food around here?"

"Well, friend, I'm going to get some chow." He flashed a broad grin back to me. "I'm never one to miss a meal, brother."

The chow line wasn't hard to find. We followed everyone else to the part of the hangar with the most noise. It was like every school food line. Instead of lunch ladies, substitute some unhappy privates wearing white fast-food caps ladling food in a serving line, and you know exactly what it was like. Somebody behind me complained it was all "Shit on a Shingle," but I had a secret. I basically liked cafeteria food. Not that I said so to friends or I'd have never heard the end of it. Yet this cafeteria was pretty poor. They asked if I wanted eggs or French toast, and for some unknown reason the guy at the end was making hamburgers. I took a burger and a glass of milk and sat at the nearest table.

My roommate joined me and plowed into his eggs. I picked up my burger and grimaced. *God Almighty*. I could have wrung a cup of grease from it. No joke. When was the last time the cook cleaned his grill? I thought about going to the back of the line and trying again, but the hundreds of guys waiting around the room discouraged me.

Shit.

Well, I wasn't here to sample the damn food anyway. Finding Ross, getting him to justice, and going back to my real life as soon as possible: that was the goal. How could I find the son of a bitch here?

"Who are you looking for?" asked my roomie as he buttered a slice of toast.

"What are you talking about?"

"Well, I ain't a detective like Sherlock Holmes, but you sure are looking for someone. No one scans a crowd like you been doing, otherwise."

For the first time I stopped and really looked at my roommate. He was about my size, black as the Ace of Spades, and with an accent I couldn't quite place. He was wearing an enameled black pin bearing corporal stripes on each of his green fatigue lapels. His nametag said Denison.

He smiled. A big smile. He knew I was looking for someone. Didn't realize I was so obvious.

"Looking for a guy I met awhile back. Name is Frank Ross. Ever hear of him?" As if I'd be that lucky, this fast, in a sea of G.I.s.

"Nope, can't say I have. You can probably track him down if you go see the admin section at the other end of the hangar." His forehead wrinkled. "Haven't you thought of that?" I shook my head and he continued. "You signed in, I signed in, everyone signs in. And everyone is going to have to sign out as well. It's the Army way." He laughed.

I excused myself, leaving behind the greasy remains of my breakfast, and hustled over to the admin area. It took several minutes to get there, what with the weaving and bobbing through hundreds of guys, all of them bored, hungry, or surly.

I found where I'd signed in the night before and stopped to think. Ross definitely should be here by now. Last night I was too frazzled to think about him signing in as I had. I needed to see if he'd shown and if he was still here. I crossed my fingers and looked for the least busy personnel clerk. Preferably someone not too high in rank. I wanted someone to answer questions, not ask them.

I spotted the best prospect. He was a PFC wearing a set of grubby fatigues clearly used several times this week. His sideburns were longer than mandated by the various pictures posted on the walls dictating the correct regulation haircut, and he wore thick glasses. Definitely not a career Army man. Probably a draftee and my best hope.

My choice was a good one. He accepted my "looking for Uncle Frank" without further explanation and let me peruse the lists.

I wasn't prepared for what I found.

Ross's name wasn't on any list. Not the sign-in list. Not the sign-out list. He was not here. He'd never been here.

There was no mistake. He definitely should be here by now. Did he have a car wreck? What happened? I shook my head. I'd come all this way, taken all these chances, done all it took to get to this point. Only to find nothing.

I was fucked.

I must have looked pretty upset because the PFC behind the desk said gently, "You know, there is one other place that processes men for Vietnam transit. Your uncle could have gone to Fort Lewis up in Washington state."

Fort Lewis? I'd assumed that since Nickels had orders to go to Vietnam through Oakland, Ross would make the same journey. Now I was in California. Apparently, he was in Washington state at Fort Lewis, just outside of Seattle, only an hour away from Lake Munson and home. What a joke.

I stood there. *Think. Think this through.* There was no chance of getting to Fort Lewis. What was I to do? Go to the local cops? Tell my story and hope they believed me? Go back to New Mexico? Run away and hide? I had no clue.

Only one thing was clear. The bastard had gotten away. Defeated, I started to slink off.

"You can probably catch up with him at Long Binh after you land, you know," said the clerk.

"What are you talking about?"

He smiled patiently. "Everyone going to Vietnam from Oakland and Fort Lewis are being sent to the 90th Replacement Battalion in Long Binh for the month of December before assignment to their final destination in-country. If he's just a day ahead of you, your chances of catching up to him there are quite good, actually."

So there was still hope. Only now it would mean going thousands of miles to a foreign country and hoping to catch him before he disappeared into the bowels of the jungle. Fate seemed to want to know just how badly I wanted Ross.

A smile came to my face. "Thanks!" I said. He looked at me uncertainly. Probably because my smile had no mirth to it.

None at all.

***

It was another twenty-four hours before I heard the name Travis Nickels called at one of the three shipping out formations we were required to attend each day.

I passed the time in between these gatherings reading old magazines and trashed newspapers. The *New York Times* was headlining the massive November anti-war march on the Pentagon. A old issue of *Newsweek* had a cover story about a concert in a place called Woodstock. The local rag featured an article about the Hells Angels serving as crowd security in exchange for free beer at the

Altamont rock concert a few weeks earlier. They killed someone when a wave of Rolling Stones fans rushed the stage.

Eventually I ran out of stuff to read. Bored, I walked around the building to waste time. The ping-pong and pool tables were all occupied. One guy was playing the harmonica and was actually pretty good. A few, safely hidden behind bunks or in a corner, were shooting craps. I stopped to watch when the constant walking made my feet ache. Money in those games seemed to be changing hands at an astounding rate. Occasionally, a pair of MPs would come by and the crowd would scatter, only to re-form about two minutes after they moved on. I had no money, no skill, and little interest if all I was going to be was a spectator.

Near the front of the building was a concrete wall with markings all over it. As I got closer I could see it contained graffiti messages from guys on their way to the war. There was Ed, who wrote a dirty limerick about what he was going to do with his girlfriend when he returned from Vietnam. Next to him was Tim, a draftee bemoaning his fate while others got to stay behind. Dave wrote how he loved his wife and hoped she would stay true. Hundreds of messages covered the wall.

I noticed two things. First, each used only a small amount of space for their scribbles, in consideration of the men still to come. Second, after listing their name, each guy also put down the date he was here and his future discharge date or maybe where he was from. A tack with a long thin string was placed in a wall crack. The string held a magic marker so you could compose what you pleased. I thought about it, took the marker and wrote "Eye for an Eye" and under it put "PFC Travis Nickels (Peterson), 30 DEC 69." That somehow made my mission more real. I didn't write down a discharge date because I had no idea when I'd find Ross. When I finished, I put the marker back for the next guy.

At the third formation of the day my new name was called and I boarded an Army bus for a ride up Interstate 80 to Travis Air Force Base. We waited for several hours before boarding a civilian 727 jet. TWA no less. With real stewardesses. This was a war?

It seemed like a trip to a tropical paradise somewhere in the Pacific, except I was seeking a murderer, and each passenger was wearing a military uniform. The Army dominated, but there was a sprinkling of airmen, marines, and even two naval officers. Most of the 184 men on board seemed to be nineteen to twenty years old. I knew how many were on board because I counted as I walked up and down the aisle several times during the flight, in case Ross magically showed up.

We did stop in a tropical paradise. Hawaii. One hour to refuel. Not permitted to leave the airport passenger area. Some guys bought items at the gift store next to a sign with a Maybellined brunette holding an ice-cold bottle of Coca-Cola and a caption saying THINGS GO BETTER WITH COKE. Other guys stared out the large glass windows and watched departing planes. I tried to sleep in the uncomfortable yellow fiberglass chairs in our waiting area.

It occurred to me I hadn't read Rita's note from a week ago. Was it really a week? No, it was eleven days now. I took out my empty wallet and looked in the folder part where I'd stuck it. It was still there.

It said: Jim, I really, really like you. I want to go steady. I want you to love me inside and out. ~ Rita.

I looked at it for a long time, carefully refolded it, and put it back in my wallet.

Twenty-four hours after leaving the mainland, we flew into Vietnamese airspace.

11

"This is your captain speaking. We'll land at Bien Hoa Air Base in approximately thirty minutes. Expect sunny skies and a temperature of one hundred ten degrees with one hundred percent humidity. As of now, with the time difference from the States, you've skipped ahead a day. It's nine in the morning, this beautiful Wednesday, January first, 1970, and the start of a new decade. Please remain seated upon touchdown. Once we are at a complete stop, an official will board the plane to explain your next steps. We hope you enjoyed your flight. Good luck in Vietnam. We wish you a speedy return home. Thanks for flying TWA."

"Hell of a way to start the seventies," muttered a tall private on my left.

The plane landed smoothly and taxied to the terminal. The roaring engines ceased and the cabin door slid open with a noise like the opening of a sardine can.

An Air Force captain strolled onto the plane with two Army MPs following close behind. Walking to the forward bulkhead, he scrutinized us and announced, "My name is Captain Hatton. Welcome to South Vietnam and Bien Hoa Air Base. As you exit the plane with your gear, you will form two lines out on the tarmac at the bottom of the ramp. Remaining in these orderly lines, you will proceed to the baggage area inside the terminal where you'll be searched for contraband by the MPs you see here with me. If you have any such items, you need to deposit them in any airline seat prior to your departure. This is your only amnesty. If anything is found on you after that, you'll be brought up on charges. Officers will deplane first and assemble in a separate line outside on the tarmac. Gentlemen, let's proceed."

A flurry of movement followed. Everyone hurried to get outside as soon as possible. The air in the plane was stale and sticky after the passenger door was opened.

I'd kept Dad's gun with the idea of using it. I realized now it was an idea from some dumb movie. Whatever happened, it was not going to be the "Shootout at the OK Corral." I felt foolish for imagining such an outcome. If I were caught with it, I'd go to jail for sure, with no possible revenge. The gun had to go.

I grabbed my duffel bag from the overhead and put it on my seat. Reaching in, I felt the hand towel with the pistol wrapped inside. Busy with their own gear, no one paid any attention as I left the towel bundle on the seat.

Plenty of others had forbidden items. Walking up the aisle, I noticed grass, pills, knives, brass knuckles, and porno mags scattered over the seats. Holy crap. How did the military dispose of all that stuff? Was my pistol the only gun on board? Five minutes earlier, I'd have said yes. Now I wasn't so sure.

A deplaning ramp was rolled up to the 727. At the exit door the stale air was replaced by sweaty heat that took your breath away. The outside world was a shimmery haze, infused with heat and smoke in all directions.

A stagnant smell mixed with the smoke was difficult to identify before I realized it was fecal matter of some kind. I tried not to gag as we moved down the ramp to our new home. Later I learned it was all the G.I. shit being burned. With 500,000 soldiers in the country and no modern sewage system, it was the preferred way to get rid of the overwhelming load of human waste.

The runways were a jumble of helicopters, civilian passenger jets, military transports, gun emplacements, sandbagged buildings, a few buses, and a line of fighter jets in taxi position for takeoff—a dizzying array of organized chaos.

Hustled off the tarmac to a small open-sided shed with bench seats, we were told to wait. A tall pole cluttered with signs pointing in the direction of major American cities stood to the side. Los Angeles was only 8,157 miles away.

Minutes ticked by in the stifling heat as we tried to breathe normally in the stinky air. After an hour, we were given forms to designate a beneficiary for our new G.I. life insurance, payable for $10,000. An imaginary name and address went on mine.

We were ushered aboard an olive-drab Army bus similar to the color of a diseased turd. Grilled mesh covered the windows. The driver said it prevented grenades flying through the windows and taking us out. Supposedly, the mesh bounced a grenade off and sent it back to the thrower. Supposedly.

Our round-faced driver was quite the tour guide. Heading to the main gate, we bounced along a potholed road he called Highway 15. Pointing to a shanty town on our right, he said "That's Turkey Row. It's closed to military personnel because it harbors Viet Cong—that's the local communist guerillas, VC for short—and their sympathizers." I was surprised the Air Force allowed hostile civilians so close to the base. On the left were untended cows munching grass by a military dorm and basketball court. Apparently that was normal, as the driver didn't remark on it while otherwise keeping up a constant stream of chatter.

The drive to our Long Binh destination ended with crossing a bridge over the Dong Nai River. Locals watched us from small huts with straw roofs. On the side of the road, a teenage girl dropped her pants, squatted, and peed.

A fellow behind me said, "Toto, I've a feeling we're not in Kansas anymore."

We passed through an entry gate and under a whitewashed half-moon overhead sign proclaiming WELCOME TO THE 90TH REPLACEMENT BATTALION, LONG BINH. The place looked like a prison. Ten-foot high fences topped with barbed wire surrounded the place. I wondered if it was to keep the VC out, us in, or both.

Several NCOs wearing crisp freshly starched fatigues with white painted helmets similar to MPs greeted us. They were distinctly different from us since our uniforms were completely soaked through with perspiration in the heat. The NCOs led us to another processing building with air conditioning. A curtained wall on one side had a series of green wooden tables with finance clerks sitting behind them. We listened to a welcome speech and had our orders checked again.

"Change your dollars into MPC, military payment certificates, now," we were told. It looked like monopoly money but professionally done. If you had no cash, they issued a pay advance of forty dollars. Both of my twenty-dollar purple certificates had a picture of Sitting Bull on the front. Actual U.S. currency was banned in Vietnam and would land a G.I. in jail. The intention was to prevent inflation and black marketing in the local economy.

Shoving my money in a pocket, I sat down as the curtain was drawn aside to reveal a large movie screen. Anticipation of a Hollywood movie release disappeared fast. Things got real quiet when a full color film about the hazards of catching venereal disease in Vietnam filled the screen. Thirty minutes of some pretty strong stuff—all in living color. Way, way, way more than you ever wanted to know. The staff passed out pamphlets warning us about the local women. By the time they finished, I was sure I'd never have sex again...or more accurately, for the first time. Not surprisingly, it was a vow that wouldn't last.

12

The 90th Replacement Battalion occupied a half-mile square area on a slight rise. It was a base within the base of Long Binh itself, which with 50,000 men was the largest Army compound in the world. It contained metal Quonset huts, barracks buildings, a swimming pool, cafe (air conditioned!), several mess halls, admin buildings, two basketball courts, a baseball diamond, post office, outdoor movie theater, post exchange (PX), barber shop, laundry, and massage parlor.

You couldn't help but be impressed. Why we hadn't won this war by now was beyond me. But then I wasn't a real soldier, just a civilian kid a long way from home.

Assigned to bunks in temporary barracks, we lined up for another formation. Through a megaphone the officer in charge said, "You have three formations a day: 0800 hours, noon, and 1600 hours. These are mandatory. Your in-country assignment will be announced during one of those formations. Miss one and you are subject to judicial punishment as being AWOL."

What the heck that meant I didn't know, but it didn't sound good. I heard a guy in the next row say in a snarky voice, "What the hell can they do, send me to Vietnam?" Soldiers around him laughed.

We marched to a hut to get our 201 files processed. For me, a clerk verified everything was there except one item.

"Where's your fingerprint card?" asked one scowling sergeant.

I pretended I had no clue, which made me appear stupid in addition to careless. He let me have it. He swore at me, called me an idiot, fool, and much, much worse, then sputtered to a halt. Exasperated and spent, he sent me to another room two buildings over to get re-fingerprinted.

"Don't lose them on the way back. How the hell is anyone going to identify your dead body if things get really bad out there?"

That brought me up short. On my return, he looked them over, had me sign, and watched as I put my fingerprints card in my folder.

We were told to take our money and hit the PX as soon as possible. On my way, the roar of a crowd drew me toward a block of barracks. Turning the corner, I saw a large green canvas tent with the sides rolled up to take advantage of stray breezes. Hundreds of G.I.s were hooting, hollering, and having a heck of a good time inside. There were no seats. Each man was standing and looking upward. No one paid me the slightest attention as I slipped my way toward the front of the crowd while scanning everywhere for Ross. Then I stopped dead in my tracks.

On an oval stage with a single walkway jutting out into the audience stood two well-endowed Asian women with long hair ending at their buttocks. No doubt existed about their being women. They were completely naked and took turns strutting down the walkway as G.I.s yelled enthusiastically and threw newly issued MPC dollars. A small Vietnamese man ran along the stage collecting the money in a green plastic bucket.

I wasn't a total newbie regarding sex. I had the urge starting at twelve in Truman's Rexall Drug Store where *Playboy* and *Esquire* magazines were kept in a side alcove in the back. If you timed it right, you could stand there, listen for someone coming down the aisle to the back area, and put the magazine back before being discovered. I don't think those magazines were placed there by accident.

One particular *Playboy* edition got my attention. The color foldout was of a beautiful, smiling redhead, lying on her side on a rug in front of a roaring fire with a bowl of popcorn strategically located. It was one hell of a sexy picture, and I had to have it. So for the first and only time, I shoplifted. I put the magazine under my coat and walked out of the store as bold as brass. Felt bad about it, but no one was going to sell a *Playboy* to a twelve-year-old. That magazine had a treasured, concealed place in my closet for the next three years. I've had a consistent hankering for popcorn ever since.

Now I was seeing a naked woman in real life. I'd imagined it plenty, but not like this. It definitely wasn't sexy. I felt embarrassed both for the girls on the stage and the guys in the audience.

Walking away, I found discarded pamphlets on the ground, the ones handed out to us after seeing the VD film. They all showed a Vietnamese woman in a short dress with a sexy smile. Below the picture it said VD IS NOTHING TO CLAP ABOUT. USE A CONDOM. The film's effect on the men lasted less than twenty-four hours. Guys are guys and some things don't change.

At the PX, I bought things on the recommendation list given to us earlier. The PX was like a small store back home, except it had civilian Vietnamese clerks overseen by Army NCOs running the place. The women were alike in being short, petite, and flat-chested. They looked like little Asian fifth graders. One good thing was that the older female tailors could adjust the jungle fatigues issued in Oakland. When they were done, I actually looked normal.

My assigned barracks was first come, first served on beds and a locker to stash your gear. I'd bought combo locks at the PX; there was a theft problem with so many guys funneled through the camp. Late arrivals ended up away from the windows and their potential breezes. A standing giant fan stood at one end of the bay, but provided little relief, only churning up hot air and blowing dust over everything.

During the day it was cooler outside if you could find shade. Concrete pads with picnic tables and carport type roofs provided a break from searching for Ross. I parked my butt at a table and closed my eyes. The heat, jet lag, and constant looking to spot a murderer were all taking a toll. Was I doing the right thing chasing after Ross or was I just a fool?

At the next table another guy talked incessantly about his assignment. He was posted to the 101st and had to report at the next scheduled formation that afternoon. He was not a happy camper.

"Damn it, why me? I've got a wife and two kids. I couldn't care less about this shithole."

His buddy tried to be sympathetic. "A draftee goes

where he's sent, man."

"Bullshit. The government is trying to screw me over again. Why in hell anyone would want to be in that outfit is beyond me. I'm not here to get my ass shot off." He ranted until his friend stopped nodding. The lack of interest made him even madder.

"Yeah, you can act all cool and stuff. You get to go to MACV. You get to be in a concrete building in Saigon during the day with air conditioning, for God's sake! You live the 'Life of Reilly' while I'm running through the jungle chasing little yellow men dressed in black pajamas." Stopping to draw a breath, his eyes narrowed as he looked across the table at his companion. "And you know what the kicker is? You get the same combat pay I do."

Holding his hands up in a surrender pose, his companion mumbled, "No one said life is fair, man."

"This isn't even close." He slammed his cap on his head and stalked off.

For the first time I wondered what would happen if I didn't find Ross here. Should I confess to an MP? Keep playing my hand poker-wise and hope for the best? I had gotten this far with some luck. What if I weren't assigned to the 101st? Nickels expected it, but maybe the Army had other plans. And what the hell would I do if I was? I had no idea how to be a real soldier.

The universe was pulling a big joke at my expense. I'd led a pretty privileged life, but the murder of my family made that a thing of the past.

13

As expected, I was assigned to the 101st. Turned out if you were a parachute qualified infantryman you went there or to the 173rd Airborne Brigade. The 101st was a full division and larger than the 173rd so it got the lion's share. The odds worked in my favor.

My name was posted on the departure board the next morning along with twelve others slated to leave in a truck in an hour. We had barely enough time to get our division patches and jump wings sewn on by the PX ladies. I bought some Marlboros and a Zippo lighter, too. I wasn't a smoker, but thought they might be handy for my nerves. I was feeling the stress. I'd decided to keep going after Ross.

From head to toe, perspiration poured from my body as I waited for the truck. Seeping moisture was inside my boots, and my fatigues were soaked. The heat and humidity were working against me. How long would it take to get used to this weather? Nothing like being hot on the outside, with a cold creeping dread on the inside to make you shudder.

Would I survive long enough to find Ross? If I did, what then? I sure as hell couldn't spend a year here. I was a soldier impersonator, not the real thing. With my lack of training, I'd no idea what to do in a real combat situation. I had to find Ross quick.

Nearby a corporal complained the Army had made a

mistake in his case. He shouldn't be going with our group. He didn't belong with us.

A sergeant looked at him with disdain and yelled, "Shut the hell up. The Army doesn't make mistakes."

I stood there thinking *Well, Sarge, I'm a big one, whether anyone knows it or not.*

The deuce-and-a-half horn sounded our imminent departure. The sergeant bellowed at the malingering corporal to get his sorry ass in the truck. Following him, I tossed my duffel bag over the side, climbed over the side rail, and sat on one of the metal side benches. The floor was lined with sandbags to protect us from road bombs. My sphincter muscles tightened up right away.

So began a two-hour ride down a dusty potholed dirt road outside Bien Hoa where the 101st had a special site for new arrivals.

Our truck parked by a large whitewashed sign with the Screaming Eagles logo. Above it was the slogan Rendezvous with Destiny. I liked the sound of that. Once I got Ross, my destiny would be fulfilled, all right.

We lined up in front of a platform where a one-star general stood.

One-star's welcome was not eloquent. It was like your grandfather reassuring you everything was going to be all right. He concluded with, "Save your money; you'll want to get that car or house or whatever upon your return. There's nothing to spend it on while you're over here anyway."

Stupid advice, given what I saw at the repo depot. I had a feeling girls and alcohol were going to milk money away from most of us pretty quick—unless you were always out in the jungle. That alternative was even worse.

Since we were processed in-country and now welcomed by the 101st, we thought we'd be assigned to our units next. Instead we arrived at the Screaming Eagles Replacement Training School (SERTS). I heard somewhere that God protects fools and idiots. In Vietnam the 101st fulfilled the role of God. We were the fools and idiots.

A captain at the front of our formation addressed us. "The purpose of SERTS is to fill in any missing holes in your infantry training so you stand a better chance of survival in the field. It helps remind you this is for real. It also allows you time to acclimate to the heat, which is brutal."

Several heads nodded involuntarily. Sweat saturated our bodies like we'd stepped out of a sauna. Not yet noon and we were dressed lightly. What the hell was it going to be like carrying a full pack while cutting our way through the jungle?

The captain was a mind reader. "For many of you, SERTS is an unexpected godsend. We run it as a crash infantry course starting with cleaning your weapon, marksmanship, moving on to mines, booby traps, and covering advanced patrol tactics. Keep focused on your instructors if you want to stay alive."

He paused and smiled before continuing. "I want each of you to look to the man on your right. Take a good look. Now look at the man on your left. Take another good look. One of those two men will not go back to the States alive."

I figured he did that for effect. The strange thing was

it had the opposite impact on me. I was immortal. I felt sorry for the two bastards on each side of me, though. I had every intention of getting out of here alive after I had settled things with Ross. Oh, sure, I might get a flesh wound of some kind but it would be non life-threatening. I was happy with my assessment of the future until the captain spoke again.

"Now, each of you is assuming the other man is going to be the one to bite the dust. But gentlemen, I assure you, he is thinking the same about you. The one who's correct is the one who keeps his eyes and ears open over the next few days. You may think you don't need this because you graduated from infantry training back in the States. But you've had four weeks of leave, and you've forgotten some things you were taught. Do yourself a favor. Pay attention to your instructors over the next week. Good luck."

I didn't need any persuading and resolved to keep my eyes and ears open. For me this was my basic training and infantry training combined. It would improve my chances for survival. Everyone else had infantry training stateside, but I suspected they were thinking along the same lines. We'd all be paying attention, previous training or not.

***

"The M-16 is the finest military rifle ever made. It's lightweight, easy to handle, and puts out a lot of lead. If you know it, respect it, and treat it right, it will be ready when you need it," said the NCO (anyone E-5 or higher).

We had each drawn an M-16 from the armory. One thing in my favor: I knew how to use a gun and was a decent shot. That was to Dad's credit as well as the hunter safety course he made me take when I was twelve. What I didn't know was how to shoot and zero an M-16. Or how to break it down and clean it. Luckily, both were reviewed in a three-hour refresher firing range course. Shooting at pop-up silhouettes was actually fun, kinda like being at a family arcade. Of course, no one was there to shoot back at me either. That would diminish the fun considerably when added into the mix.

Tearing down an M-16 and putting it back together turned out to be fairly easy. Mastering that, we had to disassemble and reassemble it blindfolded. Harder but doable. The instructor said some attacks would be at night and we'd need this skill. Parts of it were made of plastic like a Mattel toy, and only a screw and two pins held the whole thing together.

"Clean your rifle every chance you get. Four or five times a day. At all times, keep your magazine and ammo as clean and dry as possible. Cleanliness is next to godliness, gentlemen. It can save your life," bellowed the NCO. "Here's a field tip. You'll hear from some not to load a full twenty rounds in your clip—that loading only eighteen or nineteen prevents jamming. This is a myth. But it's your life. Do what you think best."

We finished the day firing a bevy of weapons including an M-79 grenade launcher, an M-60 machine gun, and a 60mm mortar along with a Russian-made AK-47, the preferred weapon of the North Vietnamese. Scary and exciting at the same time.

The AK-47 sound was distinctive from the M-16. More of a pop than the crack heard from our weapon. The bullet was the same size as the ones used in the M-60 machine gun, and its clip held ten more rounds. Knowing the enemy could get off that many more rounds was an unpleasant surprise. Their fixed bayonet folded down when not in use, which was a handy feature.

The highlight of the weapons session was the LAW (light anti-tank weapon) demonstration. A two-piece fiberglass tube rocket launcher, it fired only once and was disposable. It was thirty inches long, lightweight (five pounds), and looked similar to a World War II bazooka. Easy to shoulder-fire and the damage it could do was really tremendous. One cardinal rule: Don't stand behind the guy launching it; the backblast is hell. If you do, you'll regret it.

The North Vietnamese Army version, a rocket propelled grenade (RPG), was a green four-foot pipe with a pineapple shaped missile on the end. After it was shot, you could clearly follow the round all the way to its target via the exhaust trail. The explosion was more impressive than our LAW, too. Why the enemy had better ground weapons was a mystery.

We threw our grenades behind a four-foot concrete wall enclosure with an upside-down, bowl-shaped floor. The floor was designed to help if a nervous soldier dropped a grenade. Hopefully, he'd survive by having it roll through a hole until it emerged on the other side of the wall. At least that was the plan.

"Don't worry," said the sergeant, grinning at me. "You won't drop the grenade in the first place. Remember your throwing form. Hurl it right after pulling the pin and releasing the spoon lever. Five seconds later, it'll explode."

Seemed an awfully long time to me. What would stop someone from throwing it back?

Next on the menu were explosives. C-4 was up first. A thick, white plastic, it resembled bread dough.

"You'll use this a lot. It's a great explosive as long as you're careful. You can do almost anything with it: drop it, throw it, or whatever. It won't go off accidently. You can mold it into any shape you want, too. It's powerful and can cut a large tree in half. It's also inert until a blasting cap or detonation device sets it off."

The claymore mine followed. I was given the dubious "privilege" of staple gunning cardboard targets fifty yards away between fence posts. When they set up a claymore and set it off, the results were impressive. Targets were shredded and drilled with holes in a 130-degree arc.

"The two pounds of C-4 and hundreds of steel ball bearings inside a claymore will cut anyone to pieces," said the instructor. He demonstrated the clacker trigger. "This is foolproof unless you forget and face the mine the wrong way. There is a warning on the side, 'Face Toward Enemy,' to remind you. Remember this about all claymore mines: if you set one in the dark, and can't remember which way you pointed it, assume it's pointed at you and get the hell out of the way."

Bouncing Betties came next. Pressure mines buried in the ground, these are the kind most people think of when visualizing a mine. "Step on one and a small charge hurls the main charge up several feet to explode just below your belly button. If that baby goes off you die, lose a limb, or possibly your manhood."

Chopper protocol. In a mockup Huey without any doors, they showed how to load ourselves and our gear, and how to deplane quickly while setting up a defensive perimeter.

"Remember, a helicopter can kill you. Those rotor blades will slice you in two. Never approach the chopper from the rear. Approach only from the right-side, middle-door section or even better, the front so the pilot can see you. For God's sake, be sure and crouch as you approach. Make yourself less than five feet tall if at all possible when you board or deplane. Those chopper blades *dip*, gentlemen. That is especially important if you are climbing upward on a hill to get to your chopper. Be careful. Don't lose your head."

Landing zone (LZ) procedures, such as the proper colored smoke grenades to employ to alert the pilot to your situation and how to clear an LZ of obstacles like brush and trees, were covered next.

Every soldier is supposed to be able to read a map. But military maps aren't normal maps. They're topographical since most of the time we wouldn't be close to a road. You had to identify and use contour lines and elevation marks to know where you were. You had to use a magnetic compass to navigate. That would take practice even though we all found the markers placed in a field. I managed to pass because I followed the rule of "find the grid line and then look to your right and up." Perhaps my geometry class had some real-life applications after all. Luckily, I wasn't the only one who had trouble with this and didn't attract undue attention.

After our compass lesson, the instructor took a live chicken out of it's bamboo cage and stroked it almost lovingly. A quick move of his right hand pulled the neck taunt, and he bit off the neck with the attached chicken head in a practiced stroke, casually spitting it from his mouth. The headless chicken fell to the ground, sprang up, and ran around for thirty seconds before keeling over for good.

Staying alive in the jungle was the sergeant's specialty. He expounded on an extensive list of what to do and not to do. He followed that by reaching into a burlap sack, taking out a six-foot-long snake, and holding it by the head as the body coiled around in the open air. With a knife he sliced it in the middle along the length of its trunk. Bringing the snake to his mouth, he sucked and slurped the insides from left to right. I wasn't the only one saying, "Oh. My. God." He had our attention and for the next hour discussed the hundred different snakes found in Vietnam, various animals and vegetation you could safely eat in the jungle, and how to kill something with almost nothing.

"Drink at least twelve canteens of water per day," we were told. I thought that was excessive but decided to keep count. Turned out I averaged sixteen canteens daily and that barely replaced the water I lost through sweat. It didn't actually cure my thirst. But I was beginning to cope with the heat.

The school concluded with a patrol into the mostly pacified countryside outside our camp. There was an emphasis on keeping proper distance, moving quietly, ambushes, and setting up a night defensive position (NDP). Finally, they issued us a small blue manual titled *A Handbook for U.S. Forces in Vietnam*. It had a lot of info on military protocol and the country of Vietnam. I did my best to memorize every word.

If you left out the guns, ammo, grenades, bombs, and snake info, then SERTS resembled a big boy version of a Boy Scout camp. No one was injured and we learned a lot in a short time.

Now I could impersonate an infantryman with some confidence—at least a slow, stupid one who needed to be constantly reminded of what to do. I saw enough at SERTS to know there were plenty of others who fell into the same category.

Following SERTS graduation, we were trucked to an airstrip and loaded onto a C-123 turboprop transport plane. It was dark inside without real windows, just small glass portholes. More importantly, it was rigged for cargo and had no seats. Everyone sprawled against the sides of the plane where there was a lot of exposed wiring and pipes of some kind. I found an empty spot and sat on my duffel bag, hoping the pilot would fly the damn thing on a level course. Otherwise I figured there were going to be a lot of sick guys, including me. Lucky for us, he did. A couple of hours later we landed in Phu Bai.

On the whitewashed airport control tower a large sign proclaimed PHU BAI IS ALL RIGHT! Our plane landed ten minutes before a pelting rain came out of the lead-colored hanging clouds. A constant sheet of wetness continued for the next two hours, assaulting our faces and drenching our uniforms with a different kind of moisture than what we'd grown used to down south. It turned the hard orange dirt into fields of orange mud.

"Welcome to the Vietnam monsoon season," said the driver who showed up to take us to Camp Evans. "You guys are lucky. The rainy season in this area is almost over. Only four or five more weeks to go." He smiled like we should be happy with his pronouncement.

Huddled in the back of the truck, wet and miserable, we barreled down the road through a large urban area I later found out was Hue, the provincial capital. The rain was so bad no one paid much attention. I wondered why we were in such a hell of a hurry, even given the rain. Turned out many of the roads belonged to the Viet Cong (Charlie) after dark, and we were close to dusk. Our driver wasn't taking any chances.

An hour later we arrived at Camp Evans, the home of the 3rd Brigade of the 101st Division.

The home of the 506th.

The home of Frank Ross.

14

In classic hurry-up-and-wait tradition after barreling down the road to get there, our driver left me and two others in front of a company orderly room where we waited several hours for our assignments. The two guys with me were also PFCs. Both were draftees. Nametags identified one as Cranston, the other as Deems. We talked while waiting around in a low fog.

Roy Cranston stood six feet three inches, had bright red hair, and was from California, with a brother in the Navy back in the States. He hated being in the Army.

"People think that FTA stands for 'fuck the Army,' but lifers think it stands for 'fun, travel, and adventure.' Look at this place," he said. "What a bunch of dumb assholes."

David Deems was an inch or so shorter than me and wore black-framed, army-issued glasses that kept slipping down his freckled nose. He was a farm boy from a small town outside Minot, North Dakota, and had volunteered for the draft.

"Hell, I was bored." He shrugged. "What can I say? Wanted to try something new after living in a small town."

"How small?" I asked.

"Small enough that our main street had to be widened to paint a yellow line down the middle of it."

Deems, Cranston, and I ended up in Co F, 2/506. Translated that meant Foxtrot Company, 2nd Battalion,

506th Infantry Regiment. A wall outside the orderly room had a picture of a shield splashed with blue sky and six white parachutes descending on a green mountain as a lightning bolt flashed across the sky. The bottom of the shield had a banner with the word CURRAHEE. Later we learned it was a Cherokee word for "Stand Alone."

Our wait terminated with the arrival of First Sergeant Jackson who told us to refer to him as Top—as in the top sergeant in the company. Top was an impressive figure, six feet one inch, 250 pounds, flat crew cut with a touch of grey on the sides, and an unlit cigar in one side of his mouth. If he wore a pair of glasses you'd swear he was Vince Lombardi, coach of the Green Bay Packers. He had the aura of a guy you didn't want ticked off at you. Looking us over, he talked about Foxtrot Company, its history, and what he expected from us. He didn't seem particularly impressed with our group and sent us off with the company clerk, Houston, for a quick tour of the company area.

Our company layout was spartan. The buildings were elevated a foot off the ground and called hooches,with plywood shacks with screened windows and tin roofs sitting along a dirt road with shallow ditches on each side. Between hooches were scattered wooden sidewalks placed to escape the ankle deep monsoon mud. For protection against enemy rocket attacks, each hooch had waist-high sandbags along the outside walls. Lonely telephone poles here and there gave the place the look of a dilapidated industrial area back home.

At the supply and armory bunker, we were loaded up with a brand new M-16 with seventeen magazines, a

LAW, two claymores, four fragmentation grenades, two smoke grenades, a gas grenade and gas mask, helmet, web belt, lined poncho, entrenching tool, two field dressings, six canteens, rations, air mattress, and a rucksack. Our company was in the field, and we'd fly out to join them the next morning.

Settled in our assigned hooch, we were told we were now officially part of the second platoon. I picked out an empty canvas cot and stowed my gear in a grey metal locker by the bed.

"Top wants you guys ready at 0600 tomorrow to head out. Other than that, you're free to explore the camp," said Houston.

Deems sorted items from his duffel bag; Cranston went to see if he could rustle up a fan. I decided to do a recon of the camp. If I could find Ross now I could avoid my future as an infantryman for Uncle Sam.

Camp Evans was not nearly as big as Long Binh but still good sized. Companies were spread out, and dirt roads ran everywhere. In the middle of the camp, a road served as a main boulevard with vehicles kicking up mud as they moved along. The surrounding area was flatland with a series of faraway rolling hills in each direction. Bunkers protected the outer perimeter. On my left, choppers flew overhead. The whole camp had the appearance of a shantytown from the Great Depression I'd seen in my history textbook.

Over the next hour I scanned every man I passed, then gave up and stopped at the Enlisted Men's Club. It was a tent with picnic tables and a long wooden bar. A large

American flag served as background on the rear tent flap. A radio blared out the Rolling Stones, "You Can't Always Get What You Want." Everyone had a beer. I asked for a coke. Figured I might get ribbed, but I really wanted a soda. The bartender served it without comment. It was ice cold and tasted great, even in the drab surroundings.

I thought about my situation. Evans was big but I had no doubt I'd find Ross here. It was just a matter of time. I didn't bother scanning this bunch, though, since Ross was an NCO and they had their own club. I'd find out where it was and go there.

I was feeling pretty good about things until I passed a poster map of I Corps on a bulletin board. The individual locations of the division scattered along I Corps were all indicated with bright logos including the 101st headquarters located at Camp Eagle, forty miles away.

I'd assumed Evans was division headquarters and that I'd naturally end up in the same place as Ross. But Evans wasn't the headquarters according to the map. It had never occurred to me that Ross might not be here. What if he was at Camp Eagle? Camp Sally? Or the firebases listed on the map? A chill went through my body as I stood there looking at the poster. There was so much I didn't know about the Army. Ross could be at any of a dozen different places in the 101st besides Evans.

Panicked and hyperventilating, I bent over, placed my hands on my knees, and scrunched my eyes shut to control my hysteria. *All this way. All this way.* What had I accomplished? I was a fool.

Pacing around in circles, I tried walking off my anxiety.

Think. Think hard. Concentrate. If he's at another site you can find that out through the personnel office...or something. To get to him you can get a pass. Maybe. Did they even have passes in a war zone? Don't panic. The point is you can still make this happen. Calm down. Now.

Pacing brought me back to my hooch. Wrung out, I lay on my cot next to a screened window designed to keep out mosquitoes, a hopeless wish. The mosquito netting around my bed cut off the air circulation. I lay there sweating like a pig as dusk fell, but it beat getting eaten alive by the biggest mosquitos I'd ever seen. Even if we had found a fan, I didn't have much hope it would give any real relief.

We were asleep when a siren sounded. Was there a fire somewhere? Looking out the window, we saw men in green t-shirts and boxer shorts all running pell-mell. Without saying anything, we joined the rush. It was pure herd instinct.

Seconds later, whooshes followed by whomps and a series of explosions. We were under a rocket attack, launched from an area seven miles away called Rocket Ridge. Later we were told each missile was a Russian made 122mm armed with forty-pound warheads aimed into the heart of the camp.

As we were running, one hit the ground yards ahead of us. A rush of hot air and intense heat followed as the blast knocked me over and threw Deems six feet into the air. He dropped down like a rock. Without any dignity whatsoever, I semi-crawled and rolled into a nearby ditch. A split second later, something heavy fell on my back. I could hardly breathe. Turning over to get out from under, I saw it was Cranston on top of me. I let him stay. More cover for me seemed like a good idea.

Secondary explosions rattled the ground as two helicopters and an empty shed blew to pieces. Cranston sat there detailing what was happening as he peered over the edge of the ditch.

"That was a close one. The Reds got another shed but the other rocket aimed at the choppers was a clear miss, ladies and gentlemen. Those bastards need to go back to rocket class."

I could only hear him dimly. The blasts had deafened my ears. Listening to him was like listening to someone while wearing earplugs.

Not many rockets, maybe eight or nine, were fired. That was a good thing. The bad thing was the all-clear siren didn't sound till thirty minutes later. All the while, I lay in the ditch with Cranston on top of me. Neither one of us was injured. My ears were a bit out of whack but didn't hurt, and there wasn't any ringing. Deems had scurried to another ditch and was unharmed.

I surveyed the damage with lots of other guys, most—like us—in a state of undress. Picked up a metal fragment to keep as a souvenir, then thought better of it. I doubted I'd remember my welcome to Vietnam with any fondness later. When things died down, we trickled back to our hooch.

It was a restless night. Between the rockets, the mosquitos, humidity, doubts about Ross's whereabouts, and anticipation of moving out into the field the next day,

I didn't get much sleep.

The next morning we were filling our canteens from a green portable water tank called a water buffalo when a transport truck stopped to take us to the helicopter pad. Earlier I'd gone to the orderly room where Houston was scrunched over his typewriter, scrutinizing some form and preparing to type. I asked Houston if he could see if my "uncle," SFC Frank Ross, had processed into the brigade over the past couple of days.

"That's a pretty low item on my priority list, Nickels. I'll try once I have some free time." He didn't look up from the form he was studying. "Right now I've got to get this morning report to battalion by 0900 and it can't have any mistakes, so scram. I'll let you know when you get back from the field."

"Thanks."

"Uh, huh," he said absently. He still hadn't taken his eyes off the paperwork in the typewriter, but I left feeling better. I'd have an answer in a few days. One way or another.

Near the helicopter pad, a series of black buildings advertised themselves as the 18th Surgical Hospital. It was a sobering sight and one I preferred not to think about. Nearby sat three choppers, parked on the pad and ready to go. Not far away lay the blackened remains of the two hit by the shelling the night before. Further out was a large white metal container with glass windows, serving as a makeshift control tower. The soldier inside wearing a headset looked deadly serious, despite the large wooden cartoon cutout mounted on top of the tower of Snoopy grinning manically in his WWI leather helmet and dark aviator goggles.

A Huey helicopter emblazoned with the 101st crest on the nose sat waiting. The door gunner motioned us aboard and said to find seating around the cargo, which consisted of a large red mail sack, cases of stacked C-rations, and crates of ammo buckled down for the ride. Cranston, Deems, and I blundered around a bit before finding a spot to snuggle in. With all the gear we were carrying, it was no easy task. Observing proper chopper protocol, we sat sideways facing the non-existent doors with our weapons pointed down.

The Huey's blades turned as the engine turbines began their whine. The chopper rose six feet before the pilot dipped the nose and hurtled us forward, gathering speed and angling upward. As our speed increased so did the noise level, and the air rushing inside was terrific. I held on to some bolted C-ration belts with my left hand.

Below us rice paddies, small villages, and patches of jungle green with an occasional plateau drifted by. Dirt trails seemed to go nowhere in particular and were intermixed with waterways or ponds. Low hanging morning fog was disappearing from the mountains. The sky was the same lead color as yesterday but without the rain.

"We're at fifteen hundred feet," shouted the door gunner. Dressed in an olive drab flight suit with a green helmet and black visor that obscured his eyes, he provided a running commentary as we flew. "We're flying this high to avoid effective small arms fire from either the VC or the NVA," he said.

"When we arrive, you exit pronto. No fooling around.

We rarely land on the ground. Too much flying debris and rocks screws up the ship. We usually hover a foot or two off the ground. Stand on a skid and jump. If we're taking fire, throw your gear out and jump. Even if it's ten feet, you jump. Don't hesitate."

Deems and Cranston looked at him with huge eyes. I probably looked the same.

"No report presently of local contact so most likely you guys are in luck. We'll try to settle the skids on the ground. There were casualties earlier and you need to get off ASAP so the injured can get back to Evans." Cocking his helmeted head to the side, he looked us over. "Got that?"

We nodded.

The flight, like most of those to come, was quick. Ten minutes from Evans and there we were, hovering over our LZ and descending. It dawned on me this was a manhood test for me. I wanted to find Ross, but realized for the first time I wanted to pass this exam as well. Crazy? Yes. Yet what I was feeling was real. I didn't want to be a chickenshit again.

The LZ was a small clearing about the length of a football field and surrounded by trees. I saw men on the perimeter with another bunch clustered to one side crouched down protectively over several bodies as the chopper began its descent. The turbulence kicked up by the blades sent loose leaves, dirt, and dropped tree limbs blowing over the people on the ground, forcing them to hunch over and turn away.

"Go! Go! Go!" shouted the door gunner.

No more urging was needed. Men passing us on the

ground carried two wounded. A white bandage covered the left side of one soldier's face. His pants were shredded with little black pieces of metal, dirt, and blood mixed together. The other casualty was slung in a rubber poncho carried by four men holding the edges. Unconscious, his head and an arm flopped along at an awkward angle as he was sped by. A medic spoke to the door gunner before running back to the side where we were crouched low watching the scene.

As the chopper rose, he looked us over, nodded, and said, "Welcome to Injun Country, guys. Come with me."

15

Our platoon leader, First Lieutenant Jack Collins, was reading a copy of the *Army Times* when we were introduced. Pulling out a small cherry cigar with a plastic tip, he lit up and said, "This is I Corps. When Ho Chi Minh farts, we smell it; we're that close to the NVA. Remember that."

Stated with a definite southern drawl, we'd later find out he was a Georgia boy and product of the Army ROTC program at Georgia Tech. A small man, at about five six and 135 pounds, Collins wore black plastic-rimmed glasses attached to a rubber band around his head, ensuring they stayed on at all times. Made him look more a bookworm than a warrior. This was our fearless leader? Despite my doubts, I took note of a Combat Infantry Badge and jump wings on his fatigues. Maybe L-T, as we came to refer to him, had something, despite my misgivings.

A sergeant first class, SFC James Strode, was our platoon sergeant. Tall, bald, black, in his early forties. Sitting on a tree stump eating a can of peaches with a white plastic spoon seemed to interest him more than us. The sight of the three of us with our crisp starched fatigues and new boots garnered a grunted hello and instruction to the medic to give us to the second squad.

Our squad leader, Staff Sergeant (SSG) Charles Knight, introduced us to several guys sitting in a large shell crater eating their breakfast from C-rations. Barely glancing in our direction, their only greeting was a string of profane comments on the tastelessness of the canned eggs and ham available.

"Got any pound cake or fruit cocktail with you?" asked a lanky white PFC with a confederate flag bicep tattoo. "Any Tabasco sauce?" When we said no, it was like we didn't exist. We felt like the ugly girls at a party.

"Look, don't take it personally," said our medic guide. "They don't know you yet. You might make a stupid mistake tomorrow and get yourself killed. It's going to be a few weeks before you're worth their time. Right now you're just newbies, cherries, FNGs—which is short for fucking new guys—or whatever label they put on you."

Sergeant Knight indicated a spot to dump our gear and gave us our first chore. Cranston got to dig a shit hole for the platoon, Deems was assigned to guard duty, and Knight told me to go with the medic.

The medic's name was Harold Lee, but he said to call him Doc. "Every platoon has a medic, and they all have that same nickname," he said. Medics (Doc) and radio operators (Horn) were the nickname exceptions. Everyone else had a distinctive name, Lee explained. "You use their nickname or rank rather than given names out here. At first it'll seem strange, but you'll get used to it."

I asked what mine was going to be.

He grinned and said, "That's up to your squad. They decide. Might give you one right away or wait a few days. Just depends. You don't get to choose your own."

We stopped at a row of five black rubber body bags.

I'd seen a dead body only once before, at the open casket funeral of Mike Burgess's dad. Mike was a classmate of mine. His dad was our scout cubmaster in elementary school. I sat in the church and stared at him in that open casket for a long time. His body was so lifelike I was half convinced he'd sit up and start talking.

Pulling back the zipper on a body bag, Doc revealed a man's face. It was a chalky white mask. No doubt he was dead.

Seeing my shock, Doc said "The chalk color is due to the loss of blood."

In the next bag, the guy was shot in the throat and his dead eyes stared at the sky. He was smiling.

"I know, I know," said Doc. "You want to know what the hell causes a dead man to smile. It's not some spooky shit. Just the facial muscles tightening up after death."

Bile rose up my throat. I walked three steps to the side and vomited. Oblivious to me, Doc kept chattering on about this guy, that guy, and what to expect.

As he talked, he removed the dog tags from each man. Putting one in his own pocket for delivery to Lt. Collins, he gave the second one to me. "Watch me. Take the tip of a bootlace from each man's boot, run it through the round hole of his dog tag like this, and tie a knot on it onto the boot of the dead man." he said.

He looked up to see if I understood. I nodded.

Grunting an acknowledgement, Doc said, "This identifies the body for the graves registration unit."

I didn't see the soldiers in the last three bags. I was too busy puking to finish. Weak and embarrassed, I shivered despite the morning heat. Done, I helped move the bodies to a chopper waiting in the landing area. I could do that, since the bags were sealed.

Moving the first two went well enough. The third bag sloshed with every step, but there were no leaks. The fourth went okay, but the fifth moaned. Scared the hell out of me. I heard it clear as day.

"He's alive!" I yelled, dropping the bag to the ground.

"No, he's not," Doc said placing his hand on my shoulder. "That's a moan caused by the body being moved. It's air trapped in his lungs and throat coming out. It happens sometimes. You get used to it."

Shaking my head, I thought, *No, I'll never get used to this*. At least I hoped not.

Joining back up with Cranston and Deems, we were tasked with moving the deposited chopper supplies out to the squads. When finished, we each opened a beanie weenie C-ration and ate it cold.

With grub in me, I felt better about being there. I'd left a pack of Marlboros in my locker back at Evans, but inside my ration was a four-cig pack of non-filter Camels. Taking out my Zippo, I lit up. Ordinarily I didn't smoke but if there was ever a time it was now. It helped settle my nerves.

I reminded myself why I'd come this far. There were bound to be more ups and downs in the future. I needed to keep things in perspective. Find Ross and make him pay. That was the goal. No more, no less.

We got our nicknames that night. Cranston was dubbed "Big Red" for his six foot three inch height and red hair. Since me and Deems arrived together we were christened

"Nickels and Dimes." The guys thought that funny for some reason. It was ironic my assumed name was now my nickname as well.

"It could have been worse," said Deems. "I was sorta convinced I was going to be named 'Four Eyes' because of my glasses."

Doc started us on our malaria regimen: a daily small white pill and a weekly large orange pill each Monday. "Look guys, this is important. You don't want to catch this if you can help it. Malaria kills out here. If you take your pills there's no guarantee you won't catch it anyway, but your odds are good. Don't put it off."

As he was leaving, he turned back, reached in another pouch and said, "Oh, yeah. Take these iodine tablets, too. Put them in your canteen and let it sit for at least a half hour before drinking the water around here. It'll make it taste chalky, but it's a lot safer than the alternative. You don't want the runs out here if you can avoid it."

Big Red stared at the malaria pill. "What if I don't take it so I can get out of all this luxury?" he said, while sweeping his arm to encompass our grim surroundings.

Doc stared at him for a second and then smiled. "Well, besides the fact that you'll get deathly ill, you'll also be on the shit list with our platoon sergeant. Strode hates guys who get malaria. Thinks they're all malingerers. If you don't die and return to us...whoo boy. So be a good soldier and take your pills." He stood there while we swigged them down.

We got ready to move out so we could find a good night defensive position (NDP) before dark. First squad led the way. We, the newbies in second squad, brought up the rear so we could acclimate to how things were done on a patrol.

Spaced in line at five yard intervals, we walked scanning the area for VC along the dirt trail. Somewhere up ahead lay a village, but we were separated from it by a six-foot tall, dense thicket of elephant grass.

Took a good while for us to navigate through, but eventually we came upon a tiny graveyard outside the village. There were old tombstones with Buddhist symbols and some with Christian markings. Our squad was ordered to build foxholes next to the dead as our NDP for the night.

Leaning against the musty earthen wall of the hole I was sharing with Dimes, I tried my best not to slap the mosquitos swarming around my face and slathered on some more bug juice. It didn't do much good.

Above us, the clouds cleared and we watched the stars. An hour later, the clouds returned and the darkness was complete. The air was oppressive. Later the night turned cold, and I huddled with my rucksack to trap some body heat. I'd thought Vietnam would always be hot.

I was lonely, afraid, and wanted to cry. But men don't do that. No way I could do that with Dimes a foot away. Besides, I had my behavior at Carlsbad to make up for.

That night, after my mandatory two-hour guard shift was over, I had a dream. The family was on the upper observation deck of the *Lady of the Lake*, a ferry used to take tourists and hikers from Lake Chelan to the village of Stehekin in Washington state. During the four-hour journey, we hit an iceberg. I knew there were no icebergs in Washington, but it seemed logical as the ship pitched slightly to the left. I felt the hairs on the back of my neck and arms rise in alarm. Water seeped in slowly at first before becoming a torrent. Running downstairs, I was a few steps behind and lost sight of the three of them. I got to the lower deck as the ship began to sink. A lifeboat with oars was on my left. I got in while desperately scanning for Susie and the folks. A few seconds later the ship was gone, disappearing under the water without a trace. A low-hanging white fog rose out of the water and came toward me. I tried to row away as it kept up a steady advance. Finally, exhausted, I couldn't row anymore and it engulfed me. But instead of being enveloped in a white blanket, all was black. The darkness was total.

And somewhere far, far away, I heard someone whistling.

16

April 29, 1945
8:00 a.m.
Outside Munich, Germany

He had a soft spot for Munich. There was the park at Nymphenburg with rococo buildings and a formal garden, and the white sausage served with sweet mustard along with freshly baked pretzels and beer. It was also the Home of the Movement. To an SS man, it was one of the holy grails of Germany. Arriving on the train a month earlier, it had been a shock to see the devastation caused by the Allied air raids. The last time he was here was the summer of 1943 when he joined the military after turning eighteen. The city was bustling with life, and Germany ruled Europe. Now the historic Old City was smashed to pieces and had ceased to exist. The rest of the town was a gutted corpse of its former self. He could barely look at it.

Sent to the military hospital eleven miles outside of the city, he considered himself fortunate. The clinic was antiseptic and well stocked with medicine. The food was good, showers hot, beds firm, and sheets clean. Here he didn't have to face the reality of the coming catastrophe. Instead he'd recover from his wounds in a quiet village that had escaped the bombing in Munich. The town's small shops, churches with steeples, picturesque river, immaculately groomed flower beds, and trees were all untouched by the reality of war. The town had existed for a thousand years and made a lie of the imminent demise of Germany.

It was called Dachau.

Another benefit to recuperating at this particular hospital was its location in the SS training camp where his brother had been posted six months earlier. They were able to see each other daily after a two-year absence. They had no other relatives now except each other. The only family that existed for the past five years, an aunt and an uncle, died last October in a bombing raid on Potsdam.

Like everyone else at the Reserve Company Waffen SS Hospital, he was sent here after being wounded on the Russian Front. Actually, that was no longer true. There had been no Russian Front for months now. There was only an Eastern Front on German soil. The Russians were in Berlin, where the Führer continued to promise a final victory over the communist hordes in radio broadcasts from the capital. Every man in the hospital knew better. Even the true believers conceded the war was lost. The Americans were coming from the Western Front and due sometime today according to scouting reports brought to the hospital. Better the Amis than the Russians.

Hobbling over to the wall locker by his bed, he picked through his few belongings. A russian war-prize pistol, a Karl May novel on the American West from school, and several family photos. Despite an uncertain future, he found himself whistling. An old folk tune from the mountains, it was one his father had taught him as a child.

It always made him happy.

He examined a picture of a middle-aged couple on a park bench, smiling into the camera. His parents died in a car accident a month after the fall of France in June 1940, not before learning their oldest son Heinrich Wicker had earned the Iron Cross First Class.

Frank Wicker admired his older brother. They were close despite the four-year age difference. When Heinrich joined the SS in the fall of 1939 at the start of the war, he knew his little brother would follow him when he finished school. The SS were the elite shock troops of the Third Reich and it was an honor to enlist in the Black Corps.

Heinrich came by every day to check on him in the hospital. He appreciated it but found it unnecessary. He was walking again and going to therapy every day to regain full mobility in his battered arm and leg. Progress was slow at first, but he'd improved rapidly in the past two weeks. For several days now the cane he'd used was purposefully left behind during his daily exercises, despite the pain.

A bustling in the hallway signaled someone coming down the hall. Obviously an officer, given the clicking of heels and shouts of "Heil Hitler!" echoing in the corridor. The door opened and there stood Heinrich. Rather, SS Untersturmführer Heinrich Wicker.

His brother was a handsome giant at six feet four inches. Blond hair and blue eyes. Perfect teeth. On his tunic he wore an Iron Cross, a Infantry Close Combat Badge and wound ribbon. The wound cut him down to a lung and a half, but he was given an officer's commission and sent to an administrative post here last year after his recovery. He'd never command men in combat again, but was still the Germanic ideal, if no longer one hundred percent physically fit. Yet Heinrich's sense of humor was still intact. As usual when they met, he teased Frank.

"Ah, little brother, you are still waiting on that growth spurt, I see." Frank was both younger and stood a mere six feet one inch tall. Turning serious, Heinrich walked to the window of the second-story room, clasped his hands behind his back, and gazed out.

The window overlooked a high stone wall twenty yards away, separating the military hospital from the concentration camp beyond. The wall also served as the outer section of an empty coal yard on the camp side.

Dachau Concentration Camp was adjacent to the huge Dachau Military SS Training Barracks and grounds but separated by a small canal. The two installations were staffed by different units and did not socialize or mix. The training barracks were staffed by Waffen SS, the true elite military shock troops used in the toughest battles of the war. Concentration camps were staffed by SS Totenkopf, the Death's Head guards drafted or volunteered into such duties. Some were failed military men demoted to such a life. What happened in the camp was a mystery, and it was prudent not to inquire. Given the low quality of the camp personnel, it would not be a pleasant place. Of that he was certain.

Heinrich said nothing for a full minute, merely staring out the window. Finally he pivoted and announced, "Frank, I've been delegated to surrender the camp to the Amis when they arrive."

"Heinrich, how can that be? You're probably the most junior officer on staff, a lieutenant. Where are your superiors?"

"Our beloved leaders have all departed. Most left last night. Some of the swine even left their wives and family behind so as to better make their escape." He pulled out his ceremonial dress dagger from his belt, examining it. Inscribed on it were four words, found on every SS man's dagger. My Honor Is Loyalty. The motto of an SS man.

"My honor is loyalty, my ass," said Heinrich. His lips compressed in a thin line of contempt.

"The rats are leaving the sinking ship?"

"Yes. I'll meet the victors soon. We expect them around noon. I ordered white flags posted on all seven guard towers as of seven this morning. Reports are it will either be the American 42nd Division or the American 45th." He sheathed the dagger and hesitated. "There are some things you need to know. Matters may get...complicated."

"What do you mean?"

"Do you know what kind of camp Dachau is, exactly?"

"Well, a work camp. They also execute prisoners sometimes on the firing range back behind the tree line. There were shots until about a week ago." He knew little about what lay beyond the hospital. It never occurred to him to ask.

"Brother, you're only a corporal, not privy to things I'm going to tell you. Sit and listen."

Heinrich outlined in great detail what he learned as an invalid officer in the SS training barracks office over the past few months. Although the Waffen SS did not mingle with camp guard personnel, word got around. There were two types of camps: concentration work camps and extermination death camps. Dachau was a designated work camp. That meant inmates could be paroled and not sent to deliberately die like the ones who were gassed at Treblinka or Auschwitz in Poland.

Many did die at Dachau but not as a matter of policy. Instead they died from forced labor, disease, and even some military medical experiments. But there were no gas chambers in use at the camp.

"How many deaths are we talking about, Heinrich? Hundreds? A thousand?"

"According to the records I saw last night, approximately thirty-two thousand deaths. Inmates did hard physical labor under inhumane conditions and cruel treatment."

Frank and Heinrich had seen death in large doses for the past few years on the Eastern Front. Yet the idea of such a large number of civilian dead behind a barbed wire fence in the Fatherland was hard to grasp.

"Were there that many traitors in Germany?"

"Apparently the government thought so," said Heinrich.

"Brother, if the camp system is as large as you are saying and the deaths are even close to the same across Germany, then the Allies must have already liberated some of these camps. They know what's been going on in them. You must not assume responsibility for this. Don't go."

Heinrich smiled and patted him on the shoulder reassuringly. "Frank, if these were Russians I'd share your concern for my safety. You and I both know what they do to SS men. But these are Americans. They are civilized. Besides, you and I speak fairly good English, unlike others of our companions. It's the camp guards who will be held responsible for this mess. They're not military like us in the Waffen SS."

"Heinrich, I fear you're drawing too fine a line here. The Americans might not accept that distinction. They will see the same uniform, and the difference may escape their notice. We in Germany are supposed to be civilized also. But based on what you have just told me, look at what our own country did. How can you expect Americans to be better? Don't go."

His brother shook his head firmly. "I was left behind as the senior in command. I have no choice. It is a matter of duty. A matter of honor."

Frank knew the matter was settled.

17

January 1970
Lowlands, Vietnam

The large feces from the water buffalo thirty feet to my left floated by me in a clockwise swirling pattern. Not that I could do anything about it. I'd learned over the past few days that rice paddies were like that. The water was filthy, stagnant and heavy with mosquito larvae. It stank and when you reached solid ground again at the end of your trek, you had to check yourself for leeches.

There were only two good things about a rice paddy. One was that the water level was usually only knee deep. The other was it didn't go on forever. Eventually, you hit a dike and got to climb out of the stinking, boggy mess.

We were on patrol five kilometers outside the village where we were assigned. In the lowlands rice country you could use the trails on top of the rice dikes, cutting through the foliage around the dikes or, if the foliage was too thick, walk straight across the paddy and climb the dike to get back to land. The trails were the natural place for booby traps or ambush, so you often opted for a paddy trek, the advantage being you didn't have to worry about booby traps since the local farmers had to plod through the muck themselves, day after day.

There was a pattern to our patrols. We got up when

the sun hit the horizon, ate, and helped each other on with our packs. The typical weight was ninety pounds, so you needed the help. Placing your rucksack on the ground, you tilted it up and squatted in front of it while slipping your arms through the straps. Leaning forward to take the weight off your shoulders, you steadied your feet under you and grunted as a friend helped pull you up. After adjusting your straps, you were ready.

Carrying it the first kilometer was the worst. I wondered if I could do it. Did I have what it takes? Was I in shape? Could I handle the heat? Would those guys believe I was a real soldier? Could I endure it for the weeks or months needed to find Ross and not go insane in the meantime? My mind raced with uncomfortable feelings and my body was weighed down by the pack and the heat of the day.

All I could do was keep putting one foot in front of another. Left foot, right foot, left, right, left, right. It got monotonous. I was in real pain. I wanted to stop and quit at least a dozen times a day. But I kept walking. My mind wandered. There were long periods of silence. The sun beat down and my body screamed from head to toe. I'd get a second wind and soldier on.

Several FNGs couldn't keep up and fell by the wayside as stragglers. No one stopped to help. Here, you were on your own. It reminded me a little of football practice in August. A lot of guys quit the team during the first week when they realized how hard it was going to be. I resolved not to be one of those here. I didn't want to disappoint Strode any more than I'd wanted to disappoint Coach Diller last fall.

I did notice one thing on our daily patrols. Vietnam was green. Bright, shocking green. I mean tourist picture green. Like something out of a National Geographic magazine. It had monkeys, beautiful parrots, and elephants (although we never got close to them despite seeing several). Sergeant Knight said there were tigers up in the mountains. He saw tracks but told us they avoided contact with man.

At the end of a long day, we were back walking through the village before setting up an NDP for the night. Local kids surrounded us as we trekked. The small ones brazenly put their hands in our pockets and took anything there. If there was nothing to take, they'd sometimes shout Vietnamese cuss words and hit us with their tiny fists. The older ones tried to sell us bottled Cokes.

When we finally stopped, I was totally spent. My socks were soaked in sweat, and my feet were dotted with blisters. My shoulders, collarbone, and waist were rubbed raw from my rucksack straps. I had a throbbing headache from the hot air trapped inside my steel helmet.

Time for supper. Damn it. My rations were at the bottom of my pack. I punched it and swore. I'd have to unpack my entire kit to get to my food and then repack everything again.

Dimes sat silently, waiting for me to be over my fit. After beating my pack I crumpled to the ground, even more exhausted than before. Yet somehow I felt peaceful. My anger leaked out of me like the air from a pinhole in a balloon.

The next day I packed my rations properly. Other than that, the day was a repeat of the whole thing, all over again.

And the next day. And the next.

The pattern was set.

***

There are two theories about the point man, the first man in line in an infantry patrol. One, it's a good thing. A smart enemy allows the first man, and perhaps the second, to continue past them unharmed. This allows the bulk of the patrol to be shot in an ambush. You give up one or two to get the rest in your attack. This view holds that point is actually the safest place to be. Because of this you'll get people who volunteer to take point.

The second view is it's the most dangerous spot on a patrol. You're asking for trouble. (That's why only point gets to have his M-16 in the firing position on full auto and not on safety like the rest of us.) First contact is often unintentional, a surprise. The enemy shoots at the first person he sees and forgets about the ambush stuff. And there's the issue of stepping on a mine, snake, or booby trap when you're the first in line. Plus lucky you get to clear a path through a jungle of elephant grass, bamboo, and dense foliage so the rest of the patrol can follow.

Ninety percent of infantrymen believe point is the most dangerous spot in the line. That was my view as well. I decided I wasn't going to volunteer for anything, much less point man. That didn't mean I wouldn't get volunteered. Everyone had to take their turn unless we had someone who was of the ten percent persuasion.

"Nickels, get your sorry ass over here," said Strode. "Do you have a machete?"

"No, Sergeant."

"Well, Knight will get you one. You're point today."

"Yes, Sergeant."

What else could I say? Strode scared me a little. He never smiled. He was always squared away both militarily and gear-wise, like you expected in a professional soldier. At the same time, he wasn't prissy about us being inspection-ready and trying to impress the brass.

Two things pissed him off. The first was if he thought you were being a pussy and letting down the platoon. The second was getting malaria. He thought it was a deliberate ploy to avoid the field.

I already knew the first item was true. I saw it happen a week after I arrived. A hippy-type newbie replacement showed up in first squad—peace symbols and all. Strode was a typical lifer, but he'd cut you some slack in the field if you did your job. This new guy did not do his job. He confessed after the platoon made contact with the VC that he'd deliberately shot over the head of the enemy so as not to kill them. Strode stood there listening. Then he requested the private's M-16, grenades, and knife, and walked away.

The guy smirked and probably thought he'd be sent back to Evans and relative safety as an assistant cook or something. Well, he got it half right. Over the next several days he didn't have to shoot at anyone, but he wasn't sent back to Evans either.

As the hours passed, it dawned on him that without a

weapon he was basically defenseless. After giving him the nickname Superman, everyone else in the platoon ignored him. If he wasn't going to protect them, why should they protect him? The next day he went to Strode and asked for his weapon back. Strode refused. A day later he asked again. Strode still refused.

Superman went to the L-T. The L-T said he would take care of it but nothing happened. He went to the company commander and made the same request for his weapon back. The captain said he would look into it. Again nothing happened. Three days went by. He had no weapon and was a pariah. In tears, he went to Strode, pleading for his weapon. Strode gave it back. Nothing was said, but I was glad Superman wasn't in our squad.

We'd set out early that morning to beat the heat. Dimes was behind me in the slack position—the second man in line providing rifle cover for point and keeping your compass direction. Usually the third guy was the squad leader but, for whatever reason, Sergeant Knight was way back in line. Then came bad news. We were heading into bamboo.

Bamboo is bad stuff for infantrymen. Its shoots and leaves are food for the elephants, which were almost all gone from our area of operations by now. So the bamboo easily grows up to ten feet. It's thick enough you can't see anything beyond it, and it has sharp edges. Keeping your sleeves pulled down, you try not to get too sliced up as you chop your way through. A bamboo spine can easily puncture your hand, and it can hide snakes like the brown Bamboo Viper, commonly known as the Two Step. You get bit, take two steps, and die. Lots of fun.

I took out the machete Knight had gotten me and started hacking. My head was on a constant swivel looking for VC or snakes. In a few minutes I was exhausted. My arm felt like rubber. Sweat was rolling into my eyes, and I could taste the salt of it in my mouth. I took off my neck towel and used it to sop my face. It did little good. I had gone maybe ten yards and was lucky to get that distance.

I knew I was in trouble. If my good arm was turning to rubber, how reliable was my left going to be? I tried that arm next, but as the minutes ticked by I increased the distance by only another five yards.

Dimes hissed at me. "Hey, Knight says to get a move on; everyone's waiting."

"Well, they can damn well wait," I said. "I'm doing the best I can." A few minutes later we'd moved ahead only a few more steps. I was totally spent. It was so damn *thick.* Dimes came up and looked at the bamboo and then me. It was clear the machete and I were no longer friends. I could barely grip it, much less actually use it. At this rate we were not going anywhere. I dreaded saying that to Knight and later have it get back to Strode.

Dimes had the same fear. We were both cherries and didn't want to screw up.

"Listen, let's try this. Take off your backpack."

I looked at him quizzically but did what he said.

"Hold it in front of you," he said. "Now fall forward."

I held it to my chest, tucked in my chin. lowered my helmet to cover my eyes, and fell forward. Whoof! My body mass cleared a space of about six feet. There was some grass left over in clumps about a foot high. I stomped on that and we had a nice clearing. That took about twenty seconds, total.

It was a stupid way to get through a bamboo forest, but an enemy on the other side could hear me chopping as much as my grunting when I hit the ground. For the next couple of hours I repeated this maneuver until we got through to the plains. Doing it almost killed me. By the end I was seeing black spots and stumbling everywhere. But we made it.

Dimes never told anyone what I did, and I didn't volunteer the information. Knight later issued some rules for us in the field. One of them was: If something stupid works in the jungle, it isn't stupid. When I heard that, I knew exactly what he was talking about.

***

For three weeks things had been going pretty well. Then I messed up. Big time.

We'd established our night defensive position and I pulled the 0200 to 0400 hours guard duty shift. That's the worst. You're halfway through your sleep cycle, and you have to get up to do guard duty and then try to go back to sleep for a couple of hours.

I was groggy when they woke me, but managed to stay awake. I did it by thinking of the best wet dreams I could remember. Anything else led to sleep. I tried to avoid thinking of Ross. If I did, I would think of my family, and that was still too raw. Most of the time I blocked thinking about them by trying to keep busy. I was so successful it scared me sometimes. Were they that forgettable?

I swept my gaze back and forth in the dark in the 180-degree arc as we were taught. I could see nothing. It was pretty boring. So boring, I soon forgot all about Rita Human and fell asleep.

Something hit me on the head. My helmet flew off. The next thing I knew I was pinned to the ground. A forearm across my neck crushed my Adam's apple. I struggled then felt the point of a knife just below my right eye socket.

I stopped resisting.

"You really are a stupid son of a bitch. Hope you enjoyed your nap because everyone here could be dead. They trusted you, Nickels. They could be yesterday's news thanks to you, you idiot."

I couldn't make out the face in the dark but recognized the voice. It was Strode.

He got off of me. "Get your sorry ass up."

I was mortified. *Didn't they hang you if you slept on guard duty?* I wasn't quite sure.

"Sarge, I'm sor—"

"Shut the fuck up, Nickels. I don't want to hear it. I don't give a tinker's damn you're sorry. Neither will any man here. Get back to your hole."

I slunk back to my foxhole. I was furious, but it was my own fault. I'd made the ultimate mistake and could have got everyone killed. I was exactly where I didn't want to be: on Strode's shit list.

I had no one to blame except myself.

18

April 29, 1945
2:00 p.m.
SS Reserve Company Hospital
Dachau, Germany

Heinrich had said the Americans were expected around noon. Yet there was no word since he'd departed for the main gate at eleven with a medic dressed in a white surgical gown and carrying a large Red Cross flag. Occasional battle noises came from different directions, but it was difficult to tell from whom or exactly from where.

In the meantime, the hospital staff was organizing for a surrender and possible evacuation. The head of the hospital, Dr. Schröder, a white-haired middle-aged man with silver rimmed spectacles, led several medics through all the rooms to ensure that each occupant was ready to travel and had no weapons.

"Now is not the time or place for that," he said.

From the front of the hospital, a single gunshot echoed down the halls. It was from the luger of a legless SS major who shot himself rather than surrender. How he got a weapon, no one knew. The shot went off as Americans moved toward the hospital in battle formation. A volunteer went out the front door brandishing a white bed sheet with his good right arm. Since his left sleeve was empty, it was clear he posed no threat.

Dr. Schröder followed him and announced, "This is an unarmed hospital. We are prepared to surrender."

Two Americans approached. The first hit the one-armed man squarely in the face with his rifle butt. The man went down and did not stir. The other American hit Dr. Schröder with his submachine gun on top of his skull, breaking his glasses in half.

More Americans appeared in front of the building. An American officer came forward and demanded in a loud voice that everyone evacuate the hospital immediately. Based on what they witnessed, the occupants hurried to comply.

Patients who were crippled but could walk were separated from those who needed ambulatory help. Frank found himself in the first group and was being led away when he noticed the medic who had set out with his brother. The medic was talking to an American sergeant who spoke fluent German.

"Have you seen my brother?" Frank asked.

"Ja, the Untersturmführer surrendered the installation to the 42nd Division general. He was turned over to some men of the 45th Division and taken to the rail yard on the other end of the camp."

"Why? What would they want with him there?"

"Damned if I know."

The American sergeant listening to this took out a pack of Chesterfields and offered a cigarette to the medic, who took it happily. The sergeant didn't offer one to Frank after taking in his SS uniform. Indeed, the look the American gave him filled Frank with foreboding. He was grateful the marching column he was in didn't allow him to linger. He felt the American sergeant's eyes drilling into his back as he was marched away.

He was in a line of fifty men guarded by U.S. Army infantrymen wearing a squared bird insignia on their shoulder. They led the patients through the west side of the camp toward the railway. Freed camp prisoners were everywhere. Some wore the traditional blue and white striped prison uniforms. Most were in civilian clothes with an X sewn on the back so if they escaped they could be identified by the local authorities.

Frank watched three SS guards being deliberately shot in the legs to prevent them from escaping. Prisoners leisurely tore them limb from limb with a loaned bayonet from a watching American private. The screaming was horrible and echoed among the buildings as each limb was detached. Frank shuddered. The cheers from the group of prisoners were truly terrifying. One grasped the severed head of an SS guard and kicked it like a football, over and over. Another cut off the finger of a guard to get his ring.

Other prisoners ran around, happily waving bottles of wine looted from a nearby warehouse. A few prisoners had somehow acquired guns and wandered aimlessly. The SS patients' column passed the scattered bodies of SS camp guards that had, perhaps as a mercy, been shot execution style in the back of the neck.

Arriving at the rail yard, Frank saw a long line of train cars on one track. Some were open cars with no roofs.

Others had the usual side doors pulled open. Groups of American G.I.s looked inside the side doors or stood high up on the sides of the open cars peering down. Their faces were grim. Mounds of dead bodies lay on the ground nearby and on the train car floors.

His brother Heinrich stood by an open-sided boxcar, arguing with an American sergeant. They were surrounded by a dozen G.I.s, intent on hearing what was being said. It was clear some of the Americans were emotional and crying.

"I tell you again, Sergeant Butterfield. We are not responsible for the bodies you see in there," said Heinrich.

The American sergeant was having none of it. "That's crap, you SS bastard. Look at those bodies. Where the hell do you think they came from?"

"That's my point exactly, Sergeant. Take a look at both the bodies and the train. The bodies are emaciated. Basically, they starved to death."

"Right. Because that's what you Nazi bastards do."

Heinrich shook his head vigorously. "No, no, no. According to the records, this train was sent here from Buchenwald Camp three weeks ago."

"Shit! Listen to me, you kraut. That's a distance of about two hundred miles. Are you seriously telling me that it took them three weeks to get here?" I could see the men surrounding the two getting restless.

Heinrich walked over to the nearest open car, pointed to it, and said, "That is exactly what I am telling you. Look at the bullet holes your planes strafed into them on the trip."

The sergeant spit on the ground and looked directly at Heinrich. "So let me get this straight. You're saying it's our fault the people in there died. That we're to blame for this death train?" The sergeant almost spat out the words.

There was no mistaking the naked enmity behind the question. Frank knew Heinrich needed to be careful. Very careful.

"What I am trying to say...perhaps badly...is this," said Heinrich. "It appears from the records, mind you—and I want to state again I had nothing to do with this. The Waffen SS is a separate organization from Death's Head guard units, even though the uniforms are similar—it appears the train did indeed take a long roundabout journey. It was strafed, and the inmates inside did not get the rations or care to which they were entitled. You must understand how badly you wrecked the train system here." He stopped and looked the American sergeant in the eye. "So now the question is, what can we do together to help make it better?"

When the shot rang out it came from just outside the circle, and hit Heinrich squarely in the middle of the forehead. He spun around and pitched over into the arms of the American sergeant.

A moment of shocked silence followed. Everyone turned around and saw an American lieutenant holding his M-1 rifle at the ready. "Enough of that horseshit. There's no 'we' here. Put that SS bastard's corpse over there with the others." He motioned to a stack of bodies piled up outside a boxcar fifty feet away.

There was no disagreement among the American

troops. They hauled the body over to the pile, where one of the men grabbed his ankles and another his hands. They lifted him up, swung him side to side twice, and let go with a heave. Heinrich landed with a soft plop on the top of the pile, partially obscuring a naked woman.

19

February 1970
Lowlands, Vietnam

Dragons are real. I know. I saw one.

It happened on patrol along a brown river a few miles from the China Sea. The river smelled of brackish water and the fresh grass lining its banks. The platoon was looking forward to getting back to the local village before dark and setting up our NDP. It had been a long day.

We were on a rise, passing around a bend when someone spotted a group of locals standing at the edge of the riverbank, peering intently into the murky scum covered water. They were chattering away, pointing and ignoring us entirely, even though we were easy enough to see.

"What do you think is going on?" I asked Sergeant Knight.

"Haven't a clue, but someone needs to check it out. Take Dimes and see what's going on."

Dimes was game. We were both curious.

The sight did not disappoint. It was a monster ribbon-like fish of some kind with glittering silver and blue scales. It was still fresh and had apparently died only a few hours earlier after washing ashore. I measured it using my M-16 as a marker. It was close to fifty feet long and two feet wide in the head. What made it a dragon was a red plume running head to tail down the top of its body, along with thick six-foot long, red-and-blue tentacles that looked like whiskers or thin arms trailing from its head. A mouth with rows of sharp teeth completed the sea serpent appearance.

I was surprised the locals weren't cutting it up for food since it was still fresh, but it was clear that was a no-no. We'd been told in the Vietnamese culture class at SERTS that the locals believed dragons were once real and roamed the world before vanishing into the ocean. To them this was proof of their folklore. We had our own sailors' tales of sea serpents. The river was only a few miles from the sea. Could this be one of those? Later we were told it was probably a rare giant oarfish. I preferred, like the locals, to believe it was a dragon.

As time went on, I made a few friends among the other newbies. The old timers still called us newbies, cherries, or FNGs. We preferred newbie but knew enough to keep our mouths shut regardless of what we were called. It wasn't personal.

At mail call a few weeks earlier I noticed guys getting copies of local papers to keep up with their hometown news. I sent ten dollars I won playing Hearts for a subscription to the weekly *Munson Lake Tribune*. I wanted to see what news they had about the Peterson family starting with the January 8 issue. By the time the *Trib* processed my order and got it out to me, I received four back issues at once.

Our story was splashed on the front page of the January 8 edition. FAMILY MISSING was the headline, and there was a family photo I recognized from Dad's office desk.

The gist was we'd mysteriously disappeared somewhere in New Mexico after eating at a Stuckey's. A cashier there remembered us, but not where we were headed or anything else. Dad's plant manager told the police we'd planned to go to Disneyland. A check there confirmed we never arrived. Individuals with information were advised to contact the New Mexico State Police, or leave word with the Munson Lake Police Chief.

The second paper had more of the same but included background on Mom and Dad as locals. Susie and I were featured in a sidebar with our school photos from last year. Coach Diller said some nice things about me as did Mr. Hill, my history teacher. Mr. Alt was understandably silent. There was a much longer list of people saying good things about Susie. That gave my heart a small pang.

The third issue headlined SEARCH CONTINUES on the front page but wasn't the lead article. No bodies and no suspects according to the police.

The last issue continued the story on the front page but the focus was different. FACTORY FACES UNCERTAIN FUTURE was the headline. The emphasis was on what was going to happen to the community if Dad never returned.

I was still considered a victim and not a suspect. The larger lesson was realizing how life goes on despite tragedy. It was a concept I would become familiar with in Vietnam as well.

As March approached I was grateful. Grateful no one in our company was killed or wounded during the past weeks and the enemy was nowhere to be found. We had occasional sightings of a lone Viet Cong here and there.

As a result, we killed a grand total of three VC outside the village during daily patrols.

They died because they blundered into us. I saw no real action since they were killed by other squads than mine. Our squad did little except dive for cover and advance slowly as we heard bursts of AK-47 and M-16 fire. Each time we came forward to assist, I felt fear build in a small knot in my gut. My mouth was dry, and it was hard to swallow. My heart beat loudly. We moved forward only to discover an already dead VC with an AK-47 lying nearby.

In the lowlands, this was commonplace. Contact with the VC was sporadic at best. They came at night to terrorize the villages. We ruled the day unless we were looking to set up a night ambush. When the monsoon season ended, we'd be sent to the mountains where there were no villages. Everyone we encountered there would be NVA (regular North Vietnamese army) and they'd be wearing uniforms, not civilian clothes. There, it was an automatic shoot-to-kill situation and let God sort it out later.

I didn't know if it was God or the Flying Fickle Finger of Fate that helped us get by unscathed over the past weeks. But no injuries or deaths seemed like a good deal to me after hauling body bags. Dimes and Big Red weren't so sure. They didn't consider this real soldiering.

"Might as well be camping out at a Boy Scout Jamboree," Big Red said.

I realized how naïve I was to accept the Hollywood version of war. We hadn't disembarked from the TWA plane into a hail of gunfire. There weren't bullets flying around all the time every day, either. Forget the John Wayne stuff. It made me wonder what other misconceptions I had.

Meanwhile, Houston, our company clerk, was supposed to have tracked down the whereabouts of Ross and let me know his location. But there was nothing. No word at all. No "I'm looking hard" or "He's moved from A to B." It was driving me batty. I thought about sending a letter back on a resupply chopper but nixed that. I was an FNG and he didn't owe me a thing, except for the fact he'd promised. That ought to count for something, I thought. To resolve this, I needed a face to face. For now I had little choice but to wait. It wasn't like I could ask Strode for a couple of days off to pursue Ross, even if I got the location.

Without actual action from the enemy, we patrolled, established defensive positions, and set up ambushes for which no one showed. We ran the same routine most days but altered it at times so we weren't entirely predictable to the enemy.

Still, basically all days were the same. When we walked for hours on end, I found myself daydreaming because no one says a word. You had to fight sometimes to keep yourself from falling asleep as you walked. Sounds silly, but it's true. At first I cursed Ross every day. Now I didn't bother. It wasn't productive. Instead I rejoiced that at least it was flat land. I dreaded going to the mountains once the monsoon season was over. That was going to be a lot harder.

One notable exception to the boredom was my first encounter with the Fuck-You lizard. I'd heard about it. Supposedly, there was a lizard that could utter this phrase in the dark and fool you into thinking it was a person. Turned out to be true. Scared the shit out of me one evening when I heard it as clear as a bell. The lizard was six inches long and puffed itself up and blew air out its gills while taunting you with F-U, F-U. Seemed the ultimate Vietnam joke on the American soldier. After a while you got used to it.

The repetitive days gave me time to acclimate to the combat environment. I was comfortable—or at least used to—sleeping and shitting outdoors, getting eaten by mosquitos, being bitten by ants, having my blood sucked by leeches, and being insulted by lizards. I was used to humping the countryside with ninety pounds of gear in my pack. I was in good shape before, but I was in great shape now. What little baby fat I had when I arrived was gone.

One evening after chow Sergeant Knight told us to be grateful. "You've ticked weeks off your three hundred sixty-five day mandated tour and haven't fired a shot." He rubbed the stubble on his chin. "Thank your lucky stars. You'll face the dragon soon enough, believe me."

"Face the dragon? What's that?" asked Dimes.

"Did any of you read *The Red Badge of Courage* in high school?" He looked around at our group. It was obvious by our silence the answer was no.

"It's about an eighteen-year-old newbie in the Civil War. He's going to face his first real combat the next day and the veterans tell him he'll meet the elephant."

I laughed. "There weren't any elephants in the Civil War." I prided myself on my knowledge of history.

"You're right, Nickels, there weren't. Although there were some camels used by the Army in the 1850s out in Arizona and New Mexico."

That put me in my place.

"*The Red Badge of Courage* is a novel written thirty years after the war. The elephant saying was a real thing men talked about a century ago. A symbol of fierceness, something that could crush you to a bloody pulp, literally and figuratively."

"You mean close combat," said Dimes.

Knight nodded. "Face to face. That was meeting the elephant. That's what they called it. Here we call it facing the dragon."

"The dragon? Why not the elephant? We've got some out here," said a newbie. We all knew that was true. They were rare and avoided men but were undeniably here.

"Things change. Why are you called a grunt? In World War Two you were a G.I. In World War One you were a doughboy. In the Civil War you were a federal."

"Not me, Sarge. I was a reb and proud of it," said Peddler, our newest member. He'd joined us the week before and let everyone know he was from Mississippi.

Knight smiled. "As I was saying...when you get your Vietnam Service Medal it's going to have a dragon on it behind a grove of bamboo."

"So we'll have faced the dragon and survived," I blurted aloud.

He nodded. "So you'll have faced the dragon and survived."

A long silence followed. We were all lost in our own

thoughts about the future.

"Sarge, what happened to the newbie? In the book, I mean?" I was curious.

"He weathers his first contact well. Thinks he's got it all figured out. The next day there's another engagement; he turns and runs for his life. He even puts on a head bandage with some blood on it to fake a wound so people think he has a reason to be in the rear. Eventually he gets over his cowardice and ends up doing what he has to." Knight cleared his throat loudly and looked over each of us. "Each of you will do what you have to do when the time comes. Believe me."

He stated it in such a way I did believe. Tall and rangy, Knight looked like what he was, a Texan. Twenty-three years old, a graduate of the University of Texas draftee, he'd turned down Officer Candidate School because of the mandatory enlistment extension. But he agreed to the infantry school's "Shake and Bake" NCO course to become an instant E-5. He finished at the top of his class and received an automatic promotion to E-6 as a reward. Being a staff sergeant after being in the Army only a year was almost unheard of. When I say that he was a hell of a soldier, I mean just that.

He'd arrived in the division a year earlier, just in time for the Battle of Hamburger Hill. That assault in our future area of operations, known as the A Shau Valley, took on a mystical place in the lore of the company. The word was if you'd been there you'd seen it all. That was the scoop. Most of those veterans were rotating stateside, their yearlong tour completed.

You could tell who those guys were. They wore a wary look and attitude and only spoke to fellow short-timers—guys with less than ninety-nine days remaining in-country, a double-digit midget, hence "short." When bad things happened, they reminded themselves, "I'm so short, I only speak to midgets." I couldn't envision any of us cherries joining their ranks.

Knight didn't talk about Hamburger Hill. It was known he'd received his Silver Star and Purple Heart there. His rep and instincts were so good in combat he'd been nicknamed Prophet. He seemed to be able to sniff the wind and predict things.

While things were calm, he taught us fieldcraft: Put duct tape over the muzzle of your M-16 to keep dirt out of the barrel. Spray a ring of bug juice around you at night to keep the leeches away. If you're bitten by a scorpion, there will be a painful bite but no swelling if you get a quick shot from Doc. Avoid taking major trails with their ambushes and booby traps. Keep your socks dry by putting them against your chest at night. Bury any used ration cans since the VC are able to repurpose them into booby traps to use against you later.

Along with fieldcraft, we were also taught the Combat Laws of the Prophet. Secrets and observations Prophet lived by and wanted us to absorb to stay alive. Our squad reduced them down to ten.

1. If it seems stupid but it works, it's not stupid.
2. Assume all five-second grenade fuses will go off in three.

3. The easiest way will often get you killed.
4. Tracers work both ways.
5. Ammo is cheap; your life isn't. Empty your damn magazine if necessary.
6. A Purple Heart means you probably screwed up and are lucky to be alive.
7. If you're in a fair fight you didn't plan properly.
8. If the enemy is in range, then so are you.
9. If at first you don't succeed, call in an air strike.
10. Never think you are a superhero.

The previous week Prophet had extended his tour for a second year. I saw enough to know he wasn't a fan of the war. Why the extension while his peers were rotating home? I had no idea. He didn't volunteer the reason. He was respected enough that no one asked.

After five weeks in the field, we got word we were going back to Evans for a stand-down, a two- to five-day period of camp life where we could enjoy the goodies of the rear and some relief prior to going out again. We were hyped.

Our chopper extraction from our area of operations that morning went off without a hitch. As the breeze in the chopper rushed over me, I found myself comparing my trip coming out of Evans to going back. Back then I was scared shitless, mostly of the unknown. I was facing the unknown again heading back to Evans. But it was a good unknown. I'd get the location of Ross. I could bring this part of my life to a close. I had learned that unknowns are to be faced more than feared.

20

April 29, 1945
2:00 p.m.
Dachau Camp rail yard
Dachau, Germany

The lieutenant lowered his weapon, turned, and told the sergeant to lead the column back to where our group had come.

"Forget these men unloading bodies from those boxcars. Take them to the wall by the coal yard," he said. The German soldiers were fast-marched there as quickly as hospital wounded could go. On the way, they saw a large guard tower being torched by several freed inmates. Another prisoner was beating a guard to death with a four-foot log. No one intervened.

As they approached the coal yard, Frank recognized the Reserve Company SS hospital with its painted red cross on a white background on the roof. Camp prisoners now looked out from or sat in its rear windows. Some had wine bottles and hats or clothes that didn't fit. One waved a homemade American flag back and forth. Others leaned out his former room window and tossed items onto the ground below. It was clear they had looted the inside of the hospital while celebrating.

In the coal yard Frank was lined up with dozens of others against the ten-foot-high concrete wall. A machine gun was set up thirty yards in front of them. The men along the wall looked at each other bleakly. There was nowhere to go. The fact that they were wounded military—and not the camp guards responsible for all this—did not matter in the end. For all SS men, their time had come.

Frank was afraid many times while in action, but realized he was not afraid now. He was about to die, and this would soon be over. Maybe it was the knowledge that without Heinrich there was no one in the world who would give a damn if he lived or died, anyway. Still, he preferred a fiery Viking death of some kind, all the better to get into Valhalla or whatever lay on the other side. At least he'd die like a soldier, with a bullet, even if as a condemned man. The alternative, a noose administered by a hangman, would be the ultimate insult. He had only one regret. He wished he could avenge his brother.

"We die for Germany," said the SS sergeant to his right as the machine gun cut down the line against the wall. The sergeant fell first, falling backward onto Frank as all went black.

Frank came to sometime after the machine gun ceased firing. The first thing he heard was a single pistol shot and an American voice bellowing, "What the hell are you doing?"

Opening one eye, Frank saw an American lieutenant colonel kicking the machine gunner away from the gun.

The private was crying hysterically. "Sir, they were trying to get away."

The officer called him a coward and ordered him led off. The colonel told a medic standing by the machine gun to tend to any survivors and proceeded on to another part of the camp.

Watching all this unfold, Frank realized blood was smeared over his face and torso. The reddish black liquid was so thick he had trouble forcing his other eye to open. Fearing the worst, he took inventory. He was unharmed. The man on his right had taken the full brunt of several slugs and was bleeding profusely when he fell on Frank. The gore from the dead sergeant was smeared on him, turning him into a bloody but unhurt mess.

Frank saw the approaching medic walking among the moaning survivors. Instead of rendering medical assistance to the wounded as ordered, he threw down razor blade packets, saying "Here, finish yourself."

An American corporal followed the medic administering an execution round in the back of the head for those who declined the blades. Frank's bloody face and torso allowed him to play dead as they went by. Shot after shot rang out until the American officer who stopped the machine gunner earlier returned with Dr. Schröder. The doctor could barely stand from his earlier concussion but managed to drag Frank and several survivors over to the far side of the wall and comparative safety.

Against all odds he was alive.

The coal yard dead were left in the open for the next four days until an American Army Inspector General arrived to review the site and take witness statements. Afterwards Frank and other prisoners were ordered to confiscate any documents and dog tags on the bodies. The Americans demanded the nametags of the dead be removed before they were buried in an unknown mass grave on the night of May 3, 1945. All burial party personnel were sent to different POW camps scattered across Germany. Several men protested this violated the Geneva Convention. They were ignored.

***

Frank escaped the night of the mass burial. It wasn't difficult. No one expected POWs to wander off with the war nearly over. Where was there to go? As an SS man, he was in the automatic arrest category if found. True, he was only a corporal and not a big fish, but he didn't relish being in an Allied prison for years. He had no money, no food, and no relatives to shelter him. But after what he had seen, it was worth the risk to get away.

Four days out, he found a newly freed prisoner, drunk and passed out on a hay pile inside a country barn. He took the man's striped prison uniform and release document, leaving his own clothes in a pile next to the still sleeping drunk. Officially he was now Heinz Michaelis. The next day peace was declared. The war in Europe was over.

21

Company F Area
Camp Evans, Vietnam

L-T announced the stand-down was for three days. We cleaned our weapons and gear. All weapons were then inspected and stored with the ammo in metal conex boxes usually used as shipping containers. Next we put our clothes in garbage bags and donned robes to dump them over at the supply hut. Shredded uniforms were given to the supply sergeant and lost items replaced.

Last was personal hygiene. The showers were hot, and minutes later we were magically clean. Scrubbed up, I went to the orderly room to see Houston. Time to find out where Ross was.

The guy behind Houston's desk was a pimply-faced specialist fourth class wearing thick glasses and looking like a tall, thin, human stick. Houston was nowhere to be seen.

"Houston finished his tour a week ago," said Top.

The new clerk was the specialist and named Andrews. He transferred over from HQ to take Houston's place. I had a sinking feeling in my gut.

"Did Houston leave word for me about the whereabouts of a Sergeant Ross?"

Andrews shook his head. "Nope."

Did Houston forget? Never intended to really look, just said so to get me out of his hair? I had no clue. But I was back to square one. Bitterly disappointed, I decided I'd ask again but this time put some incentive behind it.

"Hey, Andrews. Would you like to make a hundred bucks?"

The thin stick eyed me suspiciously, "What do I have to do?"

"Nothing illegal. See if you can locate someone for me in the division. It's a relative, my Uncle Frank. Frank Ross, a sergeant first class. He's in the 101st somewhere. I want to surprise him."

It was disconcerting how easily the lie rolled off my tongue.

"For that I get a hundred bucks?" he said in a doubtful tone.

"Yep. As soon as we get paid." I didn't know how much I'd get on payday but figured it would be more than a hundred bucks. As of now I had some cash from playing Twenty-One and Crazy Eights during down time in the jungle. It was one way to make the hours go by.

"Payday is tomorrow, Nickels. You got a deal. I want fifty tomorrow and the other fifty when I find him for you."

We sealed the deal with a handshake.

"Oh, by the way, this is for you," said Andrews. He handed me a sheet of paper. It was an order granting me a Combat Infantryman Badge. It wasn't why I was in Vietnam but I had to admit it made me feel good. I knew I'd have my CIB patch sewn on all my shirts ASAP.

Coming out of the orderly room, it was time to unwind. Time to try to forget how depressed I felt by Houston letting me down. I headed to the Enlisted Men's Club.

Ordinarily I don't drink. Once, while Steve Gorwood was over at my house, I snuck some vodka and Puerto Rican 151- proof rum out of the liquor cabinet while the folks were with Susie at the movies. We got blitzed even though the taste was awful. Gorwood staggered back to his house, and I crashed in my bedroom. The next day I had a blinding headache and an aversion to food. I told Mom I wasn't feeling well and needed to rest instead of eat. Which was true.

I not only didn't like the taste of hard liquor, but more importantly, hated the loss of control. In a situation where I was impersonating someone, the least smart thing to do would be cut loose. At that moment, though, I didn't care. I told myself I'd avoid the hard stuff, order a Schlitz, and drink beer like everyone else.

At the club, someone from the company started singing a song and others joined in. The songs got louder and louder and several tables of REMFs, rear echelon mother fuckers, were clearly irritated. They were the guys who stayed in camp working supply, food, clerical duties, and the like while the real fighting took place elsewhere. With the exception of a couple of rockets logged into Evans, they might as well have been living back in the States. That, plus everyone in country getting the same combat pay regardless of location or job, meant there was little love lost between line infantry and them.

One large private came over to the table next to us and asked them to quiet down. The entire table leaped up as a group and got toe to toe with the man and in his face. The

REMF backed off, slinking back to his group where they were all scowling and tense.

This didn't go unnoticed among the rest of the company. Dimes stood and went to the center of the room. He proceeded to call out a cadence song in a loud voice. It sounded like the word of God. We all stood as one and began to return each individual line of his lyrics loudly, lustily, and defiantly, daring the REMFs to interrupt. If they so much as uttered a sound, all hell was going to break loose.

C-130 rolling down the strip,
Airborne daddy gonna take a little trip.
Stand up, hook up, shuffle to the door,
Jump right out and count to four,
My main won't open gonna use my reserve,
My reserve don't open I'll lose my nerve.
But I'm Airborne (Airborne), all right (all right),
I can ride (I can ride), I can fly (I can fly),
All day (all day), gotta go (gotta go).
One mile (one mile), easy run (easy run),
Two miles (two miles), so good (so good),
Three miles (three miles), gotta run (to the sun),
Four miles (four miles), gotta be (in the shade),
Five miles (five miles), gotta be (Airborne),
Six miles (six miles), motivated (dedicated),
Seven miles (seven miles), gotta run (gotta run),
Eight miles (eight miles), fired up (fired up),
Nine miles (nine miles), feeling good (feeling good),
Ten miles (ten miles), looking good (looking good),
Silver wings upon my chest (silver wings upon my

chest),
I can run all day (I can run all day),
I can drink all night (I can drink all night),
Feeling fine (feeling fine), drinking wine (drinking wine),
Good times (good times), feeling good (feeling good),
Fired up (fired up), Airborne! (Airborne!) ,
Airborne! (Airborne!)

Finishing, we looked around expectantly. There was total silence. You could hear a pin drop. Then, slowly, conversations began again and requests for refills filled the air. That night we ruled the EM Club and no one challenged our control.

I was feeling damn good sitting between Dimes and Big Red, shooting the breeze at our table. They smiled at me for awhile then got bored with my drunken babbling. I upped the ante and began cursing both Ross and being in Vietnam. If anyone could appreciate my situation, they could, right?

Suddenly they were quiet and looking at me strangely. The next thing I knew I must have passed out.

I awoke the next morning on my cot in the barracks. I felt the heat of the sun outside and the taste of sour sweat trickling from my face into my mouth. A peek through half-opened eyes revealed I was alone and lying on wet sheets. I didn't know if it was from body sweat or if I'd wet the bed. Right then I didn't care. My tongue felt like it had fur on it.

I staggered over to my locker and looked at myself in

a small mirror mounted inside the door. With my bleary eyes, I looked like hell. More importantly, I had a black and blue lump the size of an egg smack dab in the middle of my forehead.

The screen door to the hooch opened and slammed shut as several guys came in chatting happily and holding a handful of MPC notes. I'd forgotten it was payday. After washing up and putting on a clean uniform, I went to the company commander's office behind the orderly room.

My "PFC Nickels, reporting for pay"was given with a quick salute. L-T, who was serving as pay officer for the day, returned the salute and counted out my money. If he had any questions about my bleary eyes or the lump on my forehead, he kept them to himself.

On the way out I gave Andrews his fifty. "Do you think you can find out before we head back to the field?" I asked.

"I haven't any idea," he said while admiring my forehead. "But one way or another you'll get your answer. I want that other fifty."

Outside, men were milling around and talking about catching transport to Eagle Beach. Everyone elected to go. The route took us through Hue, and once again we passed in and out of the former provincial capital without stopping. All I saw were lots of people in the streets, crazy vehicle traffic, and street signs in French. Still, the trip proved to be well worth the effort.

We arrived at a fenced-in beach of white sand with trees and a picnic area. The beach itself was surrounded by barbed wire separating it from surrounding locals. Small hooch-like cottages with wooden sidewalks led out to the water. You could swim, water ski, or play basketball on a nice full-sized court. Many of the guys ended up playing volleyball on the sand because there were a few nurses there from the 95th Evac Hospital. A clubhouse with a jukebox, pool tables, vending machines, and a neat miniature golf course winding its way through a thicket of trees rounded out the scene.

A bandstand corralled a live rock band from the Philippines with several cute girl band members dressed in sheer black tops, gold mini-skirts, and white go-go boots. We laughed as they sang the lyrics of the songs. Their mangled English was not quite the same as ours. They tried hard, though, and the effort earned them a hearty round of applause after each number.

At the height of the day, the sand got so hot you could fry an egg on it in a few seconds. A short-timer said they measured it at 125 degrees. Thank God for the wooden sidewalks. That and some rubber flip-flops were the only safe way to get to the water.

The South China Sea was beautiful that evening as the sun set. Big Red, Dimes, and I elected to sleep on the beach instead of in a cottage. Others insisted that only dumb people slept outside when they had perfectly good beds inside. We didn't argue. The breeze kept away any flying insects, and the sand had long since cooled from the heat of the day.

I smelled marijuana drifting over the beach. Second squad preferred alcohol. No one would be busted here for dope if they were discreet, but there was no sense taking chances.

Back at Evans the next morning I went to see if Andrews had found anything. He put out his hand and said "Fifty bucks, man."

"You found him?" I was ecstatic and pulled out a fifty.

"Yes and no."

"What does that mean?"

"Well, your uncle is not with the 101st. I can tell you that for sure. I have a buddy in personnel at HQ at Camp Eagle, and he searched for me."

I shook my head negatively. "That's not possible. When I saw him he had a Screaming Eagles shoulder patch." I put the fifty back in my wallet. "No money for you."

Andrews thought a moment. "Was it on the right or left shoulder?

"What difference does that make?" I said.

Andrews laughed. "A big difference, man. If it's on his right it's permanent because it means he's a veteran of the 101st in combat. If a patch is on the left arm that tells you where someone is stationed in the here and now, and that changes." He shook his head. "You FNGs just kill me."

My face began to burn. No, I hadn't noticed. When I saw the patch on either shoulder at Evans I assumed it was wherever you felt like sewing it. Or rather, wherever the PX ladies felt like sewing it.

Thinking back to Carlsbad, yeah, it had been on his right. I remembered asking Nickels about it. That's how I learned about the 101st.

"But...he was wearing 506th background trim colors behind his jump wings, too. He has to be here."

Andrews looked at me like I was his retarded son. There

was some understanding there but also impatience at my lack of wisdom.

"He *was* here. But he completed his second tour last December. He volunteered for another unit here in Nam. When a career NCO does that, he can select any outfit he wants, as long as there's a slot available for him. Probably had yet to report to it and take off the oval when you last saw him. Did you notice another patch on his uniform?"

I thought hard for a moment. I remembered I was going to ask Nickels about another patch I saw but got distracted.

"There was another patch," I said slowly. My voice had taken on a hollow, mechanical quality. "It was on his left shoulder. A blue circle with a white arrow coming from the bottom right and going left." Andrews said something else. By then I wasn't paying attention.

Dazed, I stared behind him at the wall where an expired 1969 calendar was posted. It featured a color picture of a blonde in a red bikini, lying on the beach and sucking an RC Cola through a straw. She was fine. I could see why no one had taken it down a year later.

Returning from Never-Never Land I heard Andrews. "Didn't you hear me? You've confirmed what I found out. He's not here, but the patch you're describing...did the white arrow resemble a tilted outhouse?"

I nodded.

"Then he's with First Logistical Command, the largest unit in the whole country. They operate out of lots of posts but your uncle is at Camp Davis."

I looked at him blankly.

"Outside of Saigon. They run emergency supply convoy security all over the country," he added helpfully, seeing my stare.

"You're sure?"

"Hell, yeah. My buddy had a friend of a friend help me track him down. The patch just confirms what we found. He's there all right." Andrews hesitated. "I, uh, promised them twenty each to help locate him. You're going to, um, make that good for me, right?"

I reached into my wallet and got the fifty back out along with a couple of twenties. Logic told me to keep the company clerk on my side. There were too many ways he could screw you over regarding pay, leave, medical stuff, passes, and company news if he got pissed. I doubted he was the type to do that, but there was no sense in taking chances. I didn't thank him, though. Finding Ross in Saigon meant he might as well be on the moon. Saigon was 400 air miles south.

"Cheer up, Nickels. You're eligible in six months for a rest and recreation leave. You can take your R&R week down there and see your uncle. Things always have a way of working out."

Six months? Six months? Six months of walking patrol and trying to survive out here? I wanted to reach across the counter and wring his scrawny neck. He was so damn casual about the whole thing. Like it was no biggie. I wanted to bust up the stupid smile on his face with my fist.

What saved his ass was saying "things always have a way of working out." It was a favorite of my Dad. He believed it. As the day went on and I brooded, that's what saved me. My veil of disappointment lifted. Yeah, the can had been kicked down the road again, but the reckoning was postponed, not irretrievable.

I could still make it happen. I just needed to survive until then.

22

March 1970
Lowlands, Vietnam

"Drop your pants," said Doc.

Early morning and time for the daily ritual. Everyone in the platoon had to drop their pants and search for leeches. Notice I said pants, not underwear. No one wore underwear in the jungle. If you did, you got crotch rot and ended up scratching yourself uncontrollably. Doc had a powder that cured it after a couple of weeks but you'd be pretty miserable until then. There were also the times you'd have the runs. The Hershey squirts happened to everyone sooner or later.

In Vietnam you could get leeches on land as well as water. They came in different sizes and two colors, black or green. You could find them anywhere from your ankle to your waist. Sometimes you found them on a certain unnamed appendage.

There were two ways to remove them. Use bug juice or hold a lighted cigarette to them to get them to fall off. A nasty welt appeared where they bit into your skin but that wasn't serious.

During the morning's leech ritual, Doc discovered me feverish and shivering.

"Whoa, my man. You got malaria."

"Not possible," I said, but then my teeth chattered. "I

took all your damn pills. It's the flu."

He looked me over speculatively. It was clear he was weighing whether or not to believe me. After a few seconds, he smiled.

"Don't have to examine you, Nickels. You pissing brown urine?"

I nodded glumly.

Doc took my temperature. A cheery 104 degrees.

"Yep, you have it alright. Don't worry, kid. We'll take good care of you."

After the call was put in for a medevac chopper, he laid me down and covered me with a pile of donated blankets Dimes and Big Red collected from others in the platoon. That did little to stop the shivering and teeth chattering. Then the chills stopped and were replaced by sweating as my body grew hot again. A fever kicked in and I got dizzy. Back to cold again and I felt even sicker.

I would have been flown back to Evans, but Doc thought I was in bad enough shape to be sent directly to the 95th Evac Hospital in Da Nang. A pretty nurse there stripped me naked. I would have blushed, but I was so ill I wouldn't have cared if she was Marilyn Monroe.

The nurse had a medic bring a large basin of water with huge ice chunks in it. It smelled funny. She said it was some special water and alcohol combo designed to reduce body heat. After washing me down, they directed a large fan on me and wrapped me in ice towels to bring down my temperature.

"Don't want your brain to boil, Private," she purred.

I didn't care about my brain at that point. The ice

towel treatment coupled with the fan was unbearable, and I made no secret of it. Loudly. They must have been used to it though, because they were unmoved by my protests.

"We heard from a Sergeant Strode that you should be written up for malingering since you didn't take your pills in the field. You need to toughen up, soldier boy," said my nurse from Hell.

A flurry of curses spewed from my lips. I cursed Strode, the U.S. Army, the war, her, Ross, and God. I'd had about enough of the whole damn world and they could all kiss my ass. The nurse smiled and kept on applying more ice towels. Obviously, she'd done this many times before.

I got over the crisis hump in a few days and was sent back to Camp Evans to the Charlie Company, 326th Med Battalion clinic to recuperate for ten days. I was weak and moved slowly, but was definitely getting better.

There's one benefit to malaria. Your downtime was counted as good time toward your 365-day requirement. I was too weak to do much but glad it didn't count against me.

I hoped to read *Tribune* newspaper updates from home but no such luck. The U.S. Post Office was on strike over getting only four percent of the ten percent pay raise they wanted. That meant no mail for the past week, and it looked like the strike might last a couple more weeks. Guys in the platoon were probably feeling mighty sorry for those "poor" postal workers. Might even make a sympathy sign and mail it to them, if only they could.

I was back at Evans with nothing to do but get better. Ordinarily you'd be assigned to some small detail to keep you busy, but not so with malaria. That was a no-no. This was the one time you were allowed to do pretty much whatever you wanted. Usually a lone G.I. wandering around brought out the lifers wanting to give you something to do, so you hid. Recovering from malaria, I didn't have to hide.

Instead I read books that were lying around. None made an impact except for the thinnest one of all. I read it in just over an hour. It was called *Love Story*. Luckily, I was alone when I did because I teared up a little at the end. Must have been the effect of the malaria.

Later I went to the EM Club and had a 7Up and a burger before going over to the hospital to watch TV. Televisions were rare, but there were a few battery-powered sets in the rear areas. The only channel available in-country was the AFVN, Armed Forces Vietnam Network. All the newscasters wore uniforms and there weren't any commercials like back home, though they did run some public service announcements. From 1430 until the 2200 signoff, they had music shows, news, weather, interviews with visiting celebrities (Chris Noel, Ann Margret), contests, and reruns of popular stateside TV shows like *Have Gun Will Travel*, *Route 66*, *Beverly Hillbillies*, *Dragnet*, and *Adam 12*. I liked the *Dragnet* episodes best.

All that can only take you so far, which was why I found myself sitting on some steps out by the helicopter tarmac the next morning watching the choppers taking off. There were different types: Hueys, Cobras, Loaches, and a huge CH-47 twin propeller Chinook that was being loaded up at one end of the runway.

Bored, I wandered down to the Chinook to look inside. The crew chief was busy supervising the loading of ammo boxes for a run to a local firebase. It was quite a load. I stood at the rear ramp peering in. He saw me and grunted an acknowledgement.

"Never seen the inside of an eggbeater before?"

"Nah, can't say I have. Seen you guys carrying some heavy loads, though. Cannons and those big cargo supply nets under you. Must be challenging."

"Those are meat and potato type missions." He slapped the metal hull with one hand, but with affection. "She is one heavy duty machine. Every day an adventure." He grinned. "Hey, listen to me, I sound like a re-up commercial." He shook his head ruefully. "Sorry about that."

I laughed appreciatively, waved, and began to hike back to my seat by the runway. The tarmac was starting to heat up and the extra temps were beginning to make me dizzy and lightheaded. Last thing I needed was a relapse.

I'd parked my butt on the stairs again when they finished loading the Chinook and lifted the ramp to seal the rear shut. Slowly the twin blades began to turn. Soon they were thrashing the air furiously, and the ship took off. It flew by me at about fifty feet and was almost to the end of the runway when there was a strange horrendous sound, immediately followed by grinding noises of some type. The chopper seemed to halt in midair for a second and then plunged straight into the ground with a loud explosion and crumpling of metal. A rotor flew off in a tall arc a hundred feet high before it fell to the ground and splintered into pieces going in several directions.

People ran toward the crash, as a gigantic ball of flame erupted from what had been a mighty machine a few seconds earlier. Now it was quickly turning into molten scrap as 2,000 pounds of JP-4 fuel ignited. The ammo inside began cooking off. Two crew members were dragged out alive, but others were trapped inside and fried to death. I heard the screams, loud at first and then fading. I think one scream was cut short by a pistol shot. At least it sounded like it to me.

It took a long time before the fire died down and the victims were revealed. I didn't have the heart to see if the crew chief was one. As I walked away I tried lighting a cigarette. I was shaking so bad I had to hold the lighter with both hands. I overheard a mechanic saying it was transmission failure. Maybe. Whatever it was, it was a total rat fuck.

The next morning I got screwed, and not in the good way. I still had a week of recuperation to go, but Strode persuaded Top to put me on the shit burn detail. It was a "correction" for the malaria.

At a firebase or a line outfit camp like Evans, sanitation was always an issue. If you had to piss, you used a piss tube. You urinated into metal tubes placed in a line sticking about a foot out of the ground. The problem was your aim might be bad or you might be doing this at night and in a hurry to get back to sleep. The result was not pretty. Around every line of piss tubes was a sea of moist yellow ground and an ammonia smell.

That was nothing compared to disposing solid waste. Flush toilets were unheard of. The latrine was in a tent or a relatively open plywood building, with or without walls, housing several open-seaters without partitions. You got familiar with who had the runs or constipation.

The real problem was how to destroy the accumulated waste. The Army, in its infinite wisdom, came up with shit burning. Two unfortunates were detailed to this duty for the day. Our company latrine had ten holes carved into a long wooden bench. Under each hole was a fifty-five gallon metal drum.

Each day the two-man detail went behind the latrine and pulled out each barrel. This was done by inserting a long metal rod into two holes on the opposite sides near the top of the container. Even if the barrel was only half full, it was so heavy it required two men to tote it off. You had to carry it a good distance away, douse it with diesel fuel, and light the whole mess on fire. The flaming concoction had to be continually stirred and the fire on top kept lit until it all burned away. Then you put the barrel back to collect a fresh round of shit the next day.

Reporting for duty as a shit burner didn't make me happy. I got more unhappy when I found out I would be doing it alone. No help for me. Strode made this clear, according to the supply sergeant who gave me the diesel fuel.

Not having help meant I couldn't use the rod through the holes to pull the barrels out, since there was no one to lift up the other side. I had to drag, pull, and push it along from under the wooden bench. Then do the same to get it far enough away that an errant spark from blazing shit didn't drift back to the latrine and set the whole damn thing on fire. During the process I tried my best not to inhale.

Each time the barrel jostled, some contents sloshed over me and my boots. There were rotting feces in each container mixed with urine (not everyone used piss tubes) floating on top. After dumping diesel on top of the whole mess, I tried lighting the first barrel with a match. It wouldn't catch fire. After half a pack of matches I knew I needed a bigger flame. Grabbing a roll of toilet paper, lighting it on fire, and tossing it in resulted in a big whoosh and lots of black smoke. The smell doubled. I tried holding my breath like earlier but it was impossible. It just made you inhale deeper afterwards.

That was the easy part. I had to stir the whole evil brew continuously, while pouring in more fuel from time to time to keep the fire going. It was backbreaking work. To get a barrel to burn down to the bottom with only a few crispy charcoal-like bits left took four hours. I had to chip those out with another pipe and return the whole damn barrel to its original spot.

The heat coming off burning shit is intense. I stripped off my uniform shirt and t-shirt because I was sweating like a pig, standing next to this furnace. After twelve hours, I managed to finish only three barrels. I didn't stop to eat. I knew food would come right back up. It was just me, the barrels, and canteens of water to keep going.

When my shift was over, I dragged my sorry ass home for a shower. I reeked. Everyone stayed far from me. The smell permeated my uniform and the pores of my skin. You could smell me a block away. Even after the shower I still stank.

After five days, Top figured I was ready to head back to the field. I agreed. Better risking life and limb than burning other people's shit. I found I was looking forward to returning to the jungle.

***

During my absence the platoon acquired a Kit Carson Scout. His name was Tran. He was about twenty-two or so despite missing several front teeth.

Like all Kit Carson Scouts, Tran was a former North Vietnamese soldier who defected to the south, joining with us rather than spending the rest of the war in a South Vietnamese POW compound. He was given a special two-week course at the SERTS school, followed by a three-week basic English language school. After being given a set of jungle fatigues without any insignia except for a name patch, he was assigned to us.

Actually, Dimes was assigned by Prophet to be his mentor. Dimes was okay with that. The rest of us weren't sure Tran could be trusted. Some thought these scouts were faking their new allegiance. Dimes took the opposite view.

"Look, man, if he tries anything, he's up shit creek without a paddle. It's not like he can scamper back to the NVA. He's literally got nowhere else to go," Dimes said.

That made sense and we slowly got over our

apprehension. Eventually Tran became a valued member of the platoon. But it was all on a professional level in the jungle. We didn't socialize with him outside the field.

As time went by, Dimes and Tran spent hours of down time together. Dimes had been fascinated by Vietnam ever since we found the dragon washed up on the shore. By North Dakota standards, the country was damn exotic. He was always badgering Tran to explain the language and customs. Tran's limited English skills grew considerably, and Dimes got fairly good at speaking Vietnamese.

During our next stand-down, Dimes took off with Tran to visit Da Nang. The rest of us went to Eagle Beach, certain we had the better deal. According to Dimes when he returned, he came out on top. He was in love.

Tran had taken Dimes to visit his family in the city, and he met Tran's half sister, Nguyen Thi Be. Her given name of Be meant Baby Doll. She was tall with Western features because her father was a former French legionnaire. Dimes couldn't stop talking about her. He was smitten.

"I know you think I'm crazy, guys. But she is really hot. I kid you not. Smart, too." He looked around at us. He saw we were doubtful. He became insistent. "Look, I'm telling you. She's not a bar girl or a prostitute. It's not like that at all."

"I'm happy for you, man," said Big Red as he wrote KILL FOR PEACE with a black magic marker on the side of his helmet. "You'll have to show her off to us sometime."

I don't think Big Red was serious, but Dimes took his words at face value. Nodding enthusiastically, he agreed. We would all go with him to meet Baby Doll in Da Nang the next chance we got.

That night my sleep was plagued by another dream. Again I was with the family. It was summer and we were on vacation at Lake Chelan. I was snorkeling and looking at all the fish. The water was crystal clear from snowmelt off the mountains, which made it similar to swimming in a gigantic aquarium. The tradeoff was it was ice cold. You could only enjoy the experience for a short time before heading back for a blanket and the campfire. I approached the family campfire and sat next to Susie. She was talking to the folks. For some reason I couldn't understand them. It was like watching a silent movie. I tried to get their attention but it was no use. I was invisible.

A week later I got a hometown newspaper. The post office strike was now a distant memory, and the last several back copies had contained no news of the family at all. But this issue featured an article about us below a picture of our station wagon in Oakland. According to the article, it had been there for several months. Someone complained as the dirt and grime accumulated on the car, and it became apparent it hadn't moved for a long time. The license plates were missing, but the police identified the abandoned car by the VIN numbers.

Foul play was suspected.

"Welcome to my world," I muttered.

23

October 1945
Munich, Germany

Frank had no plans to continue being Michaelis. He walked southward out of Germany and worked as a farmhand in the Tyrol. He saved what little money he was paid and brooded. Life went on for seemingly everyone except him. His brother was dead. He was on the run. The country was in ruins. What, if anything, could be done?

It took time to come up with a plan. By autumn, Frank knew the key was Anna.

Anna was the daughter of a Lutheran cleric and had been Heinrich's fiancée. He met her during his stay at the hospital. She liked both him and his brother. If anyone would help him, she was the one.

Letters from Heinz Michaelis to Anna Straker in Dachau were sent back unopened with an official stamp reading MOVED TO MUNICH. No street address, but that wasn't unusual. Too many cities were gutted during the war, and moving meant you might end up anywhere in town before finding permanent accommodations. Still, he knew he could track her down. After arriving in the ruins of Munich, it took him two days in the pleasant fall October weather to find her lodgings.

Anna lived on the third floor of a bombed apartment building with its entire west wall missing. The interior of each apartment up to the fifth floor was visible from the street. It was like looking into a child's doll house with a cutaway wall. No privacy and exposed to the elements, but at least they had a roof over their heads. Some tenants tried to compensate by putting up thin sheets of tar paper or vinyl plastic to simulate walls and blur the workings of the people inside from random viewers on the street. Most chose to ignore the missing wall and go on with life.

Anna was not happy to see him.

"Oh, it's you." No welcome, no smiles, after not seeing each other for months. He was confused. She was always polite before. "What do you want?" she asked coldly.

"Aren't you glad to see me?'

"Not particularly. Should I be?"

Why was she so rude? He couldn't figure it out. This was not the reception he envisioned.

"Anna, I need your help. I want to avenge Heinrich's murder."

Reluctantly, she opened the door all the way and allowed him inside the room. She stuck her head into the hall and peered down the corridor to see...who? Was she expecting someone?

Satisfied, she shut the door and turned toward him, looking at him with crossed arms. "Well?" she said.

"Is something wrong?" he asked.

It was then her composure broke.

"Wrong? What could be wrong? Why do I find myself having nightmares for the past four months? All because of you and your SS buddies." Her bitter tone was unmistakable.

"What are you talking about?"

She went over to the table and opened a drawer. She took out a carton of Lucky Strikes and pulled out a pack of cigarettes. *Where the hell did she get those?* he wondered. A carton of American cigarettes was worth six months' wages on the black market. They were twenty times the cost of the stinky German tobacco.

Looking up from the carton, he saw her take a lighter from her housecoat and light the cigarette. Her hands shook. Not from fear but from suppressed anger. Toward him.

"I've had the nightmares ever since..." Her voice trailed off.

He walked forward intending to put his arms around her to comfort her. She was having none of that. Both hands came up to ward him off.

"No," she said. "Don't touch me."

"What's this about nightmares? You're talking in riddles, Anna." It had been a long day. He was tired. He took off his coat, sat down on the couch, and prepared to listen.

"I can't sleep." She shook her head vigorously. "All because of you."

24

April 1970
Firebase Veghel, Vietnam

I killed my first person today. It happened during a religious discussion.

Our platoon was temporarily placed under the operational control of the 1/501st Infantry, 2nd Brigade. Things were heating up in their area of operations and they were short of personnel. That wasn't unusual. Frequent enemy contact often whittled down a company to fifty percent or less of its authorized strength. The problem was getting 11B replacements. It was surprising how difficult that was. The Army had plenty of REMFs but always seemed short of infantrymen. Go figure. The result was sometimes you got platoons or companies loaned out to other commands for a while.

We were on a patrol six klicks outside Veghel. We stopped for lunch and a siesta at the height of the heat. After setting up a defensive perimeter in a nicely shaded spot, we ate our C-rats and talked. Talk was big in the field. In addition to reading a magazine or book, writing a letter, or playing cards, it was the favorite way to make time pass. Today, we were on the subject of religion.

"Do you believe in God?" asked Dimes. It was one of those rhetorical questions thrown out there for anyone in the squad to respond.

Big Red looked up from his *Playboy* magazine. "Damn right," he grunted.

"Really?" I said. It was hard for me to see him as a humble Christian, given his fondness for drinking, smoking, girlie magazines, and dirty jokes.

"Never said I was a priest. Never said I was a sinner. But look around at this world. Too perfectly formed and fitted to occur by luck."

I pondered this for a moment as I munched some canned fruitcake. "But is that God?"

Big Red shrugged. "Had to be a guiding intelligence behind it. Call it God or whatever. What about you, Nickels?"

"I was raised Lutheran but haven't been to church in a long time. Always thought my parents wanted me to believe but didn't seem to really believe it themselves for some reason. Never quite understood why."

"Cap, you're a Mormon, right?" asked Peddler who was eating from his fruit cocktail C-ration can. Cap was a cherry who had joined us several weeks earlier.

"Latter Day Saints is the correct term. LDS for short." The resigned expression on his face seemed to signal he knew the probable destination of Peddler's question.

"So how many wives you got back in Utah?"

"Man, you ought to know better than to ask stupid questions. First, I'm from Arizona. Second, polygamy has been outlawed by the church since 1890. Next question."

"Okay, then, what's with this 'Baptism for the Dead,' I've heard about? You guys dig up dead bodies or what?"

"No, Peddler, we don't dig up dead bodies. Baptism for the Dead is a proxy ceremony where someone stands in place of the deceased and walks through a baptism ceremony in their stead. If the dead person accepts it, then they get to go to heaven."

"You mean, if I'm a Mormon that will get me there."

"You don't have to be LDS. All the past U.S. presidents have had a proxy ceremony done for them by the church, for instance. They didn't ask for it, and the general public probably doesn't know. But if they led good lives and accepted this blessing, they're now in heaven, even though none of them were LDS."

"Crap, you guys done that for every president?"

"Yep. Just another part of the presidential benefit package."

"So, if I die you could do that for me? Even though I'm a Jew?"

"Sure." Cap frowned. "But I thought Jews didn't believe in the Christian idea of heaven."

"We don't." Peddler shrugged. "But we might be wrong. A little extra insurance could prove valuable. You did say we could accept it or reject it as needed, right?"

Cap smiled. "Now I see where this is going. If you buy the farm you want me to take care of it?"

Peddler finished his fruit cocktail and proceeded to walk over to our trash hole to dump his can in it.

"Sure, why not. Who knows? Might come in handy." He wiped the sticky fruit juice on his hands onto his pants.

Cap looked around at the squad. "Any other requests?" Smiling, he chanted "Going once, going twice—"

That's when we heard the pop, pop, pop of small arms fire. Superman, walking by from first squad five feet away from me, clutched his throat and fell to the ground. His back jerked up in a bow off the ground and flattened out. After that he didn't move.

Utter chaos. Guys yelled to get down or hide. Others demanded to know what the hell was going on.

A second series of pop, pop, pop. Down went a newbie named Blanchard. He was with us for a week. Nice smile and a bit of a jokester. Half of his head was lying several feet away from his body. No more jokes from Blanchard.

"Anyone see anything?" demanded Prophet. His request settled us down. Everyone scanned our surroundings.

"Somewhere to our left," shouted Dimes, as a claymore mine detonated in that direction with a massive explosion. Dust drifted up from the area.

I heard a thump and saw a mortar shell shoot in a high arc from beyond the trees. At first I was enthralled watching its graceful flight. As it headed in my direction it dawned on me I was the intended target. *Oh, shit.*

The mortar hit about ten yards away with a resounding crump. I hugged the ground like Prophet said to do in case of mortar attack. "The shell blast will generally go upward, so hug the ground and leave your mouth open to adjust for the concussion," had been his advice. His advice was pretty good. I was showered by the dirt and debris the explosion threw up but unharmed.

The next thought in my head was: *Those little yellow bastards are trying to kill me.* That made it personal. Yet if I could have crawled into my helmet and waited out the next few minutes, I'd have gladly done so. Neither Strode nor Prophet would have it.

"Get your asses in gear! Move it! Now!" shouted Strode.

I saw Prophet out of the corner of my right eye running along the line kicking guys trying to hide in the dirt. "Move it or die here," he yelled.

He didn't have to tell us where to move. We all instinctively headed in the direction of the enemy. I heard bullets buzz and hum as they sped by me. Some made a cracking sound as they thudded into tree trunks. Before, I somehow had it in my mind I could dodge or see bullets heading toward me and avoid them. What a joke. They went by at what seemed like twice the speed of sound.

I was running and shooting into the trees where the enemy fire was coming from. I was scared, yes. At the same time, I never felt more alive. There is nothing like someone shooting at you, and missing, for you to feel alive. Weird.

I found cover behind a ruined tree trunk and looked around. Green tracers came from the brush in front. Wood splinters were flying from my cover as an AK-47 spewed bullets, chewing up the trunk. I took a grenade, pulled the pin, and held it for a couple of seconds. The last thing I wanted was them tossing it back at me. I heaved it as far as I could. An explosion followed, and the crack of the enemy gun ceased.

Someone yelled for a medic.

With no incoming fire, we began to advance outward from our perimeter. We found three bodies wearing pith helmets and the green uniform of the North Vietnam

Army.

Two were shot. One was killed by grenade fragments that had split off one side of his body and left a red spongy mass of exposed tissue and blood. It wasn't difficult to know which kill was mine.

I'd been dreading this moment. Now that it was here I felt strangely apathetic. Maybe because I'd anticipated and worried about it for so long or maybe because I felt like it was "better him than me." In any case, I'd crossed the threshold of some boundary, and there was no going back.

Big Red had shot one of the other two. He came up and spit in the dead man's face. Big Red liked Blanchard's jokes. We lost two men for nothing other than these three getting in some shots at us. The NVA team shooting the mortar had disappeared.

Afterwards Dimes had Doc put some ointment on a deep cut above his right eye. He had run into a tree branch during the firefight.

Dimes flinched as Doc applied the salve.

"Don't be a pussy," said Big Red.

Dimes shot him the finger, but grinned.

"Hey, Doc, does this qualify me for a Purple Heart?"

Doc didn't reply. Just kept lathering on the greasy stuff.

Big Red went back to where we were holding our religion discussion earlier and located his *Playboy* magazine in the dirt. He cleaned it off and tore out the monthly centerfold featuring Miss March. Walking over to a nearby tree he impaled it on a branch for all the world to see.

"When the bastards come back here I want them to know what they're missing," he said. "God Bless America."

25

April 24, 1970
315th Tactical Air Wing
II Corps, Vietnam

The C-130 stank. It stank of sweat. It stank of aviation fuel. When the jumpmaster signaled the six-minute warning, it stank of my fear as I stood in line waiting to make my first parachute jump.

Our platoon was rotated from Veghel and back to our company two days before when we received orders for all paratroopers to report to Top. The division had gone off jump status months ago, but the 101st still had hundreds of paratroopers drawing jump pay. To keep your jump status, Top said, everyone had to re-qualify. Not a combat jump, but a practice one.

Dimes, Big Red, Cap, Peddler, and I—along with a collection of several dozen others—were crammed in a plane being flown, courtesy of the U.S. Air Force, by the 315th Tactical Air Wing, II Corps. Their mission was to fly soldiers and supplies all over Vietnam. This was a milk run for them.

Some of our guys treated this as a lark, a nice escape from the jungle. "Watch out for that first step, it's a doozy" was a joke I heard over and over as we boarded. Others were less enthused.

After the order to report, I didn't know what to do. Everyone else had actually completed a jump. Not once, but at least five times to earn their wings. I, on the other hand, was a fraud. If I didn't handle it right, I'd soon be a dead fraud. How would I fake this? Actually fake wasn't the right word. This could not be faked. You either did it or you didn't. Yet there was no in-country SERTS for this. So I did what any sensible person would do. I went to the camp library.

Like much of the U.S. setup in Vietnam, this was a bastardized version of the real thing. Instead of a real library we had a green library bus that came by every day from Camp Eagle with a new shipment of books from the division library. I didn't know if it would help, but decided to give it a try.

Did they, I asked, have anything on Screaming Eagle history or parachuting? Turned out they had a small shelf on 101st history and several books on skydiving as a sport. The skydiving books proved useful only in making me aware that civilian programs qualified everyone in one day, unlike the Army. Maybe I could pull this off after all.

The books didn't answer other questions. What's a static line? How long did I have to pull the chute? Was there a spare chute? How did I put on a chute? Was the chute the same type as shown in the skydiving photos? Were you supposed to yell Geronimo as you exited as I had seen in the movies? How do you steer the damn thing? Most importantly, how do you land safely?

Reading the books, I despaired. Most were filled with pictures of smiling civilian jumpers, showed the differences between a T-7 and T-10 parachute, or talked about maintaining a jump log.

Picking up the last volume on the shelf, I'd almost given up hope of finding any useful information. That last book was titled *Blood on the Risers*. It showed what a paratrooper did in training, the hook up procedures inside the plane, how to exit and execute a proper PLF (parachute landing fall). The book finished with the lyrics to some paratrooper beer songs and even showed pictures of a prop blast party given to celebrate a successful jump. I pored over it, trying to memorize every detail.

Sneaking behind the mess hall after dinner, I found two large crates and piled them on top of each other. Taking several sandbags from the wall, I untied them and scattered the sand in front of the crates to make a landing pit. The book's pictures showed an airborne shuffle, hookup commands, and a diagram of the PLF drop and roll I needed to practice. The rest of the evening that's what I did, climbing on top of the crates, practicing commands, shuffling, and jumping down into the sand and rolling.

Great practice. But 1,200 feet above ground and in a plane going 150 miles per hour, I was about to find out how accurate that book was.

I felt the plane lurch to the left. My breakfast almost went with it. Who the hell thought being a paratrooper was glamorous? What was I doing here? I didn't want to die splattered all over the landscape.

The jumpmaster gave the commands:

"Unfasten Seatbelts! Get Ready!" Grab the cable over my snap fastener and hold it in my right hand.

"Stand Up!" Grab the cable line overhead with my left hand and turn toward the back of the plane.

"Hook Up!" Reach up and snap the fastener over the cable line.

"Check Equipment!" Check the trooper pack in front of me following the checklist in the book. A shout countdown began with individuals in line shouting "15 okay, 14 okay, 13 okay..." until each man in line sounded off and slapped the shoulder of the man in front.

"Stand In Door!" Do the airborne shuffle toward door, like a pregnant waddling penguin loaded with gear. If first man at door, position yourself with hands gripping each door side and look at the horizon.

"One Minute!" First jumper in door stays put until given the signal. The rest of us keep our eyes on the green and red lights by the door.

"Go!" The green light comes on and the line begins to move with each man shuffling along and pushing the man in front of him.

Reflexes took over. I stopped questioning if I should jump and instead moved forward as fast as possible. If I hesitated, common sense would return and I'd freeze up. Holding my head forward and leaping out the door, I swung my left leg over and tried to make the recommended fifteen degree body turn when the prop blast hit me and threw me down and sideways.

I was supposed to shout "Currahee!" and count to two. The chute would open automatically. Caught up in everything, I forgot. I was reminded when the chute snapped open with a tremendous jolt, and popped my shoulders like a puppet on a string. Everything seemed to come to a screeching halt. I knew it was an illusion. I was still descending fast, but I also seemed suspended in air.

Looking up, my white canopy floated overhead. Everything seemed fine. No need to deploy the reserve chute. Below me were several other jumpers, all far enough apart there was no danger of colliding or landing on each other.

The ground approached fast. Looking toward the horizon, I took hold of the risers per my book instructions. I was forgetting something and briefly panicked before I remembered: feet together, knees slightly bent, and execute a PLF roll unless you want a broken back or legs.

I hit the ground hard. My roll was not a thing of beauty. On the ground, the chute filled with air and pulled me across the field still strapped in and lying on my back. Dragged twenty yards, I struggled to release myself and get free. Then I had to chase down and collapse the canopy. I sat on it for a while, exhausted but grinning. All my body parts still worked. I'd done it.

A truck pulled up as jumpers rolled up their chutes and headed toward it for the ride back to camp. Joining them, I thought of the old pilot's adage: any landing you can walk away from is a good landing.

Back at base, the EM Club had a prop blast party for us. Sitting at a table with Big Red and Dimes, we toasted each other and the 101st, damned all non-paratroopers, and watched as everyone got sloshed. I nurtured my beer. The last thing I needed was to get loose lipped around these guys again. I still didn't know what happened to my forehead the last time and didn't want a repeat.

In mid-party form, we were approached by Prophet. NCOs didn't go into an EM club, nor did officers. This was an exception and the only time I ever saw him tipsy—not drunk, but feeling good.

He walked by, slapped me on the back, and said, "So, how are The Three Musketeers?" He wasn't interested in an answer, and moved on to another table. We all looked at each other and smiled.

Dimes raised his Budweiser and said, "Here's to The Three Musketeers!"

Grinning back, we clinked bottles to make it official. We had a new name and liked it.

The party closed down about 0100, and as we stumbled out the door, Big Red yelled, "Halt." He drunkenly peered at us eye to eye and said, "You know what falls from the sky, don't you? Birdshit and idiots."

"Nah," said Dimes. "That's wrong. It's birdshit, idiots, and The Three Musketeers."

Six months earlier I'd received a varsity letter for football at Lake Munson High. As a freshman that was damned rare. I was happy to get it as my parents watched in the audience. At this moment that achievement paled. I'd jumped from an airplane, cheated death, and earned the wings on my uniform for real. The only drawback: my parents, would never know about it. Still, for the first time, I felt like I belonged somewhere again.

26

May 6, 1945
Dachau, Germany

She was at the Lutheran Church helping her father prepare for Sunday service when word arrived. After being in town for the past week, the Americans posted a large flyer at the public square and on all government buildings. It was signed by General Patton and addressed to all citizens.

The order said everyone age eight and up must assemble at designated points the next day at eight in the morning. No luggage or foodstuffs, just themselves. Buses and trucks would meet them at the transit points. Mothers with children under the age of eight could leave them at the designated shipping points where they would be taken care of until their parents' return. What the Americans planned to do was unknown. It would not be good. Speculation was rife in the town.

She wavered about reporting that day. She didn't trust the Americans. Yet her father, the pastor, was going along with his congregation, so not participating was out of the question. At the appointed hour over 200 people waited outside the church to be picked up. They were taken out to the SS training compound parade ground. Prior to entering the concentration camp itself, they were put in two long lines single file. Each visitor was then deloused inside their blouse or shirt from a small hose attached to a DDT cylinder. It was to prevent the spread of typhus, which had been raging through the camp the past several weeks. Soldiers stood with guns at various points along the column to ensure no one failed to participate.

She didn't know what to expect. Civilians were never allowed on the training grounds unless married to SS men. And no one visited the concentration camp next door, where the undesirables, the prisoners, were held.

An American Army major arrived with a small staff behind him, went to the front of the line, and mounted a small platform. Taking a sheet of paper from his back pocket he read it aloud in fluent German and in a nasal voice.

"By order of the Supreme Commander of Allied Forces, General Dwight D. Eisenhower: All civilian inhabitants aged eight or older who are within a thirty-mile radius of any liberated German concentration camp, or the sub-units thereof, will be required to take a mandated tour of such installations. What exists there must never be forgotten. Such visits will be coordinated and recorded with local authorities. Commanders are given wide discretion in carrying out this order. There will be no exceptions."

The major folded the order and put it back in his pocket. He sniffed the air, grimaced, and said, "You really are a miserable bunch of bastards." He walked with his staff over to a waiting jeep and left.

The crowd was broken into groups and directed to different entry points. Her father went with half the congregation in one entrance while she and the others went through the west gate. A main boulevard had separate barrack buildings on both sides. Clusters of ape-like looking men in prison striped garb gathered in doorways and windows. Others stood on the street. Overhead the lead-colored sky and low-hanging clouds seemed to reflect the sullen mood of the ex-prisoners who stared back at them. Neither side spoke as the civilians filed past. The coughing of the sick and the squeaking of civilian shoe leather on the rainy pavement was the only sound as they moved on.

Some staring prisoners were like walking skeletons. Their shaved heads were normal only if normal can be defined as large eyes and sunken cheeks on top of a waxy yellow body. They wore little in the way of clothes. Every rib and vertebra was seen through their translucent skin. Many were covered in huge festering sores and had no teeth.

The civilians were stopped by the guards at a brick building surrounded by large piles of dirt. Some of the children began to play with the stuff—stomping in it, tossing it around, and playing King of the Mountain on various piles until their parents told them to stop.

The building turned out to be the camp crematorium. Forced to peer inside the ovens, she saw bones and skulls. In the corners by the ovens, bodies were stacked in piles waiting for disposal. She estimated sixty dead corpses with intertwined limbs. Realizing the white piles of dirt outside were not really dirt, but human ash from the ovens, frantic mothers beat the white dust off the clothes of their bewildered children.

The tour took them to an area where the raw smell of the camp hit them. Previously they were upwind; now the stench was unavoidable with its odor of feces, urine, body sweat, rotten flesh, soiled clothing, and garbage.

"My God, the smell!" said Anna.

People struggled to find handkerchiefs or other cloth to plug up their noses and mouths to keep from gagging. Some lost the battle and retched or vomited ashamedly. The source of the stench lay hidden just beyond the rise in front of them. Against their will they trudged forward.

27

May 1970
A Shau Valley, Vietnam

We flew in at tree level. Yellow smoke popped up, marking the landing zone and guiding us to the open meadow. Red and white tracers bounced off trees down below, and enemy mortar rounds fell inside the LZ. The grass was on fire in spots, and gray patches of drifting smoke made my eyes water as the Huey's door gunner shot suppressive fire into bushes and hedgerows outside the perimeter.

The NVA had a lock on us. Tracer rounds flew through the open areas of the chopper and it shuddered as several hit metal. The last few yards till touchdown took forever, and we couldn't do much more than pray.

Time to jump from the hovering chopper. I tossed out my load, followed with a five-foot leap, and tried my best to turn it into a tumble of sorts. Around us various explosions threw up dirt, plants, and grass. The smoke from the grass fire made breathing hard.

A man with dirt-matted hair and dusty raccoon eyes lay close by, bleeding heavily. Dragging him by the arms over to the settling helicopter, I hoisted him under his armpits and threw him in like a sack of potatoes. Several guys were throwing others in with no ceremony as well. The chopper took off, its skids clipping the tops of trees before making good an escape.

I grabbed for my rifle but it slipped away. A copper smell of blood soaked both my hands and the front of my shirt. Frantically wiping my hands on the grass, I grabbed my gun and gear and ran toward cover behind an earthen berm about three feet high, landing next to another guy. Turned out he was dead. His body, riddled with holes, meant my "safety" behind the berm didn't mean much. Making myself as small as possible with bullets and shrapnel flying around me, I hopped up and ran to a small ditch further on.

A newbie started screaming after being hit in the leg. I grabbed a rock and threw it at the idiot, yelling for him to shut up if he wanted to live. He got the message, changing to a quiet whimper.

A Cobra flew directly over the enemy position spraying its cannon and rocket firepower. Awesome. If anything was alive after that I'd eat my shorts. I actually felt a bit sorry for the poor bastards.

Everything went quiet. The enemy was either all dead or retreating silently into the surrounding jungle. We'd find out with a sweep over the area in the next few minutes. Our dead and wounded would be sorted out and sent back to Evans.

This was my tenth air assault in the mountains. Some were hot with contact; on others nothing happened.

At lunch I found I'd lost my P-38 can opener and struggled to open a can of spaghetti and meatballs with my bayonet. Prophet walked by and laughed at my clumsiness.

"Whoa, whoa. You're going to hurt yourself. Here." He took my can, scanned our surroundings, and walked over to squat by a flat rock. Placing the can lid down on the rock, he held the other end firmly while rubbing the lid briskly against the coarse surface of the rock for twenty seconds. Finished, he flipped the can back upright, and the lid popped upward. He bent it back until it snapped off, then held both the lid and the can out to me. "Be careful of the lid. The friction makes it extra sharp and it can cut you pretty badly."

"Thanks for the demo. Didn't know it could be done that easy."

"Make sure it's on a coarse rock or rough concrete surface. Otherwise it won't work."

I filed his latest tip in my Prophet fieldcraft knowledge kit.

After our meal, there was a siesta for two hours. Some guys didn't sleep. They read a magazine, comic book, or a letter. The lucky ones had perfumed letters from their girl back home. Sometimes they'd pass around the envelopes for everyone to sniff. Sounds pervy but a whiff reminded us of what we were missing.

At the end of the day we hunkered down in a NDP with claymores, trip flares, and interlocking fire lanes. Darkness fell fast and was pitch black in the mountains.

Sometimes we moved outside the perimeter to conduct a night ambush. I'd learned to put my left index finger at the end of my rifle barrel to give me something to guide on in the dark since I couldn't use the sights. I'd also discovered that if I touched my M-16 dust cover in the dark and it was closed, then I still had a round in the chamber, even if my magazine was empty. Good to know.

This time the NVA sent sappers into our perimeter and we endured a ten-minute firefight before they withdrew. Two of those left behind we'd shot in the legs.

"Newbies have a tendency to fire high in the dark, but you guys are firing low. Adjust accordingly," said Strode.

We got word to carry out a Mad Minute at 0400. For sixty seconds everyone shot off an entire magazine and tossed a grenade in front of their position. They called for Mad Minutes in the dark every once in awhile. It was designed to keep the NVA off balance. Did it work? Who the hell knows?

All in all, it was just another day at the office.

***

A few days later we were at Firebase Veghel.

I read in the *Stars and Stripes* newspaper about the fallout in the States over the invasion of Cambodia. President Nixon explained it as a temporary measure to cut off the supply line to the NVA in South Vietnam and not a widening of the war. No one back home was listening. Several Kent State University students protested in a demonstration turned riot a couple of days earlier. The National Guard was called out and opened fire on the crowd, killing four students.

Our platoon was all in favor of the invasion even if

it was a limited foray. "About damn time" was the usual comment.

There was less unity on the killing of the protestors.

"Man, anyone calls an armed guardsman names and throws stuff at him must know he can snap. You take your chances. That's my view," said Peddler.

"What do you expect from the gutless wonders?" asked a newbie. "National Guardsmen only enlist to stay away from here, anyway."

Heads nodded in unison. Avoiding the draft and Vietnam by enrolling in your hometown unit with a ninety-nine percent probability you'd never leave the States created a distaste for National Guardsmen, a.k.a. No Guts, in everyone's mouth. This was regardless of if you were in Vietnam as a draftee or enlisted man.

"Still, they didn't have to fire. Everyone has a right to demonstrate, and that doesn't mean getting shot," Cap said.

"I beg to differ, my good man," Big Red huffed. "Any person who throws crap at me and calls me names can expect a response."

"Really?" said Cap. "You'd shoot a college kid? Maybe twenty years old and unarmed?"

"That's just it. I'm twenty and armed." He chuckled. "Courtesy of Uncle Sam. Here I am fighting to let assholes like that enjoy their sex, drugs, and rock 'n roll while I'm over here to defend democracy." He turned serious. "Lucky me." Then he looked around at each guy and said, "Lucky us."

Prophet walked by and told us a resupply chopper was

coming in thirty minutes. "Get ready."

We were slow to respond until he added, "Oh, yeah. There's some Doughnut Dollies on the chopper. You'll get some time with them if you look good for the L-T."

That did the trick. Doughnut Dollies were civilian Red Cross volunteers who spent a year in-country as morale boosters. If a firebase was deemed safe by the brass at any given time, you might get a visit.

"Real live American women? I know how they could boost my morale," Big Red said.

"You should be so lucky," said Cap. "They only go for officers, not jungle rats like us."

That was probably true. Still, the idea of seeing round-eyed women, hearing their voices, and—God forbid—smelling them, would be like manna from heaven.

Thirty minutes later we formed up to welcome the chopper as it arrived with supplies, fresh clothes, and mail. Four American girls from the Land of the Free emerged, wearing light-blue Red Cross uniforms. A redhead, a blonde, and two brunettes.

"I'd give my left testicle for a chance to see the breasts on that blonde," said Big Red.

"Partial to the redhead, myself," I blurted.

"The brunettes will do just fine," said Peddler.

Escorted by five officers, mostly captains and majors, the girls made their way down our welcoming line as handshakes and comments were exchanged.

"Hi, there. Where are y'all from?" asked the blonde.

I muttered, "Seattle," confused why I was so intimidated by this woman in front of me.

"Oh, yes. The place with all the rain." She smiled to put me at ease. The smell of her perfume was wonderful.

The other dollies were having the same effect on the rest of the platoon, who eagerly surged forward.

All except Prophet.

He stood off to the side with a disapproving look on his face.

"What's the matter, Sarge?" I asked.

"They shouldn't be here. They don't belong in Vietnam. They need to go back home and stay there."

"But Sarge, that's why they're here. To remind us of home. Isn't that a good thing?"

Prophet shook his head and walked away.

We spent the next few hours playing games. I kid you not. Word games, card games, and a TV theme song game where they held up a TV show name card and the first guy to stand and hum (or sing it out loud if brave enough) won a candy bar.

The highlight was Twister. I was one of ten selected to participate. The platoon cheered us on as the girls spun the color clock and we took turns struggling to put our feet and hands on the right colored dot. We looked ridiculous with our butts in the air, teetering and tangling up with each other as our squads cheered. For a short while, we were boys again.

Eventually the girls said their goodbyes and flew off. Something occurred to me. I asked Strode why they were named Doughnut Dollies. I hadn't seen any doughnuts.

"They got the nickname in World War Two when they operated doughnut machines and brought them out to guys in the field. Don't do it here, though. Too damn hot to use doughnut machines in Vietnam." He smiled. "Or so I've been told."

We didn't get any doughnuts. But nobody complained.

***

The Army had a weird policy for infantry officers in Vietnam. They served in the field for six months and then rotated to staff positions back in the rear for six months. Didn't make much sense to us grunts. As soon as you had a leader with experience, he was replaced by a newbie. Big Red said it was a classic example of a right way, a wrong way, and the Army way.

Our L-T left us the last week of May. Collins turned out to be a good leader despite his looks. He completed his missions (pleasing his superiors) without endangering his men unnecessarily (pleasing us). He relied on the experience of those around him and didn't let his ego get in the way. I met other officers as time went by who should have followed his example. One was his replacement, Stuart Harrington III.

The new L-T was a ring knocker. That's the term for West Point grads who wear their class rings out here. They're big and impressive. The wearer emphasizes certain points during an argument by knocking the ring against a desk, truck, post, gun, or something else solid. Like it's a magical talisman of some kind. If you could win a war with the size of those rings, we'd have won this fracas way before now.

***

It was noon when we found a stairway carved into the mountainside. It was a thing of beauty, really, with carefully chiseled steps and wooden handrails which obviously took a great deal of time and effort. The jungle foliage and tree canopy hid it from us as we walked by, ten yards away.

Big Red was razzing Dimes about small towns in North Dakota. "I bet you all gather downtown on Saturdays to watch the one parking meter in town violate itself."

Dimes was about to reply when we saw something moving in the bush. Scared the hell out of us, but turned out to be a wild pig. That's when we spotted the steps.

Harrington radioed for artillery assistance from a nearby firebase to soften up the hilltop prior to our upward assault.

Climbing up the steps with Cap, we heard a burst of gunfire from a tree about fifty yards ahead.

Cap said, "I'm hit," dropped like a rag doll, and died right there. Like a candle snuffed out in one poof. Big Red looked at me in a silent inquiry. I shook my head negatively.

"Too bad. I hope he's in Mormon heaven. He was a good guy," he said.

An RPG roared past our position and a newbie behind me disappeared.

Fucking A! I felt AK-47 rounds slicing through the air near my head.

The assault took three hours and cost the company

twelve dead and five wounded. At the top we threw smoke grenades in each bunker we found, but they were all empty. Blood trails led into the jungle. As usual, few bodies were left behind.

We'd found 1,500 pounds of rice from the black market marked with the USAID handshake logo, courtesy of the U.S. taxpayer. There was also fifty pounds of TNT, an operational telephone line, running water brought via bamboo pipes, a substantial weapons cache, several uniforms drying on a clothesline, medical supplies, a cornfield, and five old pig pens.

Most importantly, Dimes and I found a hooch with maps and documents with communist stamps. The new L-T was ecstatic.

Harrington, grinning from ear to ear, swaggered over to the NVA flagpole where their flag was fluttering in the breeze. He reached up to grab and pull it down.

Big Red was twenty yards away, saw what he was about to do, and yelled "Lieutenant, don't!" just as the booby trap went off. The explosion blew L-T ten feet before he landed on his side. When we got to him he looked like a piece of overdone meat topped with ketchup. I thought I heard a mewing sound, but maybe it was my imagination, because Strode pronounced him dead. Big Red was far enough away to survive the blast with only a few shrapnel pieces in his lower legs.

A medevac took our wounded and dead while we stacked the ammo and guns in a large pit and blew them up. We burned the supplies and food, hiked to a nearby hillside, and called in a B-52 strike to flatten the place forever. We watched from two miles away and felt the ground shake underneath us as the bombs fell.

It was a hell of a show.

***

Dimes and I got a promotion to Specialist (E-4) and a three-day pass for finding the papers. We decided to swing by the 18th Surgical to check on Big Red and then continue over to Da Nang to see Tran's family. There was no transport, so we didn't get to leave until late in the afternoon. We managed to bum a ride from Evans to the hospital, which had relocated twenty miles north of us.

Big Red was in a large open ward, recovering well and glad to see us. He flashed a two-fingered peace sign along with a big grin. Pinned to his pillow was a Purple Heart—or what he called his "Honey, I Forgot to Duck" medal.

We brought him magazines, but he really wanted to hear about the guys in the platoon. Everyone was fine, we said. No killed or wounded since he left. We did have a new cherry, who got heat stroke and was taken back to Camp Evans. They said he'd recover.

"Holy shit. I'd hate to be him when he comes back. Strode will not be happy," Big Red said. He turned and winked at me. "You might need to teach the kid how to move those shit can drums singlehandedly. Sounds like that's in his near future."

We swapped stories and lies for about an hour before the nurse came and shooed us out so Big Red could have dinner. Dimes went to flag down another ride. I went out the door closest to the chopper pad to have a smoke while waiting. Next to the exit was a sign directing transports of the dead over to the graves registration unit in the next building.

Outside, I wasn't alone. A black hospital medic with an Afro was smoking a Winston. It was clear in his eyes how he saw me. A grunt with a deep tan in a sun-bleached uniform sporting a Combat Infantryman Badge and jump wings. Probably a little crazy. It was the first time I realized I was no longer an FNG. I'd moved up in the world.

He nodded and I nodded back. Reaching in my upper pocket, I pulled out my crumpled pack of Camels. I hated unfiltered cigarettes. No matter what the brand, you always ended up picking loose bits of tobacco off the tongue with your fingers. Filtered cigs were the way to go. A Winston would taste pretty good right then, but I was stuck with a couple of unfiltered Camels. Still, it was better than nothing. The nicotine felt good and gave me a quick buzz. All was calm and peaceful. We both enjoyed the relative coolness as dusk approached.

Hospital staff was holding a ceremonial event of some kind on the far end of the chopper pad. Lined up in single file, each gave a high five and a handshake to a nurse making her way down the line.

I asked my fellow smoker, "What's the occasion?"

"It's Passover time," he said. "Everyone who is ready to DEROS back to the Real World gets one."

The nurse reached the end of the line, turned, waved, and ran to a nearby jeep. Hopping in, she barely had time to settle before it took off like a bat out of hell, circling the pad twice while emitting bright red smoke from the tailpipe. It ended up by a Huey on the helipad. The smoke disappeared, and she scurried onto the helicopter. It took off, heading directly over the hospital crowd. She leaned out and tossed her boonie hat out, like a bride at a wedding. A frenzy erupted as everyone attempted to catch it. The winner, a tall blonde fellow, snatched it and danced an Irish jig.

"Impressive," I said to my fellow smoker. "I still don't get the Passover connection."

"Wait."

Two Hueys quickly caught up to the departing chopper. Attendants to the departing ship, all three made a circular turn passing over our heads in tight formation about fifty feet above. Another tight turn followed along with a second pass. Then the middle chopper headed straight in the direction of home while the other two peeled off and disappeared. As their noise faded away, the crowd dispersed. My smoke buddy left with them. All was still once again.

Finishing my second cigarette, I saw something approaching on the horizon. It was a Chinook CH-47. Remembering the crash of the other bird weeks ago, I found myself shuddering involuntarily, then told myself to man up. Shit happens. Get used to it.

Taking a final drag, I threw the butt on the ground, grinding it out with my boot. The Chinook loomed larger, and I saw a hanging cargo net loaded with tanned bodies. One large pile of heads, legs, arms and other odds and ends sticking out at strange awkward angles through the rope lacings.

Hovering over the pad, the pilot no doubt intended to gently lower the bodies onto the tarmac. Misjudging the altitude, he dropped the cargo net too high. The massive load hit the concrete with a resounding wet splat. Think rotten tomatoes hitting a wall and you have the idea. The remains and body parts flew in all different directions.

Graves registration soldiers from the building next door moved toward the mess. Their job? Scoop it up and sort it out. For the first time, I was grateful I was in the infantry. Maybe not every REMF had it easy after all.

I found out later the bodies were casualties from a battle at Firebase Henderson two days earlier. Bad weather prevented their removal by chopper. They ripened in the moist heat, accounting for the wet splat.

In any case, they deserved better.

28

May 6, 1945
Dachau, Germany

Anna's line halted at the top of the rise. Beyond it lay another world, a rail yard with boxcars lined up far into the distance. The stench increased as they trudged downward toward the train. Some guards pulled out gas masks from their belts and put them on. Others stuffed their uniformed arms against their faces to guard against the smell.

Inside the boxcars were people of every shape and size. Dead people. Dead for a long time, many decomposed and rotted into unimaginable shapes. As Anna walked by the side of the train she saw boxcar after boxcar of the dead. Some cars were stuffed, others almost empty. Some had bodies falling halfway out. Piles of fresh corpses brought from other parts of the camp lay on the ground everywhere. Most of these were covered in flies.

People cried at the ghastly sight. None were staying there voluntarily.

One woman motioned toward the children. "They had no part in this, what are they doing here?"

Anna shook her head. She didn't know, either. The guards made it clear they couldn't leave.

As they were marched down the side of the train, she

saw something to her left on a pile of bodies. For an instant her mind denied it, but the illusion could not hold. It was Heinrich, sprawled out at an unnatural angle on top of a woman and thirty or more other bodies stacked like logs. She smelled the rotting flesh and saw his lifeless sunken eyes staring at the sky. Something inside her went dead. Finally, she began to cry.

The American guards took them to a shed where every third person was issued a shovel. Marched over to a tremendous pile of bodies, they were told to divide into three groups. The first was assigned to dig a pit one hundred feet long, four feet deep, and six feet wide. The second group was issued rubber gloves and assigned to moving the bodies from the piles onto makeshift wooden stretchers and then to the newly dug mass graves. The third group also received rubber gloves and was tasked with placing the dead in the grave with some modicum of dignity. Bulldozers filled the graves with dirt after the locals completed their tasks. Children under ten were not assigned to a group but told to watch their parents.

Some refused to join a group. "We had no part in this," they said.

The guards accepted the refusals calmly. "You don't have to participate, if you'd rather not. Instead you can spend the night with your family in one of the Polish or Russian prisoners' barracks. The inmates will be happy to show you what it was like here. Your family would find it quite an educational experience."

After that, everyone participated.

It took all day for the piles assigned to her group to be

properly placed in the ground. Men, women, and children. Eighty-three bodies. She counted them. Their faces would stay with her forever.

29

June 2, 1970
Da Nang, Vietnam

Da Nang is an Asian version of Seattle: close to the water, a blue bay with freighters waiting to unload cargo, some high rises (only a few higher than five stories), and people scurrying everywhere. Then again, Seattle didn't have a curfew where you'd be shot on sight by an MP if found in the street. It didn't have sections with dirt roads like Da Nang's slum area, referred to as Dogpatch. It wasn't nicknamed Rocket City, for how often the NVA shelled it so everyone knew they were still active in the mountains a few miles away.

Dimes and I spent the night at the U.S.O. Their slogan over the door, A Home Away From Home, proved to be pretty accurate. They had pool tables, pinball, a library, gift shop, overseas telephones, cafeteria, a few sleeping cots, and hot showers. More important, they had three American girl employees. They were forbidden to wear pants in-country. They were required to wear mini-skirts. Most guys were there just to get a look. The girls didn't seem to mind as long as you were polite and didn't act like an ass.

We each got a gift for our visit the next day at Tran's house. Dimes said local custom required one. I bought a

Timex watch and he got a bottle of Jack Daniels whiskey. One of the girls gift wrapped them for us.

"Anything we can do for you, just let me know," she said.

I grinned. "Anything?"

She blushed, stood a little taller, and beamed back. "Well, almost anything."

We both laughed. It felt good to flirt with a girl.

Next morning, we took a battered VW bug taxi to an old colonial French villa, painted a light green and surrounded by a high whitewashed concrete fence with a wrought iron gate. Dimes said something in Vietnamese to the driver as he paid our fare, causing the old man to smile.

I asked him what he said.

He shrugged. "Just 'Father, you can keep the change.'" He looked at me. His glasses, as usual, were falling forward down his nose, giving him a professor look. He pushed them back up with a finger. "It's amazing how people react when you speak the language and treat them with respect, eh?"

Walking toward the two-story house, it was hard to miss the long mirror mounted on the front door.

Seeing my puzzled look, Dimes said, "That's to fool a dragon thinking of entering and causing trouble. Seeing his own reflection, he thinks a dragon is already there and moves on."

After seeing that dragon in the field, I understood, at least a little, the hold that dragons had on the Vietnamese imagination.

The door opened, framing a tall middle-aged white

man with grey hair, wearing a short-sleeved white shirt and black slacks. I must have looked surprised. I expected a native. He smiled briefly at Dimes and extended a hand to me.

"Good evening. I'm John Paul. Please, do come in."

I shook his hand and he ushered us into the foyer where we gave him our presents.

"Chou ong (Hello, sir)" said Dimes.

The man smiled. "Your Vietnamese is getting better, young man," he replied.

He laid our presents in front of an altar on a table against the wall by the front door. Dimes warned me not to be offended if he didn't open them. Tradition was for wrapped gifts to be opened after your departure. We followed him down a corridor into the main room of the house, where the family was seated. They stood and bowed as we entered.

Tran was flanked by a woman on each side. On his right was his mother. On the left was one of the most gorgeous girls I'd ever seen. Tran's half sister was tall for a Vietnamese woman—at five feet eight inches—and wore a sheer blue ao dai with painted cranes on its front, hanging over her silk pants. She had a shiny mane of long black hair, wonderful round breasts, and a tiny waist. With green eyes, high cheekbones, and full lips, she was a knockout. Dimes hadn't exaggerated. She put the U.S.O. ladies to shame.

"Let's have some entertainment for our guests," John Paul said, nodding toward his daughter.

This must have been prearranged, as she reached behind the couch and pulled out a crude looking wooden guitar. But it wasn't a guitar. It was more like a four-foot-long hand harp. She sat on the floor, laid it on her lap, and introduced it as a dantranh. As she played for us I was spellbound. Here was a beautiful woman: talented, refined, and living in a nice house. None of this was what I expected to find. Dimes was a lucky guy. I was an idiot.

After several musical pieces there was quick chatter with their high-pitched sing-song language. A decision of some sort was made.

"Agreed. Come," said John Paul. "Time to eat."

As we moved to the next room I admired the grace of Baby Doll's body. She moved almost in a glide that was strangely calming.

The table was prepared with bowls of food. As we sat, I noticed plates of rice and chopsticks in front of two unoccupied seats.

"Are we expecting more people?" I asked.

"Not at all," said our host. "Those are a courtesy for the Dead."

John Paul's wife carried in a dish and ceremoniously placed it in front of Dimes. It was a plate of chicken heads—an honor reserved for the eldest of the male guests. Dimes waited while the rest of us were served fish, beef, chicken, rice, and vegetable dishes—but no chicken heads, thank God. Then he ate the heads with gusto as we began our meal. Obviously he'd had this "honor" at their house before.

Taken aback at seeing Dimes crunch and swallow several heads in a row, I turned to our host and asked if he was a contractor from the States.

"No, I came to this country with the French Foreign Legion. I stayed after their defeat in 1954." I must have looked confused because he quickly added, "No, I'm not French, young man. I was an Austrian who joined the Legion after World War Two, just one of many men in Europe with no future after that disaster. The Legion offered me a new name, a job, and life in Asia in return for five years of my life. For men with no hope and nowhere else to go, it was a fair bargain at the time."

Dimes finished, put his plate aside, and stared at Baby Doll. She blushed and the others at the table pretended not to notice either of them.

We moved to the outside patio to have tea. Actually, the ladies had tea. We men had a "33," a local beer served in a small green Coke-sized bottle. I was watched as I drank it. Apparently foreigners sometimes didn't like the taste, since it was made of rice. It was about the same as a Schlitz. I smiled and lifted the bottle in appreciation.

Curious about John Paul, I asked why he stayed in Vietnam.

"I met my wife." He nodded in her direction and she smiled back. "I knew she would be more comfortable here than in a devastated Europe. If I wanted her and to be a stepfather to Tran, I had to stay."

"Did you have trouble becoming part of the community here?" I was wondering how accepted Dimes and Baby Doll would be. Probably better than in North Dakota, but maybe not.

"A Westerner is never truly accepted in Vietnam, young man." He smiled at my naïveté.

"Let me give you an example." He pointed to his wife. "When she agreed to marry me, I had to of course meet her parents. We went to their house, where she introduced me. She said, 'Mother, Father, I would like you to meet It. I love It. It and I are going to be married. Both It and I ask for your blessing.'"

"She called you 'It'?"

"Indeed she did. In Vietnamese culture I wasn't a real person. I wasn't Vietnamese. It's a casual sort of racism Asians practice. They have their own hierarchy, and each Asian society—be it Japanese, Chinese, Korean, Cambodian, Thai, or Vietnamese— regards the others as inferior. All of the others are 'It.' I took no offense. I knew she loved me."

That was hard to wrap my head around. In America, only whites were considered prejudiced. Yet I'd noticed black Americans here called the Vietnamese names like gook and slant-eyes more than the whites. The notion that other races could be prejudiced as well was an eye opener. Was it human nature to need someone to be inferior so you could feel better about yourself?

I was going to ask Dimes, but he and Baby Doll were quietly murmuring back and forth to each other. They weren't paying any attention to us. I turned back to John Paul.

"Was that the only barrier?" I asked.

"Of course not. I had a shaved head when I was in the Legion. In Vietnam that's considered bad luck, unless you're a monk. I had to grow it back if I wanted to stay here." He rubbed his hand against the top of his head.

"There were plenty of other barriers as well. But one puts up with many things for love." He turned and patted his wife's hand affectionately.

We talked about other things, but those are the ones I remembered as we rode back to Evans that night.

30

June 14, 1970
A Shau Valley, Vietnam

There is a saying on the blue Morton salt container back home: When it rains, it pours. That applied in what Big Red called the "Aw Shit Valley" as well.

When it rained there, it was a deluge, a solid sheet of water. You couldn't see more than a few yards ahead. The upside was you didn't have to worry about taking a shower in the mountains. Wait, and a good rain would come and clean you off, clothes and all. The downside: when the rains persisted, choppers didn't fly. No air support, no resupply of fresh clothes. Food and water ran short. That could go on for a week or more.

On patrol in valleys, you'd find large craters often fifty feet deep and a hundred feet across, the result of B-52 bomber strikes. Rain filled them up. They would have made great swimming pools except the soil was loose so they resembled gigantic mud holes more than anything.

The two biggest problems were jungle rot and boredom.

The first was easier to handle than the second. Pull off your boots and your skin peeled off in greenish-black sheets, like a shedding snakeskin. One guy shed so much wrinkled skin I saw the actual bones on the bottom of his feet. They stank real bad, and he was lucky not to lose a foot. But keeping your feet dry wasn't easy. You and a buddy could try and link ponchos overhead into some kind of shelter. More often than not, it didn't work out, and you ended up soaked anyway. The best you could do was air out your feet daily, have dry socks filled with white foot powder in your ruck, and change them every day.

The real enemy was boredom and how to pass the time. We had a couple decks of waterproof cards and played a lot of card games. I'm decent at Twenty-One and Crazy Eights, but suck at Poker.

The best boredom antidote was sharing stories and shooting the bull about novels you read, real life experiences, or philosophy. Anything to make the time pass. As a result, guys told you things they would never share ordinarily. It just came out. During one of these breaks, we found out Tran's life story.

Tran was a student at Hue University three years earlier. Despite having an American English professor whom he liked, he was a nationalist. The Americans were occupiers, and like the earlier French, needed to go home. Looking back, maybe he was trying to make up for his Austrian stepfather. Without telling anyone, he left the university in October 1967 and traveled north with a classmate where they joined the North Vietnamese Army. He had finished his training in January 1968 when his unit was sent to participate in the Tet Offensive outside Hue.

He was happy. The NVA were going to liberate the city, free all political prisoners, and deport the foreigners. Supporters of the Saigon government would be housed in special camps and reeducated before being freed in the new socialist country. He would be a liberator and show his family the true way.

The city fell faster than anyone anticipated. The South Vietnamese army (ARVN) units defending the city fled or quickly surrendered. Tran and the others were exhilarated. They thought the people were with them.

At the end of the first day, they were given lists of those to be arrested. The lists were detailed. Names, addresses, occupations, and relatives were all named. Special attention was given to school teachers, clergy, civil servants, American civilians. This was no last-minute plan. It was well thought out.

Tran recognized the name of his American English professor. Thinking it would be best if his teacher saw a familiar face, Tran went with his squad to arrest him. His teacher was taken with his hands bound behind him to a local Catholic church school to be held. Several hundred men, women, and children were there, all scared and wondering about their fate. Tran reassured the professor it would be all right, but he was ashamed. The professor and he knew better.

The next day a communist party commissar ordered Tran's unit toward the wharf along the An Cuu River. Trucks with mounted loudspeakers patrolled the city, announcing the names of people on the lists and telling them to turn themselves in at designated buildings. Most complied. Others tried to sneak out of the city and were caught.

They were combined into a large group of prisoners and given the task of digging a long ditch next to the river.

They were forced to stand alongside it. Each was bound by the feet and had their hands tied behind them. A rag was stuffed into their mouths and all were thrown down into the ditch. Several of them struggled to climb out as a bulldozer was brought up. Those who managed to get to the top of the ditch were struck by the guards AK-47s and tumbled back into the hole. Then the bulldozer began its work and buried everyone alive.

Tran was horrified but kept silent. Dissent, and he'd be in the next group. This happened again the next day, in the same way. His professor was in that group.

The day after, they were given a new list of names including Tran's stepfather, mother, and sister. His commander did not realize Tran was related to them. Tran volunteered to bring them in. Reunited with his family, he told them what was waiting for them if they stayed. He smuggled them out on a stolen oxcart, and drove it to the nearest ARVN outpost. After surrendering he was sent to Con Son Island prison camp. He languished there for over a year until selected for the Kit Carson scout program.

He still wanted us gone. "Vietnam for the Vietnamese" was his slogan. It was just that he thought it had to be under the Saigon government. They made a lot of mistakes but they weren't as bad as the North, he said. Slaughtering innocents on a list was not South Vietnamese or American policy.

Finishing his story, Tran grinned. "Besides, I have met you Americans. None of you want to be here. We will get the country back for the people," he said.

After his tale, none of us said anything for a long time.

Personally, I thought, *What a country. What a mess.*

***

Somehow over the next two weeks, I become a parent. Didn't plan on it, didn't want it. Got it all the same.

I was throwing the remains of my C-ration into the scat hole when I was introduced to PFC Hiram Webb of Pine Bluff, Arkansas. Big goofy smile. Eager to please. Aside from being a cherry requiring the usual learning curve, I thought he would fit in well enough as time passed, until I noticed some things. Little things that didn't add up.

Webb could only follow basic directions. You needed to reinforce those often or he forgot and wandered off elsewhere. He wanted to carry a yo-yo to do tricks like Walk the Dog or Round the World while on patrol. Every morning we took his yo-yo away until the end of the day. He had me read a letter aloud from Loretta, his girlfriend back home whom he referred to as his Valentine. Turned out he couldn't read or write. He got in the Army by having a witness watch him sign an X on his enlistment form. I'd never met anyone who was illiterate, before. He was like a big, overgrown, grateful puppy. He didn't lay his head on your lap while you were eating at the table, but it was close.

After the eighth day of this, I asked Prophet what was up with the guy.

"He's a Project 100,000 recruit," Prophet said, as if that explained everything. When I didn't respond, he went into more detail.

"Here's the deal. The government decided to share the misery of this war. Someone noticed that a lot of men who couldn't pass the military entry tests were poor and uneducated. Why not allow them to see the world, earn a wage, and fill out the ranks over here? So they started a program called Project 100,000. The military was granted the right to enlist up to one hundred thousand of these guys who otherwise would have never gotten in."

"You're basically saying they allowed the retarded in the Army?" I couldn't believe it.

"They're not retarded. They're slow. There's a difference. They can function and obey directions. They can't do more than one thing at a time, as you found out."

"But Sarge, he's going to get hurt. Or maybe get someone else killed. He's not going to be a plus for the platoon, that's for sure."

Prophet nodded his head in agreement. "Already talked to Strode about it. We need to get him out. We can't refuse him, though, or the Army will get on us. Best way to handle it is watch him like a hawk for the next two months. At that point, he'll have enough time in service to reenlist for a three-year hitch. You know what that means."

I knew. If a guy reenlisted for three years while in the field it got him out of combat and into a rear echelon job as a supply clerk or the like. Several guys did that during my time there. No one criticized them for it. You did what you thought you had to.

"Shit, Sarge. Is there even a job he can do? One that will keep him out of trouble? The guy can't read or write. Hard

to be a supply or admin guy. Maybe he could be a cook?"
Prophet shook his head. "Maybe. But even a cook has to be able to read directions. When we go on stand-down, I want you to see the re-up NCO on his behalf."

"Why me? I'm not his mother."

Prophet laughed. "In this case I'm making you one." He grew serious. "The poor bastard deserves better than what will probably happen to him out here. Your job is to make sure Project has some kind of future." He picked up his M-16 and took a bottle of LSA oil to begin cleaning his weapon.

It was clear I was dismissed. Webb had a nickname and I'd been appointed his mother.

We got a four-day stand-down a week later. I did the usual cleanup requirements regarding gun, ammo, clothes, and shower and got drunk. It wasn't until the afternoon of the next day I remembered my "son" and headed to see the re-up NCO.

His office was easy to find outside the battalion headquarters building. Reenlistment posters in full color were displayed along the inside corridor leading to his office. There was JOIN THE PEOPLE WHO'VE JOINED THE ARMY and WORK IN THE SKY, featuring a paratrooper descending in his chute. The one that caught my eye was CHOOSE YOUR VOCATIONAL TRAINING.

I knocked on the door. "Come in," commanded a booming voice. SFC Johnson sat behind a large mahogany desk with a large nameplate proclaiming his name, rank, and title of re-up NCO. Beside the desk was a tall pole with an American flag. On the wall was a framed picture of President Nixon and others of various enlisted men holding one hand in the air and swearing the new enlistment oath for the camera.

It took me a minute to explain I wasn't there to reenlist but was feeling things out for a friend. At first he didn't believe me. As we got into details, he saw I was serious.

"Let me get this straight. You want to know if there's something available for this Category IV guy? Job-wise? Something that allows him to stay in the Army but keeps him out of harm's way?" Johnson did not look enthusiastic. "Specialist Nickels, you have to understand the Army doesn't see these guys as career material. Hell, we don't want them here in the first place."

"Sarge, if we don't get him out of the field he's going to get himself killed. There's gotta be something he can qualify for." I nodded toward the Sign Up for Vocational Training poster on the wall.

"Only one real possibility exists, as I see it," said Johnson. He took paper and pencil from a drawer and began to draw a map. "There's a building several streets over from where we are. Go and see the major in charge. If he agrees, I'll sign the guy up. But only if he agrees."

Building 4141 was unlike the majority of the buildings at Evans. This one had concrete blocks and wasn't elevated off the ground. Inside, I saw a front counter running the entire length of the room, with a small waist high swinging door to allow entry. Behind was a pair of double doors with a clear smell of something strong coming from behind them.

A PV2 was sitting on a stool and reading a *Casper the*

Friendly Ghost comic. He was so engrossed in his story I cleared my throat to announce my presence.

"I'm here to see the major."

"Okay." He tucked his comic in his rear pocket and went through the back doors. A minute later he returned, sat back down on his stool, took his comic back out from his pocket, and began to read it again. I was about to ask what was going on when the major appeared.

Only he wasn't a major. He was wearing an E-6 insignia, and his nametag said Talbot. He looked at me expectantly.

"Sergeant, I think there's been a mix-up." I took out the map drawn by Johnson and gave it to him. "I'm here to see the major about the possibility of having a friend of mine sign up to work here. Sergeant Johnson said he'd sign the guy only if the major agrees." I shrugged.

"Johnson gave me a call when you left his office. Been expecting you." He squinted as he analyzed me from head to foot.

"Okay...I guess." I still didn't have a clue what was going on but decided to play along. "Do I get to see the major now?"

Talbot's face was expressionless.

"Come along, I'll give you the tour. You can ask questions as needed." He turned around and proceeded through the double doors in the back. I followed.

Behind the doors was a huge open space, probably at one time a large garage and motor pool area for trucks. Now it was a laundry, the biggest I'd ever seen. Dozens of industrial washing machines were located on the right side of the concrete floor. The strong smell I identified earlier was Clorox and detergents being used to clean the heavy loads. Large grocery carts like you'd see at Safeway were in the middle. On the left were dozens of dryers. Men were putting clothes into them or taking them out. Others carted finished wash loads over to the dryers or were folding clothes and placing them in large bins with a designated company and unit painted on the side.

I emitted a long appreciative whistle. "I had no idea. Thought when you gave us back our fatigues and other laundry through supply that it was done by the local women."

"No, we do it all right here. Those men you see here are all in MOS 57E." He saw my puzzled look and laughed. "Means Impregnation Specialist. Hell of a title for laundryman, I know." He shook his head. "I can guarantee you half the Army has no idea such an MOS exists. But the question is do you think your friend would flourish here? Can he do this job?"

"Yeah, he can do this. There's nothing too difficult here."

I hesitated.

"Well?"

"I might be stretching my luck, but is this a career path MOS? In other words, if he wanted to stay in for twenty years and qualify for a pension, could he do that here?"

He stared back at me. "What did Johnson tell you about me?"

"Nothing. Why?"

"You're sure?" He seemed skeptical.

"He didn't say a thing."

He contemplated that a few seconds before saying "Okay."

As he walked away, he said to me over his shoulder "Tell Johnson it's a go. The major says yes." Then he disappeared amid the maze of machines. Our conversation was over.

I wasn't sure what had happened but went back to the re-up office and told Johnson it was a go. I asked him why I wasn't allowed to see the major.

"You did see him. He gave you permission for your friend."

"No, Sarge, that was an E-6 named Talbot."

"One and the same, kid. Talbot is both a major and an E-6. Until six months ago, Talbot was a major flying a Huey. It was his third tour here. At some point he woke up one morning and couldn't get out of bed. Couldn't get into that chopper anymore. Just couldn't do it. Seen too much and it broke him. He was ten months away from getting in his twenty years and a well-deserved retirement."

Johnson shrugged.

"It put the Army in a quandary as to what to do. On one hand, you can't have an officer refusing to do his duty. On the other hand, he was close to retirement. Something had to be done. He was demoted to an E-6 and transferred to the laundry detachment. Putting his last year in there means he'll be allowed to officially retire as a major and collect an officer pension instead of getting nothing. Pretty good deal, but humiliating even so. That's why he wondered about you. Thought you might be there to twist the knife in him, somehow. When he decided you were on the level, he wanted to help. Probably sees some of your friend in his situation, I suspect."

Johnson yawned and scratched the side of his face. "People are basically good, Nickels. Even lifers in the Army." He smiled and then opened his top desk drawer and pulled out some paperwork forms, put them in a manila folder, and handed them to me.

"Keep these. In two months have your friend bring them back to me completed and signed. That means you'll be doing the completing, I know. Make sure both of you are here when he swears in for his new term. I need to know this is really his idea and not you forcing him into something he doesn't want."

Back at my hooch, I stored the folder away. Like a good parent I had protected my "son" the best I knew how. I just hoped it was good enough.

31

October 7, 1945
Munich, Germany

Anna stubbed out her cigarette. She had smoked continually during her tale. Now that tale was over.

She stood up. Since she told him what happened, it was clear he was expected to go.

For the first time, he was angry with her.

"That's it?"

"That's it," she said glumly.

"What has that got to do with me?"

"You don't get it, Frank? I want nothing to do with anyone associated with Dachau."

He tried reassurance. "Anna, you know I had nothing to do with that. It was the Death's Head units."

"I don't care. Papa died of a heart attack two weeks after we toured the camp. I lost my faith that day. A world in which such things are allowed to happen means there is no God. I had to leave the parish and move here."

She shuddered. "I have terrible dreams now. I'm thrown naked in a pit and I see those faces all the way down while screaming. I don't know what I could have done when that camp was running, but I know I want out of this godforsaken country. I want to go somewhere new. Somewhere fresh."

"Just like that?" He felt the bitterness of the words even as he spoke them. Germany was in ruins. He was on the run. Now his brother's fiancée was denying her heritage and talking about going to a new place. A new world.

A sudden thought occurred to him.

"Anna, where did you get that carton of cigarettes?"

She got defensive. "I think you should go, Frank."

"Answer the question."

"That is none of your business."

"Oh, I think if the fiancée of my brother is now a whore, it's definitely my business." He felt himself getting angrier.

She slapped him across the face. The sound it made was loud.

He stared at her. Her eyes had always been a metallic blue. Now they seemed to ice over as he looked at her.

"I ask again. Are you now a whore, Anna?"

"You sorry bastard. You're a member of a criminal organization and you're calling me names? I lost my innocence that day because of men like you!" She fairly shrieked the last sentence.

She calmed down and said quietly "When I was there viewing the handiwork of your Nazi state, I realized I felt both anger and compassion at what I saw, but also guilt and shame at viewing it. I want to run away and put distance between me and this charnel house of a country. I will get out of here, Frank. How I do so is no longer a concern of yours."

He stared at her for a long moment. She disgusted him. But Heinrich had loved her. He owed him that but no more.

"Very well. You go your way, I go mine." He drew close to her face. She flinched and he smiled. Bending to the side he whispered in her ear. "For my brother's sake, I leave you. But if you are ever in the way of my avenging his murder, you will pay. Remember that."

32

July 4, 1970
Firebase Ripcord, Vietnam

Happy Birthday, America. We have our own fireworks for free out here. At Firebase Ripcord, every day is the Fourth of July.

We arrived three days ago. Ripcord turned out to be about the size of a football field and located on the top of a tall bald hill. It existed to fire 155mm artillery toward the Ho Chi Minh Trail to disrupt the NVA supply trains and block the enemy from Hue. Forward fire support for infantry companies operating in the A Shau Valley was especially needed when the helicopters couldn't fly due to bad weather. The population varied from 150 to 400 men at any given time. Units of the 506th took turns providing security.

Our 155mm cannons shot a distance of twenty-nine miles, while four 105mm pieces had a shorter ten-mile range. We had a fire pit for 4.2 inch mortars shooting shells for eight miles, along with some 80mm mortars with a two-mile range for close-in support. Only if this barrage of artillery wasn't effective, would an infantry unit in the field call for air support. This safety blanket meant few companies moved out beyond the range of firebase artillery support.

Security at Ripcord was a line of bunkers with interlocking fields of fire and rows of wire and traps put in depth further out. None of the bunkers were of the sandbagged, aboveground, easy target types, and our positions were built-in L-shaped fighting pits that were dug deep. A bulldozer carved out a trench for steel conex containers for a battalion HQ and medical station. There were four helipads at various points.

Some guys loved firebase duty, since it often kept you out of direct contact with the enemy in unknown territory. You usually got a hot meal and there was no humping up or down trails, except for occasional patrols. The downside? If things were calm you got to work guard shifts, laying lots of triple layered concertina wire, trip flares, claymores, and detonating wires connected to mines, repairing barbed wire fences, garbage detail, shit-burn detail, and that Army favorite: filling sixty-pound sandbags with the local dirt.

My "son" actually seemed to enjoy it. For the rest of us, it felt like being on a prison chain gang. If the enemy wanted to come after you, you were often a sitting duck on top of that hill. I found myself thinking the war here was like a game—a deadly one, but a game nevertheless. We sent day patrols out on trails through the wire. NVA sappers tried to sneak in through the wire at night and blow things up. Tit for tat.

The insides of our bunker had a musty basement smell. Rats the size of cats came in to escape the sound of the artillery or to feed on G.I. leftovers. I slept with a blanket over my face because they would run right over you in the dark. You had to be careful, because the snakes liked to eat the rats and both could be found nesting under or on your cot. To kill the rats, we mixed a bit of C-4 with peanut butter and left it out at night.

If you had free time and a call came in for some artillery rounds, you might go watch a salvo. If it was a morning round, you watched the ground as the dirt came alive with thousands of insects and fire ants coming up from under the ground to flee the blast. At the same time, you could see the sound of a round as the shock wave traveled through the air and hit you, causing an involuntary blink. The real trick was sleeping when they fired rounds at night. It took a good week to adjust. Eventually, I could sleep thirty feet away and ignore the whole shebang.

We were there two weeks when a Chinook, hovering to drop a sling load of 105 ammo, was hit by an NVA long range 12.7mm machine gun. It crashed on top of the ammo bunker and spilled burning JP-4 aviation fuel into the ammo dump. Over the next eight hours hundreds of artillery rounds went off. They shattered the six tubes of 105-artillery and burned out the medical aid station and ops center. There wasn't a thing we could do except wait it out, huddled in our bunkers. Stick your head out and all you saw was a cloudy atmosphere, like heavy smog in Los Angeles.

When the explosions ceased, we emerged into a total mess. The only artillery to survive were the 155mm howitzers. The rest were twisted scrap metal thrown around like toy playthings. Yet the firebase perimeter was intact. We figured they would remove the destroyed material and resupply.

Prophet figured otherwise.

"Infantry doctrine dictates not to commit infantry to direct combat without close-in artillery support. Only 105s deliver enough rapid close-in support to dislodge well dug-in or concealed enemy troops. Pay attention to the 105 Redlegs. If those guys are removed, this place will shut down."

The next day the 105 artillerymen were evacuated. We took bets as to Prophet's prediction.

We'd been shelled by mortars every day for the past three weeks. Starting the last week, we were shelled hundreds of times a day. On one day alone we had twelve casualties. No one was happy about being a sitting target. Hell, trying to go outside to take a crap in the latrine turned into a game of Russian Roulette. I got so I could hold it in for three days so as not to take a chance. Morale was starting to hit bottom.

"I'd hate to be the captain these days," said Big Red. "Imagine if someone bites the farm while attending to his business. The C.O. has to write a condolence letter like 'Dear Mrs. Smith, I'm sorry to inform you Billy was killed in action yesterday as he sat heroically on our shitter bench in the latrine.' Hell, the mothers of America get letters like that, and this war would end pretty damn quick."

Two days later we got word Ripcord was closing down. A live NVA field telephone wire in the jungle was discovered by Delta Company, who tapped into their conversations for five hours. Turned out we were now surrounded by four NVA regiments. That meant 12,000 of them and less than 400 of us.

Nobody wanted to leave ground that had been fought for and won. Men died and we needed to have something to show for it. But there it was. We were the hole in the doughnut. To stay was suicide.

It was time to go.

***

At first light on July 23, 1970, fourteen Chinook CH-47s hovered in line against the bright, beautiful, cloudless sky, coming to airlift us out. Each could carry thirty men per trip back to Evans, and we anticipated all of us getting out over the next several hours. One by one they came in to take their turn landing on Ripcord's large lower pad. It was the only pad large enough to accommodate a Chinook landing. Several choppers were outfitted with gear to take out the remaining six 155mm howitzers, the inoperable 105mm cannons, the two bulldozers and the commo equip with us.

The first few evacs went well, despite taking some hits. Our platoon was in place to take the next available Chinook after the current one was loaded. In spite of the heat and gusty winds, we were all wearing flak vests as the NVA shelling grew more intense. Groups of men huddled in lines, hunched over, faces down, grabbing the back of the man in front, and boarding the helicopter in a prop wash whirlwind of dust and rocks whipped up by the chopper blades. Looking inside the cigar-like fuselage, we saw soldiers kneeling against the cot seating or clutching cargo nets on the floor for handholds on takeoff. Everyone wanted to put this godforsaken place behind them as quick as possible.

They say bad luck runs in threes. It's a lie. I'd already seen three Chinook disasters since I was in-country. Now I saw a fourth. Just before 0800 an NVA .51 anti-aircraft shell hit our CH-47 as it was hovering over the pad prior to our boarding. We ran for our lives as it crashed down in flames near the area of the destroyed 105 artillery pieces from five days earlier. Hundreds of rounds went off again in a chain reaction of loud, sustained explosions. The neatly assembled squads awaiting evacuation scattered like leaves blown all over our side of Ripcord, huddling behind whatever cover they could find.

As the minutes ticked by, the explosions continued. The earth shook and metal shards flew in every direction. The resulting wreckage prevented other CH-47s from using the only pad large enough to accommodate them. Now useless, the eggbeaters returned to base leaving over half of us behind. Only Hueys could fit on the three remaining smaller pads at Ripcord. It would take time for them to get to the firebase, and they could only take out six men each as opposed to a Chinook's thirty.

Our squad ran to the nearby command bunker when the crash occurred. Waiting out the explosions, we heard the radio and calls for the division to send all Hueys to Ripcord *now*. Within a half hour, there were sixty appearing on the horizon, all heading for us.

The mortar fire and artillery shells hitting us were so thick they dared land only one Huey at a time at each pad for a second or two, as desperate men ran for their lives from the bunker areas and threw themselves inside. All organized withdrawal by platoon disappeared. It was every man for himself. Overhead, the remaining Hueys formed a single line and circled the mountaintop, waiting their turn in line to dodge the NVA shells, grab their six-man load in seconds, and get out as quick as possible.

Not all of the helicopters made their pickup successfully. One was shot down on the steep southern side, but another hovered over it and managed to get the crew out and back to safety despite numerous mortar explosions near the wreckage. That rescue crew had balls of steel.

Prophet found me outside the command bunker with Big Red, Dimes, Tran, Peddler, and Project. We were separated from the rest of the platoon. "We're going there," he said, pointing to the uppermost helicopter pad on the hill taking the least mortar fire of the three evacuation points. It seemed an insane choice given the distance of eighty yards and the number of incoming shells, but we had faith in Prophet. He would know where to go. I looked at the others. They were nodding and getting ready.

The boom, boom, boom of the NVA artillery was constant. Prophet started out and we followed, passing a wrecked Huey that had crashed minutes earlier with its load of men. Inside, charred outlines of bodies were surrounded by leaping flames. Smoke was everywhere. Mixed in were white clouds of NVA tear gas to disorient the Huey pilots. Each of us teared up, and I could feel salty tears and snot pouring out of my nose. None of us was carrying a gas mask. Luckily, the constant winds carried most of it away.

Below us on the valley floor, I saw artillery shells from Firebase Barnett and Firebase O'Reilly hitting masses of advancing NVA, all mixed together with the streams of green and gold enemy tracers, the shriek of jets swooping low to drop 500-pound bombs on the NVA, the screams of the wounded on both sides, and the rockets of the Cobra gunships as they fired their ordinance on attackers outside the wire perimeter.

To slow down the enemy attack, Prophet had us shoot from different angles to convince the incoming NVA there were more of us left in our sector. No time to get scared. Survival instinct kicked in.

Halfway to the upper pad, the fuel dump was hit by a mortar shell and set off the remaining 155mm ordinance. The resulting blast was gigantic, and we were forced to take whatever cover we could find. As the blaze burned down, it produced a brown haze blocking the sun. The ground everywhere was now either gray or charcoal colored dirt. Coupled with the noise, screaming, and shelling, it was the closest to Hell we were going to get on earth.

Below us the NVA were coming up the mountain like a swarm of ants. If we didn't do something quick, we'd see the real underworld soon enough. Prophet set up a final security perimeter on the northern slope. Some gooks were past the lower perimeter wire.

"Now I know how Davy Crockett felt at the Alamo!" yelled Big Red.

A Phantom jet roared in at less than a hundred feet off the ground toward the NVA swarm, and the noise was both deafening and painful at the same time. We threw ourselves flat on the ground and covered our ears. A massive explosion of dirt, vegetation, and body parts passed over us. I had dust in my eyes and could barely see, but crawled away from the slapping sounds of bullets all around me. A concussion from another blast hit me in the right shoulder and I rolled to my left involuntarily. I kept rolling. Anything to get away from the noise and confusion. A mortar round hit close, causing me to stop tumbling, and I tried to collect my thoughts. An RPG round whistled through the air and came down near my right, creating a small ditch before the actual explosion.

To my left some guy with a blonde crew cut and wide-open green eyes sat upright, staring at me. I crawled to him and pulled him flat to the ground.

"Get down, dumbass." I shook him thinking he was in shock, but there was no response other than his head rolling to the side. I saw a small hole in his chest. No visible blood. Just that hole.

In front of us, hundreds of NVA climbed the hillside. They were like silent ghosts, except for an occasional high whistle from an officer directing the NVA assault. When they got within the last hundred yards they fired their automatic weapons. At thirty yards they threw grenades and screamed insults.

"G.I., you die today!" one screeched.

We yelled our own insults back.

"Come and get us you slant-eyed sons of bitches!"

We threw grenades at them, eliciting high-pitched howls. It was like a playground fight at lunchtime, except this was a death match.

Running out of grenades, we threw rocks. This actually worked. Gooks would hear or see the object thrown, duck, and then peer over to see why it didn't go off. We'd take a single shot at them as our ammo was low. A quick verbal inventory revealed we averaged five rounds each, with only three grenades scattered among us.

The big question was whether we could get a rescue before being overrun. Fighting was now at twenty yards or so. We worked our way backwards up the side of the hill to the last chopper pad. My helmet flew off when a round hit it, penetrating and following the curvature inside before going out the other side, leaving me with a nicked ear. I had four rounds left.

We headed toward a pile of large boulders to plan our final dash to the top of the ridge. Behind the rocks were six men from Bravo Company. I don't know who was happier, us or them. With more hands on deck, we might have a chance to get out of this mess.

Prophet took over despite Bravo having their own staff sergeant. He didn't ask and the Bravo E-6 didn't object. "Here's what we're going to do. When the next wave of jets strafe and bomb the valley floor, we run a zigzag pattern up the final fifty feet of the slope to the crest. When the jets come in to bomb, the NVA close to us will duck. It's instinctive. That gives us time to bolt uphill. Got it?"

Sure enough, when the next wave of jets flew overhead our attackers ducked. We ran like hell to the top. I was spent when I got there and rolled over the crest to temporary safety. I had two rounds left. At that moment we heard the whoosh, whoosh, whoosh of a Huey, showing up like cavalry to the rescue in a John Wayne movie.

"Thank God," said Dimes.

That was premature.

As the chopper set down on the pad, it was hit near the rear rotor. It wobbled awkwardly, reared up like a horse, and did a flying wheelie heading directly toward us. At the last second, the pilot pulled it up and it flew ten yards overhead. He traveled another fifty yards before the rotor snapped off with a high-pitched squeal. The Huey fell to the ground in two separate pieces, and disappeared in a ball of fire, smoke, and dirt. There weren't any survivors.

There was no time to feel sorry for our would-be rescuers. 60mm mortar shells smashed down on us, throwing metal shrapnel and rock splinters everywhere. It was hopeless.

Swooping in from behind the hill, another Huey stopped and hovered a yard above the ground twenty yards away. We ran like madmen and threw ourselves onto the aircraft floor as AK-47 rounds pinged through the skin of the craft. The pilot raced to 2,000 feet and circled to look back.

Below us we saw the last six-man team from Bravo taking off in a separate Huey. A solid wall of neon-green .51 caliber anti-aircraft fire followed it with basketball-size exploding shells, trying to get in one last knockout blow as they flew away.

We watched with bated breath till they were out of range and then burst into cheers and backslaps like we scored the winning touchdown. Later we found out those guys had been among the first to arrive at Ripcord three months earlier. Now they were the last to leave. Karma, I guess.

As for us? Exhausted and in a daze, we said little on the flight back to Evans. What was there to say? We were alive.

***

Once we settled back in our hooch at Evans, the subject of R&R leave came up. You could apply for it after you had six months in country. I had almost seven and it was time to do what I'd come for—settle things with Ross. I would have tried a few weeks earlier but I knew with Ripcord going on it wouldn't be approved.

"I'm putting in for my R&R this afternoon."

"Where to?" asked Dimes.

"Saigon."

Both Dimes and Big Red looked at each other.

"You sure you wouldn't rather go spend your week in Thailand? Australia? Hong Kong? Hawaii? I'd want to get the hell out of this country," said Big Red.

"No, I've got some business to take care of down there."

"Positive?" said Dimes.

"I'm sure."

They looked at each other again. "Nickels, there's something we need to discuss with you," said Dimes. He adjusted his glasses as he looked over at Big Red for agreement.

Big Red nodded. "Tell him."

Dimes looked me squarely in the eyes. "We know."

"You know what?" I'd finished changing clothes and was putting the dirty ones in a green laundry bag to take to supply to be cleaned.

"Frank Ross."

Time stopped.

"How...wait...what?" Had I heard correctly? I dumbly looked at them both.

"Remember the time you got drunk and woke up with that big bump on your forehead?"

"Sure..."

"Well, Big Red gave it to you." Dimes glanced over to him and he shrugged back in return.

"Hey, it seemed like the best way to handle things at the time," said Big Red. "You were drunk and talking your fool head off. Once we figured out you were serious, I rammed your head into the table to knock you out and keep your secret."

I flopped down on my cot, totally embarrassed. I didn't dare look at them but lay back down on my pillow and stared at the ceiling.

"Why didn't you rat me out?"

"We talked about it all night," said Dimes. "Figured if you'd come this far we'd keep your secret. But we decided to watch out for you, too," he added hastily. "We almost turned you in when the jump requirement was announced. We found that paratrooper book on your bed and saw you after dinner practicing PLFs off some crates. Figured you knew what you were doing." He hesitated. "Look, if you're really determined to do this, we'll take our R&R with you to Saigon. We'll find Ross together. After all, we're The Three Musketeers."

"All for one, one for all, and all that crap," said Big Red.

I was flabbergasted and turned to face them. "I don't know what to say..."

"Wait," said Dimes. He held up his hand to stop me. "I've asked Be to marry me and she's said yes." His pride practically dripped off him.

"Congratulations." I meant it, too. I was happy for him.

"Thanks. But here's the catch. Army policy on local marriages states you can't file the paperwork until you have ninety days left in-county. Then your civil marriage paperwork is only good for the one day you select. I discussed it with her family and we selected the week of 20 October for my R&R. That's the earliest I can get in under the ninety day window. The betrothal ceremony is the twentieth. I'll get married on the twenty-first and come with you and Big Red on the twenty-third. If we all take the week on leave together, we'll have three days to fix things with Ross once we get down to Saigon. Will that work for you?"

Work for me? Two friends to help me take on Ross if I delayed for three months? It was a no brainer.

"You've got a deal."

33

November 11, 1945
Munich, Germany

Huddled in a doorway, Frank was trying to get some relief from the cold wind gusts when the car pulled up to the mansion. It was an American officer's vehicle, the usual green pea soup color with a white star on each side. A corporal chauffeur was behind the wheel, and the man Frank was looking for sat ramrod straight in the back seat: Colonel Anthony Ryan, U.S. Army, of the 157th Infantry Regiment, 45th Infantry Division.

Frank recognized Ryan from the file picture provided by a contact. He'd paid good money for the file so he'd know Ryan's background. It was money he couldn't afford, and it wasn't to be wasted.

Most of Ryan's division had returned to America in September, temporarily stationed in New York while awaiting deactivation. Frank's source was clear about that. They'd be scattered to the high winds by the end of December. That's why getting to the man in the car was important. Ryan was scheduled to rotate back to America tomorrow. This was Frank's only chance to get what he needed.

Frank knew if he walked by the colonel, he'd probably be ignored. There were too many like him in Germany to attract much notice from the American. Homeless tramps, men without money, prospects, or jobs. Men who lived by their wits alone in an occupied country. His country...or at least it had been. Now it was a vassal state to the new conquerors. Not that he felt any loyalty to, or sorrow for, the German people who survived. The best fell during the struggle.

What did that make him? He hadn't figured that out yet, and chose not to think of it now. The task ahead was too important.

The colonel entered his villa. It was the former mansion of a high-ranking Nazi party official, one of the "Golden Pheasants" who flew off like frightened birds at the approach of the Allies. *Probably living the good life in Argentina by now*, he thought bitterly.

Frank had no illusions about what he planned to do tonight. It was an irrevocable decision with no turning back. If he carried it out, he would become what he was already accused of being; he'd be a murderer. Even as he thought about it, Frank knew the decision was already made.

The driver opened the garage door and got back in the vehicle. Frank was unobserved as he slid along the hedge by the edge of the garage, sidling up to the car's side door. Crouching low, Frank followed the car as it moved ten yards forward and parked in the garage.

In less than a minute he eliminated the surprised driver with a knife. Frank put the knife back in his right pocket and entered through the servants' quarters connecting the garage and house. No servants on duty. They were dismissed yesterday in anticipation of the colonel leaving for America.

Ryan sat in the study with the door partially ajar. The room was magnificently adorned in black walnut panels, along with a large wall of filled bookshelves, several mirrors, paintings, and mounted golden adornments that sparkled in the light of the overhead chandelier. The carpet was plush and cushioned the sound of his approaching footsteps. Frank stopped in front of the desk and stood holding his hands together in front of his body in a casual pose, as if a bystander watching an everyday occurrence.

Ryan didn't look up. The American was reading correspondence from a pile of papers sitting next to an empty whiskey bottle and a recently poured glass. Frank knew the officer was aware of his presence, but mistook him for the driver. Finishing the letter, Ryan looked up as he lifted the glass to his lips.

"Who the hell are you?"

Frank saw the colonel's eyes widen slightly, but like a good officer the man kept his composure.

"Someone who has wanted to meet you for some time, Colonel Ryan." Frank smiled tightly.

The American relaxed visibly. "I'm not interested in whatever you're selling. Have the corporal show you out."

"Oh, I'm not here to sell anything. Rather, I'm here to take." He took two quick steps forward, seized the whiskey bottle in his right hand, and smashed it against the edge of the table. Leaning across, he grabbed the colonel's ear with his left hand and held the jagged edges of the bottle under the man's chin.

"Listen to me carefully, Colonel. If you do what I say, you might live. Do you understand?"

Sweat appeared on Ryan's brow. "I, uh, understand."

"Where is the I.G. report on Dachau?"

"I don't know what you're talking about."

Frank pushed the bottle forward a quarter inch, and the American gasped.

"The inspector general's report. One last time. Where is it?" He knew Ryan felt the rivulets of blood trickling down the outside of his throat.

"The safe. Behind the wall painting on the right." The words rushed out.

The painting was there.

"Now, no tricks or you will die by a thousand cuts. What is the combination?"

"14-12-25-33," wheezed Ryan. The sweat on his brow formed huge droplets.

"Are you sure, Colonel? If you're wrong it's going to get much more unpleasant for you."

"I'm sure, I'm sure. God help me, please," he pleaded.

It was the last thing the colonel would say. Frank Wicker drove the jagged edges of the shattered bottle up under the chin as far as they would go. Blood spurted out in a rush, drenching the papers, the desk, the colonel's tunic, and the killer's hand. Watching Ryan writhe and become still filled Frank with the bittersweet taste of vengeance. He began to whistle.

34

August 30, 1970
A Shau Valley, Vietnam

The unexpected happened.

We'd been humping up and down mountainsides of three and four thousand feet in elevation for several weeks. It was hard work. We walked the ridgelines so we could have the high ground and avoid the draws and small valleys below. Some ridge trails you dared not take for fear of landmines. The safest way was to go up the sides off the trail. Some were so steep they resembled cliffs. Pulling a strap of a ninety-pound load and weapon behind you while you were looking for handholds to grab onto was exhausting. If you couldn't hold on or lost your ruck, you or it would go crashing down in an ungainly fashion to the bottom. On the way down you hoped like hell you didn't roll into a tree, large boulder, or a buddy. Then you rested and started all over again. It was especially bad if it rained. The hillside turned to slick mud and it took twice as long to get to the top.

Sometimes we had to sleep on these steep hillsides. To keep from rolling downhill in your sleep you found a large rock or tree. Then you dug a shallow trench around it to lie in and hugged your body around it as a barrier to prevent you from tumbling down. Worked pretty well if you could find a tree or rock.

The jungle was so thick in the valleys sometimes helicopters couldn't see us to land supplies. Instead they dropped heavy pallets over us, sight unseen. Several times they had come crashing through the trees and almost hit us below. They basically exploded and we gathered the food cans, ammo cases, and medical supplies from the remains.

Our wounded were evacuated by a helicopter lowering a jungle penetrator, a wire basket connected to a metal wire and lowered from a Huey. Place your wounded guy in and he'd be hauled through the foliage and trees up into the chopper. It was so thick there'd be a lot of jostling and sometimes the guy fell out and crashed back down to the ground. It was worth the risk to get out if you were hurt, though.

With all that, we still managed to do some good out there. Firefights with the NVA produced a high body count, so the higher ups were happy. We found bunker complexes with food, ammo, and other supplies and destroyed same. As a reward we were given coordinates to establish an LZ for chopper evacuation.

When we got there we knew it was going to be a long day. It was full of trees to be cleared for the Hueys to have room to land. Sometimes when this happened chainsaws were lowered by rope to chop the trees down. Today we did it with C-4. You wrapped some around a tree trunk and set it off. It does the job quite nicely. Call us G.I. loggers.

It was late afternoon when we got the area cleared enough for two choppers to land at the same time. They landed in pairs while others flew overhead waiting their turn. When it came time for the last two birds to lift off, I was standing with Dimes, Big Red, Doc, and Strode. Prophet was directing a newbie toward the other chopper as our group began to board. Then came the first explosion.

It didn't take a genius to know it was a mortar shell. Seconds later there was another one. And another. They were walking the rounds toward the second helicopter where Prophet had directed the newbie. The guy was standing there frozen, watching the advancing rounds like a theatergoer. Prophet sprinted toward him and ran into him with a full body slam as another round struck nearby. We were relieved to see both unhurt as we bundled into our chopper for takeoff.

Below, Prophet and the newbie hustled the final yards toward the last bird. A round fragment hit the left skid, causing it to tilt. Everything from that point on was like watching a slow motion movie from our vantage point overhead.

As the Huey tilted left, its blade dipped down. It caught Prophet and the newbie in mid-run. There was no chance to duck or dive out of the way. None. The blade was like a large meat cleaver, lopping off the head of the newbie and splitting Prophet in half. The bottom part of Prophet's body stood upright for several seconds before it collapsed. The next round impacted directly on the chopper, and it burst into flames.

It happened so fast none of us could believe it. If there was one person we thought would survive it was him. I would have been shocked, except I'd already learned life isn't always fair.

35

November 11, 1945
Munich, Germany

Frank spent an hour looking at the I.G. report on Dachau from Ryan's safe. Dated June 8 and embossed with a TOP SECRET stamp on the front, it was compiled by the Inspector General's Office into the investigation of the massacre of SS soldiers during the liberation of the camp. Headed *Investigation of Alleged Mistreatment of German Guards at Dachau*, it was conducted at the site from May 3 through May 8, 1945.

The report indicated who was be charged with the killing of guards and hospital prisoners. Twenty-three men from the 157th Infantry Regiment, 45th Division, both officers and enlisted, were named. Recommended charges were indicated for each individual based on his involvement.

The last page was the most interesting.

A letter from the newly appointed Military Governor of Bavaria asked that all reports of the incident be collected and brought to his office. According to one of the scribbled notes in the margin by a Colonel James Whitaker, head of the investigation, the governor tore up the papers. He then tossed them in a metal wastepaper basket and set it on fire.

There would be no charges. Officially, it never

happened. The letter was signed by General George S. Patton, Commander of the U.S. Third Army and Military Governor of Bavaria.

Frank hurled the report across the room. It hit the wall and fell to the floor. "So," he muttered, "this was never to come out."

Angered by his brother's death, he was even more outraged that the Allies had turned Dachau into a camp called War Crimes Enclosure No.1 back in July. It was a prison for German war criminals to be tried by an American Military Tribunal on the SS training grounds next door. All those imprisoned were charged with violating the Laws and Rules of War under the 1929 Geneva Convention, regardless of personal responsibility. Just being an SS member made you guilty.

He didn't doubt some SS committed atrocities. As a former member, though, he felt no responsibility for those actions. Why should he? Let the guilty be punished.

The first trials had begun the previous week. There would be more. Yet the men who murdered his brother and tried to kill him were going to be free.

Unless he did something about it.

The rest of the evening he mulled over how to achieve justice. The 45th Division had been scheduled to rotate to the Pacific Theater to partake in the invasion of Japan. The new atomic bomb halted that. With everyone back in America awaiting discharge, tracking these men would be difficult in the vastness of America.

According to Ryan's file, the 45th was an Oklahoma City National Guard unit before the war. In the ultimate irony, the division patch was originally a red square with a yellow swastika, a tribute to the use of the swastika as a good luck charm by local Indian tribes. The division switched to a tribal thunderbird symbol when the war began in 1939.

Knowing the 45th was a National Guard division was important. He knew from Waffen SS wounded facing Amis that National Guardsmen weren't full-time soldiers but reservists. They reported for monthly weekend training at local armories. They probably had some obligation during the summer as well, a week or two at most.

On the bookshelf, he found an atlas. Flipping it open to the United States, he zeroed in on Oklahoma, since most of the men would be from there. That narrowed the search area.

Twenty-three men. It was a considerable number. It would take time but could be done, if he was careful. The question was how to get there. His name was on an automatic arrest list as a former SS member.

Analyzing the problem from every angle, he came to a conclusion he first refused to acknowledge. It made his skin crawl. Pondering his dilemma, Frank finally faced facts.

If he was going to go to America to find these men, there was only one way to do it.

He would become an American.

36

September 5, 1970
Camp Evans, Vietnam

Preacher was a black man from Alabama. He served as a lay preacher in a small rural church. The word of God was literal and exact. He never let you forget it. At least at first. He arrived full of the conversion spirit, figuring in a war there would be plenty of souls willing to be saved. As time went on, the flames cooled. His faith didn't carry him through the day anymore, and we didn't realize he needed something else to take its place.

Because he was a good soldier, Preacher was tolerated in the platoon despite his Bible thumping. He had few friends, and not many paid attention when he got a transfer back to Camp Evans as an assistant mess hall cook. No one knew how that happened. One day he was with us; the next day he was gone.

I'd noticed things changing since the spring. Guys were wearing mustaches and long sideburns. Hippy necklaces became popular. If you wanted to go to college, you could apply for a three-month early out of your enlistment, or a five-month one in other circumstances upon returning to the States after your tour.

With the Vietnamization program underway, we weren't dedicated to winning the war, just not losing it. A stalemate like the one in Korea seemed to be the new goal.

The hooch next door had self-segregated into a blacks-only REMF enclave a couple of months earlier. They called themselves the Camp Evans Black Forum. Preacher began hanging out there and was rarely seen with us. When he did see us, he was still friendly at first. Then he began wearing black sunglasses like a Black Panther revolutionary, affecting clenched fist Black Power salutes, and sporting so-called slave bracelets or necklaces made of black shoestrings. He talked constantly of the coming revolution. Coupled with this was a growing surliness directed toward people he called Chucks.

Chuck was the black counterpart of a white person calling someone a nigger. It was a step up from calling you a cracker. (The comparison would be a white guy calling a black man a boy). It was used when blacks got together, started flashing signs, and giving each other the dap. The dap was a complicated ritual of hand-gripping and slaps, coupled with fist bumping and body slams. Didn't make any difference to white soldiers except for one thing. These black gangs delighted in doing the dap in mess lines, on buses when you were trying to get to your seat, or in doorways, deliberately blocking your entry as they completed their elaborate dapping ritual. Go around them and cut ahead, then all hell would break loose since you were now guilty of showing disrespect. Any place you could be inconvenienced, and taught that as a white man you would have to wait, was fair game.

Relaxed hair regulations had taken effect several months earlier. Now some REMF blacks were wearing Afros with pick combs sticking out of their hair and not having to shave by getting a medical profile excuse stating their skin could not take a razor. All this while collecting Uncle Sam's dollar and complaining about the "white man's war."

White soldiers felt that the higher ups were intimidated by the revolt, and there was some truth to that. If an NCO or officer cracked down, they faced fallout naming them a racist, and their career prospects were impacted. The Army started including a line on the bottom of your annual efficiency report stating you supported affirmative action programs in the military. You were required to sign. It was not optional.

We didn't deal with this much in the field where we relied on each other or faced possible death. Foolishness in the field didn't last long and wasn't tolerated. Back in the rear, it was a different story. No one could quite make out why Preacher fell for this bunk. It was clear he had, and it came to a head one night.

Big Red was sitting by the window, trying to catch a breeze and read a book. Dimes and Tran were visiting Baby Doll. I was playing a desultory game of Twenty-One with Peddler and Project for a penny a hand. Our concentration wasn't helped by the blasting of music coming from the black barracks next door. It wasn't just that the music was cranked up or that it had been on for the past four hours. It was what they were playing. Over the speakers the record kept repeating "The Niggers are coming, the Niggers are coming," as the lyric refrain. Repeated requests to lower the volume or change the song were ignored.

Finally Big Red snapped. "I can't take this shit. I've had it." He went to his locker, took out his entrenching tool, and twisted the shovel head into place. "I'm going to put an end to this." He marched out the door and headed to their hooch.

I followed him, beseeching him to stop. "Look, what do you think you're going to do? You're going to get yourself in trouble."

He paid me no mind and kept up a steady pace toward their door.

"Oh, crap." I knew more than one or two guys were in that barracks. Things were going to go south pretty quickly. But he was my friend so I followed him in.

Ten feet ahead of me, Big Red slipped silently through their screen door. Catching up, I saw the offending stereo on the second locker to the left. The inmates of the asylum were playing poker in the middle of the hooch, not paying attention as Big Red entered. They paid attention only when his shovel smashed the record player and speaker to smithereens. Then he tore down a red, black, and green striped Black Liberation flag hanging on the wall next to a Malcolm X poster.

All hell broke loose.

Ten black soldiers advanced toward us. Someone yelled, "Kill the rabbits!" as I tried to pull Big Red toward the door. Six piled on him, taking him down as the remaining four swerved for me. I thought, *I'm dead,* then hit the first guy squarely in the nose, feeling a satisfying crunch of cartilage as blood spurted. I grabbed the second man in a chokehold, threw him to the ground, and made sure to land on top of him as heavily as I could. I hit him hard and fast in the mouth three times with my right. I wanted to hurt him as quick as possible because I knew I wasn't going to win this thing.

Sure enough, I didn't.

As I was hitting the second guy, Preacher grabbed a metal mortar marker pole and swung it at my back and head. I felt pain behind my left ear where the skin split and knew I was bleeding from the first blow. The second strike hit the back of my head. If I didn't get out of there immediately, I was going to die. Big Red was on his own.

Pushing through the throng by the screen door, I stumbled out the entrance and slammed down hard on the wooden sidewalk. Splinters entered my skin all over, but I was out of the hellhole. Two seconds later Big Red came flying outside. He grabbed me by my left shoulder in one fluid motion and hauled me stumbling and dragging out to the middle of the road. A barrage of catcalls and rock missiles flew at us. We were dodging and throwing rocks back when several MP jeeps showed up and surrounded the place.

The would-be revolutionaries barricaded themselves inside their hooch. A shot was fired from inside, followed by obscenities and dares for the MPs to come in and get them. No takers. Minutes went by. A jeep pulled up with the battalion commander and other officers. Words were exchanged. An M-60 machine gun was stationed in front and back of the building with a two man crew. Sanity prevailed and the Camp Evans Black Forum surrendered.

I was getting my ear and the back of my head sewn up with eleven stitches by a medic at the clinic when Strode came by. He asked what happened, and I gave him the details. I was livid about being attacked and fully expected Strode to agree with me. I knew his no-nonsense attitude. I was surprised when there was a long pause. I asked about the charges to be brought.

Leaning his back against the wall, Strode crossed his arms and looked at me. "Nickels, did I ever tell you about my experiences with the 555th Airborne during World War Two?"

"No, Sergeant." My head hurt like hell and I didn't feel like a nostalgia trip right then.

"Well, when the war began I was gung ho. Who wouldn't be against the Nazis? They were such a bunch of evil racist bastards. I couldn't wait to give it to them so I joined a paratrooper outfit. It was the 555th. We called ourselves the Triple Nickels. Thought you might appreciate the name."

Taking a pack of Kools from his front pocket, he offered me one. I shook my busted head in a painful no. He lit up, sucked in a long drag, and blew it out while staring up at the ceiling for a moment. "The Army was still segregated in those days. The 555th was a black outfit with black officers. But it was quite clear who was actually in charge." He smiled ruefully. "Quite clear."

He shook his head as if clearing his thoughts. "Anyway, we sweated through training and the typical army harassment to get a chance to see how good we truly were. A chance to prove ourselves. When the Normandy landings took place and we saw the 82nd Airborne, the 101st Airborne and the others, we knew we would be right behind them. We were ready."

"Okay." I had no idea where this was going.

"We never left the States. Never saw combat. World War Two was a white man's war with blacks used almost exclusively in support roles. The only time we got to jump was when the U.S. Forest Services was short of smoke jumpers in the summer of 1945. Instead of confronting the enemy, we spent time fighting forest fires." He grimaced. "Just like Smokey the Bear."

"What's that have to do with tonight, Sarge?"

"Oh, it has a lot to do with it, Nickels. What I'm trying to explain, black man to white, is there was a time when black people were more than willing to shed blood for this country. Now, not so much."

"But you're here. The Army is fifteen percent black." I shook my head. "I don't understand."

"Son, I'm here because I took an oath to serve this country and she sent me here. I did so voluntarily. With draftees, black draftees I guess I should say, well, it's more complicated. When you keep getting knocked down by someone you love, eventually you may choose not to love them anymore."

"So the U.S. is to blame for what happened tonight?" I couldn't keep the exasperation out of my voice.

"Yes, in a way. Now don't get me wrong. Those fools outside will get what's coming to them. I just want you to remember that while they might be thugs, it doesn't mean there's not some truth behind their feelings."

"With all due respect, Sergeant, that is the dumbest thing I've heard today. They tried to *kill* me. I find that hard to forgive."

Strode held his cigarette up to his face and turned it sideways seeming to inspect it. "I'm not asking you to forgive. I'm saying you need to understand why this is happening."

"All right, let's say this is all the sin of the white man. How do we cure it? Where does it end?"

"Nickels, if I knew that I'd be God. I'm not, even if I play one here in the platoon." With that said, he departed and left me to my throbbing head.

The next day Big Red was busted back to PFC and fined fifty dollars. The blacks were flown to the Long Binh Jail outside Saigon to await trial for attempted murder, among a myriad of other charges.

Everyone in Vietnam had heard tales about Long Binh Jail. It was nicknamed LBJ as an ironic nod to former President Johnson and was known for the strikes and riots that occurred there. The worst part was said to be the maximum security area known as Silver City. That's where they were going to end up.

I didn't envy the bastards.

37

September 14, 1970
A Shau Valley, Vietnam

"Strode wants you," said Doc.

What the hell did I do now? Or not do? Whenever I got called into his presence, I felt like I was being hauled in front of the school principal.

This time was different.

"There's an E-5 slot open. Want the job?"

I was dumbstruck for several seconds.

"Me?"

"You."

"There's better people than me. Big Red, Dimes..."

Strode shook his head. His bald black pate shone in the sun like an ebony pearl.

"Red would have a slot except for his getting busted. Can't promote an E-3 to an E-5. I'm not God." His eyes twinkled. I got the reference from our past conversation and nodded.

"Yeah, but Dimes is more capable than me."

Strode frowned. Maybe he thought I was challenging his expertise.

"Don't flatter yourself. He *is* better than you. There are

two slots. He's getting the first, you're getting the second. You both can thank your lucky stars there's a war on. Otherwise you two would be hard pressed to make PFC. Now scram."

I found Dimes, and he'd already been given the news. We felt bad about Big Red, though. He was the most deserving of us. When we told him, he would have none of it.

"Look, I screwed up. I shouldn't have done what I did. Strode was right, although I sure as hell won't ever tell him that. Besides, I'll get my rank back in time."

Strode gave us three infantry field manuals to read and practically memorize in two days so we could pass the monthly secondary zone promotion board back at Evans. That proved easy. Every question by the board's officers came right out of the manuals. As soon as our interviews were over we were back at the chopper pad and out to the field. We bitched about not getting a hot dinner or getting to spend the night on our cots in our hooch. Still, we figured we'd come out ahead.

It wasn't till we landed back with the squad that I remembered it was my birthday. My real birthday, as Jim Peterson. Big Red gave me his pound cake. Dimes contributed a can of peaches to pour over it. I bought a Baby Ruth candy bar from Project which I crumpled and scattered all over the top of my homemade dessert.

It was my sweet sixteen.

***

Toward the end of the month, five days of continuous rain drenched everything. The monsoon season was back with a vengeance. My fingers had that pruney look like you get from too much time in the swimming pool. It was so cold at night that I slept sitting up with my rucksack on my lap to keep the rain from totally soaking my body. Thankfully, we'd soon be leaving the mountains and returning to the lowlands.

A fist fight almost broke out between Linc and Doc. Doc was passing around the white cardboard box the Red Cross sent each platoon monthly. It was filled with goodies like real American hard candy, smokes, toiletries, and even a can of WD-40. The last was the most prized item of all since it was great for maintaining our weapons.

The rule with the box was that it had to be shared equally and a drawing held for the WD-40. This was one time when not having a full platoon came in handy. The Red Cross operated on the assumption we were at forty or so men at any given time. Now we were stood only at twenty-three, so there were extras for everybody.

Taking more than your share from the box was a no-no. The box represented home and not being forgotten. You didn't screw around with that. Unless you were Linc.

Linc was short and homely and looked somewhat like Abe Lincoln without the beard, thus the nickname. He was also the entitled type of guy who believes the world revolves around him and is always looking for a sucker. My first week with the platoon, he conned me into taking his guard shift. Said he was sick. Cherry that I was, I said okay. But he continually asked people for favors without giving back. Once I had the lowdown on Linc, I avoided him like the plague and was grateful he wasn't in second squad. Lucky for him, we had a constant stream of new guys coming in the platoon along with people he'd taken advantage of departing, giving him a constant pick of innocent newbies to target.

When Linc tried to take more than his share, Doc called him on it. Words were exchanged. Doc broke it off, went over to his pack, and grabbed his weapon.

In the movies, medics don't carry a weapon. That's Hollywood. Out here they all had either a .45 pistol or an M-16. Their choice. The only exception was if they were conscientious objectors, who won't kill under any circumstances. I'd never met a C.O. medic. The medics were great in the field, but wanted to survive like the rest of us.

Doc took his M-16, walked over to Linc, placed the muzzle in Linc's ear, and told him to "put it all back." Linc treated it as a joke. But when Doc pulled back the charging handle and chambered a round, we all knew he was serious. Linc replaced everything he'd taken.

There was a long pause. Doc said "Alrighty," and went back to his rucksack. He began sorting medical supplies as if nothing had happened.

Everyone in the platoon was getting worried about Doc. He hadn't been his usual self. He was moody and easily irritated. He'd cut back on his own food and water in order to carry more medical supplies. His interactions with people seemed ragged, as if the effort to explain things was more than he could tolerate. He was jumpy, a shadow of his former self.

The 101st required medics to rotate out of the field at seven months and serve the rest of their time at a clinic or hospital. The rationale was that medics ran the risk of getting so wrapped up in others they often stopped taking care of themselves. With the shortage of field medics, Doc had been with us for ten months.

I overheard Strode and L-T discussing Doc a few minutes later. Strode said Doc had reached burnout.

"The good thing about medics is they end up going all out for the platoon because they see themselves as the family GP. The bad thing is they start to depend on that respect and affection so much they neglect themselves. They stop realizing there's a world beyond this."

"What do you recommend?" said L-T.

Strode shook his head. "Not a lot we can do except ask battalion to replace him as per policy. Not sure how Doc will take it, though."

They never had to ask for Doc's rotation.

That afternoon we were walking down a trail, and I stepped to the side to re-tie my right boot. Project and Linc passed me. As I rejoined the patrol line, I heard a loud explosion. Someone up ahead had triggered a mine.

Advancing, we realized it wasn't a who. It was a them. Project and Linc were lying on the ground. Sort of.

Project's right leg was impaled on a tree branch, dangling upside down like a trophy hoisted high by an angry God. He was conscious and didn't seem in any pain. There wasn't a lot of blood. The blast sealed off his right thigh with almost surgical precision where the leg was blown off. In shock, he kept on muttering, “Oh, no,” in a low voice.

Linc was worse. Hit in the head, the top portion of his skull was sheared off. Blood, tissue, and brain matter was splattered all around. He never knew what hit him.

L-T called a medevac for Project. Doc administered morphine and started albumin. Loading him on the chopper, I asked Doc if he’d make it.

“If a man is alive on the chopper he’ll usually survive,” said Doc. “But in this case...”

His diagnosis was hard to accept. It could have been me on that chopper but for tying my boot. On one hand I was relieved. Yet why was I alive and not him? So much out here was sheer chance.

I went over to Doc and got a body bag. He didn’t say anything. I think he knew what I was feeling. Back up the trail Linc’s body and skull remains had been collected by the squad and wrapped in another bag. I placed mine by the tree, shimmed up the trunk, and climbed out to the branch holding Project’s leg by his boot. It took several jerks before it dislodged and tumbled to the ground. I bagged it and took it over to where Doc and Strode were sitting on a large boulder.

“I’m done,” said Doc glumly to Strode.

“I know,” said Strode.

Neither of them looked at each other.

We got a new medic the next day. Project died of shock back at Evans. Doc was transferred to the 95th Evac Hospital. We never saw him again.

I wrote a letter to Project’s girl. His folks would get

one from our company commander. Army regulations required it. Girlfriends get nothing. So I wrote her. Told her how Project served well and honorably. How we'd miss his yo-yo tricks and how often he talked of her. She was his Valentine. I told her this would be hard, but I knew she'd survive. I wished her a happy life.

Two weeks later I got an unexpected reply. Except when the *Munson Lake Tribune* arrived, it was the only time my name was mentioned at mail call. The letter was a light blue. Her cursive was sort of childish, but the letter was not. She thanked me for helping Project. Unknown to me he'd had someone else in the platoon help him write letters to her, praising me and how much he admired me. He was proud to be my friend.

After reading that, I went out and found a spot where no one was around and cried for the first time since the Bluebird Cafe. It went on a long time. I'd lost not only my family but now a "son."

38

Early in 1946 Frank assumed the identity of another displaced person, this time a dead former German political prisoner he befriended at a homeless shelter. He was careful to find someone his age and physical stature, but also someone with a known condition and very little time left to live.

Cancer. His new friend was diagnosed a month before. No doctors were available, and no records were kept of his condition. The relationship had lasted almost a year, when the man passed on. Assuming Hans Keppler's mantle, Frank moved far away from where they were known.

Getting to America was a slow wait. The line to emigrate was long, the process laborious, the quotas small. If he impersonated a Jew or a Pole, he'd make the approved list quicker. But there were lines a good German did not cross.

Frank's break came in the spring of 1949 when the Allies recognized West Germany as a new political entity and an American ally. The floodgates opened and his papers were approved that fall. He listed his occupation as a baker, the trade of the real Hans Keppler. He pursued it while waiting for his chance to leave and became fairly proficient. Frank knew that being a baker was not the solution to his quest, though. He needed a job with stability, travel opportunities, and some modicum of respect in America. A baker would not do.

The Korean War in the summer of 1950 came to Frank's rescue. The Americans were routed by the North Koreans, and the authorities looked everywhere for new recruits. Being a soldier in the United States Army was the perfect disguise. The manpower shortage allowed him to enlist as a non-citizen with a fast track to citizenship a year later.

It was then, at the age of twenty-six, he became Frank Ross. All it required was a court appearance, seventy-five dollars, and a signed affidavit stating he was not using the new name for criminal purposes. He hated the name Hans Keppler. Frank Ross sounded like an American name, not that of a foreigner. Regaining his real name of Frank Wicker would tempt Fate, though he did briefly consider it. Using his actual first name would have to do.

Winters in Korea as an infantryman reminded him of winters in Russia. He'd survived those and knew he'd survive these as well. Combat experience in Russia transferred well in Korea. Promotions and awards were quick for knowledgeable men. When the war ended he got the chance to go to Officer Candidate School. It meant more money and prestige, but he declined the offer. An enlisted man did not undergo the background scrutiny an officer would. Frank didn't want anyone nosing into his past.

While an E-5 sergeant stationed at Fort Sill, Oklahoma, Frank marked his first man off the list, Alvin Eubanks, a car mechanic. Easy to find in the Oklahoma City phonebook.

According to the I.G. report, Eubanks loaned his weapon to prisoners and allowed them to shoot any SS men they wanted for an hour before taking his weapon back. Frank shot him in each kneecap, and listened to his anguished cries as he bled out on a lonely prairie mesa outside of town. When the cries ceased, he found himself whistling as he buried Eubanks in an unmarked grave.

Nine years had passed before he could start trimming down the list of names he'd copied down before placing the report back in the safe.

Over time Frank preferred dispatching each man with a long switchblade bought in Korea. It was more personal than a gun. A special leather sheath with a long cord kept the blade wrapped around his right thigh, unnoticeable under his uniform. A hole in his pocket allowed him to remove the knife smoothly.

Frank was methodical in eliminating the men on his list. He was careful not to be seen scouting them. Forced by time constraints to employ private investigators to find some, he left his target alone for a year or more so as not to arouse suspicion. He made sure no bodies were found.

The pattern continued over fifteen years. On a pass or a leave from wherever he was stationed, Frank would identify and kill a man on his list. He got lucky occasionally and executed two instead of one, when they were friends or lived close to each other. It all depended on the logistics and ensuring he had identified them correctly. That was important. Honor dictated he didn't kill the innocent.

As an honorable person, he always tried to get the individual alone and away from family when making a kill.

If that proved impossible due to time constraints or the details involved, he was not above killing the whole family. Honor did not apply in that situation.

It had happened twice. The first time he questioned himself, but only that once. They stole his brother from him, tried to execute Frank at the coal yard wall, and cost him his country. He would take their lives and anything else that got in the way, right down to the root if needed. In such a situation, the family was not really innocent. He didn't feel any qualms about it. He still found himself whistling afterwards.

In the fall of 1969, Frank came to the last name on his list, the man who shot his brother. He'd saved it for the finale of his quest. Like others, this man had moved to another region of the country after the war. Tracking him down took time and money. But it was worth it to settle things with Lieutenant Tom Peterson of Munson Lake, Washington.

39

October 1, 1970
A Shau Valley, Vietnam

Whack.

Attacked by the NVA at our Command Post position, something hit my right thigh. Felt like a combination hot metal poker and baseball bat slamming against my leg. Ten yards ahead was a shallow depression. I staggered toward it, looking for a place to hide.

Don't fall, I told myself. *Don't fall. If you do, you won't be able to get back up.* I couldn't help it though. Wobbling a few steps, I fell sprawling to the earth. I saw the kind of stars seen in cartoons. *You're hit. You're hit,* my brain announced like a loudspeaker. I felt something inside my leg. Couldn't believe it—this happened to other people, not me. I was supposed to live forever. I pressed my hands on my leg to put pressure on the wound. Both hands ended up wet and sticky. I knew it was blood. Lots of it. I was on my back looking at the sky (*had it always been that blue?*) and laughing out loud. For all I knew, I was going to die, and yet I was laughing like it was an absurd joke.

"Medic!" someone yelled. Took a second to register it was my voice.

Forget Ross. More than anything else, I wanted to go home and sleep in my own bed. I wanted Mom to make me waffles for breakfast. I wanted to see my sister do her fire baton routine. I wanted to play football again and hear the crowd roar as I ran for a touchdown. I wanted to make love to Rita Human. I wanted to see my dad and tell him I was sorry I was such a disappointment. I'd even apologize to Principal Alt.

"Please, Lord, I'll do anything you want. Don't let me die. Please."

I blacked out.

***

I awoke in Da Nang, specifically the surgical ward of the 95th Evac Hospital, a huge place with 350 beds. White walls, starched sheets on clean beds, low lights, and black tiled floors. Every so often a uniformed nurse or medic hurried along down the corridor between the beds.

My right leg hurt like a son of a bitch. I slowly looked down the length of my body. If part of my leg was missing, and I was feeling phantom pains like I'd seen in war movies, I didn't want to know. Yet my eyes were drawn downward toward my limb, despite the fear. My leg was still there under the sheet. Happily, I rotated it slightly to the right and then to the left. My eyes weren't deceiving me. Hurt like crazy, but it was attached.

"What the hell do you think you're doing?"

A Specialist 7 male medic stood by my bed. Hands on

his hips, he stared at me with an irritated look.

"Seeing if it was still there," I gasped. My leg movements caused beads of sweat to break out on my face.

"Well, stop it," he said. "You'll loosen your wired stitches. If that happens you're going to smell a really foul odor as blood and pus seeps out. You'll have a green and yellow mess, and you could still lose the leg."

Seeing my alarm at his last statement, he smiled. "Don't worry, we're not going to let that happen. We'll watch you like a hawk for the next week or so."

"Do I have to go home?"

Surprised by the question, he asked, "Don't you want to go home?"

"Want doesn't enter into it. Can't." I gritted my teeth as I shifted on the mattress.

"Then you're one lucky bastard. Your wound is a clean one. You lost a lot of blood, but the bullet didn't hit any bone. You ended up with a flesh wound minus some muscle. The end result is, no, you won't be going home. They're going to send you back to your unit."

I must have looked doubtful.

He leaned forward and continued in a quiet voice. "Look around you. Why are you in a bed in the surgical ward at the farthest edge? Means you're expected to survive. The doubtful ones are closest to the double door ops room area."

He shook my hand and said "Good luck." Turning to leave, he stopped. Nodding to my right, he added, "Congratulations," in an ironic voice and departed.

Confused, I looked at the side of my pillow but saw

nothing. Then I felt the scrape of cool metal cutting into my lower chin. A Purple Heart medal had been pinned to the pillow while I was asleep.

For the first week, my leg was flushed twice daily with hydrogen peroxide to prevent infection. A nurse came by every four hours to examine my wire stitches and see if they were still tight. Apparently, others deliberately aggravated their wounds so they didn't have to return to their units. Any temptation on my part was stopped by knowing I'd never find Ross as a result.

My second week included rounds of physical therapy, bending my leg and getting it to move despite my aching muscles. The PT guy was either a sadist or one of the most dedicated persons I ever met. Some sessions I felt he was the former; others I swore he was the latter.

Later they pronounced me fit to be transferred back to Evans and Charlie Med for more rehab. I was given a wooden cane and told to start walking as much as possible to strengthen my leg and thigh muscles.

While hobbling around I got the latest edition of the *Munson Lake Tribune*. Dated two weeks earlier, the front page featured a large photo of the MLHS homecoming court with Sophomore Princess Rita Human. She seemed happy with her beaming smile and appeared not to have a care in the world. I looked at that photo a long time.

Dad once said "It's too bad youth is wasted on the young. They don't appreciate it." It made no sense to me then. Now it was an insight I thought I understood. I found myself envying her. Life was pretty simple there.

Putting the paper aside, I lit up a Marlboro, and did

some serious thinking. Thousands of miles away Rita was living a normal life. Could I live a normal life after this was over? I'd been so focused on Ross, I had never considered the aftermath. What would I do with my life after taking care of the bastard?

I finished my cigarette and began field stripping it for disposal. I knew one thing for sure. Rita wasn't going to be a part of my future. I took out my leather wallet and found her note.

Reading it again, I wondered if she even remembered writing it.

I tore it up.

40

October 20, 1970
Da Nang, Vietnam

Most Vietnam weddings take place in the fall. This tradition, explained John Paul, comes from getting the harvest over before celebrating.

The actual date for the nuptials was set by a family astrologer months ago. Big Red and I gave Dimes flak about getting married according to an astrology forecast. Be, like most Vietnamese, believed in both astrology and fortune-telling. The astrologer grumbled that their choice was not a good date, just the best one given that our R&R was the week of the twentieth. The betrothal ceremony would take place today, the actual wedding tomorrow. Our Ross adventure in Saigon would be two days after that.

The betrothal ceremony, an hoi, involved gift-giving. The groom and his family (me and Big Red) visit the bride's home bearing round red lacquered boxes full of tea, wines, cake, fruit, plus areca leaves and betel nuts. Because it was a lucky color, the boxes were draped in red silk and carried by a local boy and a girl clad in red clothes and hired for the occasion. This was meticulously outlined by Tran, and Dimes did his best to comply. Based on the smiling faces of the family after our arrival, he'd done well. I even saw John Paul wink at Dimes at one point.

Gifts were placed on the ancestral altar along the wall inside the front door, with the edible gifts divided into two equal portions. One was given back to Dimes.

"It's to demonstrate her family isn't greedy," he told me.

Personally, I thought Dimes and Be were young to be getting married. But the average marriage age in Vietnam was thirteen for the girl and sixteen for the groom. Cripes, I was sixteen now, and I wasn't ready for this. Hoped they were.

Dimes elected to stay at the house and room with Tran for the night. I got the feeling, he wanted to ask some personal questions. Big Red and I decided to spend the night at the U.S.O.

We awoke to the sound of our windows rattling. A salvo of rockets was striking the city somewhere.

"Hell of a way to start a wedding," said Big Red.

"Oh, I don't know. Think of it as a bunch of celebration fireworks," I said yawning. "Just another day in Rocket City."

I was wrong.

At the house we were stunned to see a flattened, smoking ruin. Outside were ambulances, fire trucks, dead bodies, and shocked onlookers. At first I thought it was from the rocket attack an hour earlier. But that made no sense. The houses around were untouched. NVA rockets don't pinpoint individual homes with such accuracy that there isn't collateral damage. They have to bracket their fire to achieve a particular result. No, this was not a rocket attack.

Big Red grunted approval over my take on what had happened. He canvassed the area, speaking to the locals while I stood there in shock.

"You're right. It wasn't a rocket. According to the neighbors, it was a car bomb. Someone drove a French Citroën through the gate and straight into the front door, then set it off. The family was targeted." He motioned over to where a clump of officials stood. "I'll go see what else I can find out."

I didn't bother going with him. Didn't take a genius to figure out who set off the bomb. A family headed by a foreigner, a daughter engaged to an American soldier, and a son who deserted the NVA to serve with the enemy was a high value propaganda target for local communists.

"Any survivors?" I asked when he returned, hoping against hope.

He shook his head negatively. "Everyone at home was killed. The only family member left is Baby Doll. She was at the fish market this morning getting supplies. Another ten minutes and she would have been inside as well."

"Dimes?"

Big Red shook his head again. "We've lost our third musketeer."

We'd never see Dimes again. At least in this world.

"How's Be coping?" I asked. I wanted to know but also wanted to stop thinking about losing a good friend.

"See for yourself. She's over behind the ambulance where the bodies are being loaded."

With her Eurasian heritage, she towered above most of the local ambulance crew.

Be was sobbing as I approached and paid me no mind. I stood there for several minutes, saying nothing as the pieces of her family were assembled, put into body bags by the ambulance crew, and placed on the car floor for transport. Only when the vehicle vanished down the street with its grisly cargo, and the onlookers began to disperse, did she stop her sobs and notice me.

"Forgive me, Sergeant Nickels." She daubed her eyes with a lace handkerchief.

I didn't know what to say. "I'm sorry for what's happened here. Your family were good people. Can I help?" I didn't know what I could do, but it seemed appropriate to offer.

Baby Doll ignored me and started walking down the street. It was as if she was willing the ambulance and cargo to come back to her. I trailed along, slightly behind, as the next few minutes ticked by. Nothing was said by either of us. My leg had been feeling good the past two days, and I'd ceased using my cane. But I could feel a twinge as we kept walking.

Suddenly she stopped and turned around. Her face was looking down at the ground and not at me when she spoke.

"I would like to ask you for a favor, Sergeant Nickels. A very big favor."

I'd almost forgotten my offer of assistance. "Anything I can do, I will," I said.

She looked up at me and held up her hand in a stop

talking dismissal motion before saying, “I’ll understand if you refuse.” She dropped her head again and stared at the ground for the next few seconds seeming to gather her thoughts. Finally she looked directly into my eyes and made her request.

“Sergeant Nickels, will you marry me?”

I couldn’t have been more surprised if the Apollo 11 astronauts had come back from the moon last year and told us it was made of cheese.

“Why would you want to marry me?”

Her answer fit her personality, straightforward and practical.

“I now have no one in this country. No money, no home, no family. I will need to start over. You are here. I repeat: will you marry me?”

I began to list all the reasons why I couldn’t—no marriage permit, no real relationship with her, we weren’t in love—when I saw her shake her head and flash me a sad smile.

“No, Sergeant. I think you misunderstand my request. I do want to be married, but not to you. To Dimes.”

“But he’s dead.”

“That was unfortunate for both of us. Now I need your help to fix things.”

“Okay,” I said questioningly. “But I don’t know how we...” I found my thoughts trailing off at the absurdity of it all.

“Sergeant, I need you to marry me as Dimes. We were to get married this afternoon and the paperwork is in order. It needs to be today or the papers will be no good. I need you to be Dimes, my groom."

She stared at me for several seconds noting my hesitation.

"Well, I don't know if—"

"I'm three months pregnant, Sergeant Nickels. Without your assistance, I will be penniless, unmarried, and the mother of a half-caste American bastard baby." Now her request took on an urgent tone of finality. "Will you help me or not?"

Dimes told me once that charity wasn't a feature of Vietnamese society. Instead they depended on the family to provide and found the idea of charity—as we practiced it in the U.S.A.—a silly concept. Without family, what she said had the ring of truth. If she was married to Dimes, she'd get his G.I. life insurance of $10,000. She would be a widow, not a slut. She would have a chance to survive.

I owed it to Dimes to help her any way I could.

"Yes," I said. "I'll marry you."

***

The civil ceremony took place as scheduled that afternoon, October 21, in the courtroom at Da Nang City Hall. Since her traditional red bridal ao dai and silk pants were destroyed in the fire, Baby Doll wore a white dress we bought at a local shop after lunch. White was the traditional color for young unmarried women, as well as the color of mourning in Vietnam. Seemed appropriate.

Big Red was our witness after first going back to Evans

to get a khaki dress uniform for both of us. He brought Dimes's nametag for me, along with two wedding rings he found in a small pawn shop close to City Hall.

The ceremony took less than five minutes. We stood before a Vietnamese judge sitting behind a heavy wooden desk. A bright vase of flowers was on the right side of the desk, perhaps as a nod to this being more than the usual civil transaction. Our judge read some questions from the civil marriage manual, an interpreter translated, and I answered each one in the affirmative. Baby Doll did the same. Formal "I do's" followed and rings were exchanged. The paperwork was signed, stamped by the judge, and Baby Doll was officially married to "David Deems" of North Dakota.

When she said her new name to the recording clerk, it was given with an edge of sadness in her voice. Meanwhile, she arranged a bribe for Dimes's body to be transferred from the civil authorities and reported to the military the next day, the day after his "wedding." His official death (by rocket attack) would be recorded twenty-four hours later than what actually happened.

I started to wonder who I really was. I had been Jim Peterson, was Travis Nickels, and now (at least for a few hours) I was David Deems. I was "married" to a beautiful woman I didn't really know. Was anything in my life real these days?

After the ceremony was finished and the papers signed, Big Red left for Camp Evans. Once I got Baby Doll squared away, I would meet him back at Evans and we would depart for Saigon and the rest of our leave. I told Baby

Doll I'd take her to a hotel to have a place to stay. In the taxi on the way I gave her an envelope containing $1,721. I had withdrawn it from the finance office at I Corps HQ in town earlier while she got her dress.

"It's not a lot, but it's all I have. I hope it'll keep you safe until you get his life insurance."

I didn't know how much money she had access to, but it couldn't be much. Scuttlebutt was it took ninety days before a surviving spouse got their G.I. settlement money.

Shortly after this she asked our driver to stop in front of one of the shops and stalls lining the main street in Da Nang. According to the posters on the glass window, it specialized in local herbs along one wall and high-priced cameras on the other. I'd no idea what was going on, yet she seemed determined.

"Sergeant Nickels, do you trust me?"

I was confused but nodded.

She placed her hands in a praying position and bowed to me.

"You are my mighty dragon," she said. "I want you to come with me but not say anything. Can you do that?"

I nodded once again.

"When one is married in my country, it is often wise to consult a fortune teller. That is what we are here to do." She gripped me by the arm and led me into the shop.

A small wizened woman stood behind the vegetables and herbs lined up in rows of small boxes. She looked like a witch, with her walnut-wrinkled face. Or maybe in this case a fortune teller. She was almost blind, with milky cataracts and blackened teeth from the stacks of unwashed empty cups of tea behind the counter.

Words were exchanged and I saw the flash of cash. A sharp command erupted from the little witch, and seconds later another woman emerged from the back of the shop. She was definitely not a witch. She was tall, middle-aged, wearing a Western style dress and a pearl necklace. The witch woman engaged her in a flurry of conversation during which they kept referring to us with arm gestures and glances back to where we stood. Finally a conclusion of some sort was reached and Western Woman approached us.

"Do you have the money?" she asked in English. Baby Doll paid her and she tucked it into a side pocket on her dress and motioned for us to follow her to the back.

In the rear of the shop where there was an expensive set of mahogany furniture in a nicely decorated Western style living/dining room. On the dining table was a box about the size of a briefcase. Sitting down at the table, Western Woman pulled the box toward her and opened it.

From my angle I couldn't see inside, but she reached in, rummaged about, and pulled out a small Pringles-size can. It was full of pickup sticks, the kind elementary kids play with back in the States. I might have thought this was for fun, but the faces of both the fortune teller and Baby Doll made clear this was serious business.

Western Woman shook the can briskly and threw the contents onto the table. They spilled into a messy pile which Baby Doll examined intently. Western Woman allowed her to do so and waited by lighting up a Ruby Queen cigarette she took out of a turquoise pack. The smell was bitter.

Soon Baby Doll looked back up and nodded approvingly.

Our fortune teller removed the top stick. It had some markings she showed Baby Doll amid a flurry of chatter as my "wife" listened silently.

With the first stick explained, Western Woman carefully pulled the next one out of the jumbled pile. Again she showed Baby Doll the result amid another burst of Vietnamese. This procedure was repeated many times until she pulled out a solid black stick. It was the only one in the pile.

Baby Doll was deathly still as Western Woman spoke. I didn't know the content, but it was clear it ended with a question. When the question was asked, Western Woman looked at Baby Doll intently, who in turn looked over at me. It was as if she were seeing me for the first time. Eventually, she turned her glance back to Western Woman and gave an affirmative reply.

Western Woman's face was impassive, although I thought I saw the raising of an eyebrow with Baby Doll's answer. It must have satisfied her, because she pulled out another stick and placed it next to the black one. Baby Doll emitted a sigh and looked at me once again for a long time. She reached into her purse and pulled out several bills and paid her a second time. Western Woman put the money away in the box, chattered with Be, then they both stood up. Whatever had been decided was now over. It was time for us to go.

The sun was almost blinding on the sidewalk compared with the relative darkness and coolness of the back room. I asked Baby Doll what happened.

She smiled tightly and shook her head. "It was nothing," she said. "Nothing at all."

With the curfew, I couldn't catch a ride back to Evans after turning in the marriage paperwork at I Corps HQ. I got a hotel room down the hall from where I had arranged to put Baby Doll.

That night I was asleep when I heard a quiet knock on my door. I stumbled groggily toward the entryway while glancing at the luminous green glow from my watch. It was past midnight.

Outside was Baby Doll. Standing there in her hotel robe, she seemed scared, flustered, and excited, all at the same time.

She didn't ask to come in. She slipped into the room without a sound as soon as I opened the door, putting a finger to my lips in a shushing move. Standing on her toes, she put her arms around my neck and pulled my face down to hers. She looked at me for several seconds, kissed me tenderly, and led me over to the bed.

Any sleepiness vanished. My breath became ragged as she quickly disrobed. Soft, deep kisses smelling of sandalwood followed. I found myself trembling as she tumbled down on the bed, pulling me into her softness. When she slid her hands over my buttocks, the blood rushed in my temples. She guided me to where I needed to go.

Afterwards, as we lay there, I found myself staring into her eyes. She said nothing but smiled as she stroked my chest with her long fingernails.

So this is what it was like, I thought. *No wonder it's such a big deal.* Her final kiss was soft and sweet, and helped me drift off into a deep sleep.

When I awoke the next morning she was gone, not just from the bed but her room as well. Somehow I sensed we weren't going to see each other again. Why this happened I didn't know.

But I was grateful.

41

October 22, 1970
Camp Evans, Vietnam

Sometimes I'm a dumbass.

No matter how I try, it happens at times. Especially about things obvious to others. For instance, I didn't find out until a month ago that pickles are really cucumbers cured in vinegar. Or that bar girls fart just like guys. These things never occurred to me so I gave them no thought, just as I never gave the concept of medals any real attention.

I always believed they were given out rationally for valor. The idea that they could be awarded for merely doing your job, as a favor to someone the brass liked, or as a bribe to keep your mouth shut never entered my mind. Here I was, the day after the still unreported death of Dimes, waiting to get a medal. Actually two.

Like I said, sometimes I'm a dumbass.

A typhoon hit off the coast two days earlier but had moved on. The result was sixty-degree cold weather coupled with rain and fog. I was lined up, shivering with twelve others, to receive various decorations outside battalion HQ. Both Big Red and I were getting a Bronze Star for Ripcord and an Air Medal for accumulating twenty combat helicopter assaults during our tour. Even though we were technically still on leave, Big Red and I decided to attend the ceremony before leaving for Saigon to deal with Ross.

Strode told me I was also eligible for another Purple Heart for Ripcord but I declined. Told him three stitches in a nicked ear does not a Purple Heart make. I think it was the first time I got his approval, though he didn't say anything.

"Your country is proud of you, Sergeant Nickels. Keep up the good work," said Lieutenant Colonel Paterson. As our new assistant battalion commander, he pinned both the Bronze Star and Air Medal on the front pocket of my fatigues. I saluted; he returned it.

Time was when I'd have been bursting with pride for such awards. Now all I felt was emptiness. It was pretty clear we were no longer here to win this war. Instead we were playing for a tie. Our mission had changed during the summer, from Search and Destroy to Search and Clear. The result was a fiasco like Ripcord and people dying for a newly deserted hilltop. War was such a waste. It didn't deserve to be celebrated.

I was also depressed about Dimes but looked forward to getting Ross. Our R&R leaves had officially begun two days ago and we had planned on leaving for Saigon tonight. It was the whole point of my being here—and long overdue. Despite the loss of Dimes, Big Red had agreed to meet later in the afternoon. Our trip to Saigon was still a go.

As our new commander turned to leave, I spotted a

45th Division Thunderbird patch on his right shoulder. It was the only one I'd seen since arriving overseas.

Without even thinking, I blurted out, "Sir, did you ever meet my dad? He was a 1st Lieutenant in the 157th Regiment of the 45th in the War."

The colonel stopped, turned, and looked at me. He'd been going through the motions of military ceremony and we probably all looked alike to him. Young men far from home. For the first time, he really saw me, searching my face for a familiar resemblance. Looking down at my name patch, he saw the name Nickels. I realized that name would not match up with Dad.

"Sir, his name was Tom Peterson."

The colonel's eyes noticeably widened. He nodded affirmatively. "You're damn right I knew him." He paused for a moment as if about to say something more, then remembered we were both in a military ceremony and surrounded by others.

"See me in my office after the ceremony, Sergeant. We'll talk."

He moved on down the line.

***

Colonel Paterson sat in his office chair looking at me with a wondering, bemused smile on his face.

"So you're Tom's kid." He shook his head as if he couldn't believe it. "Sorry, thinking about things that happened a long time ago. I was the best man at your folks' wedding. What would you like to know?"

"Well, sir, I'd like to know what you and he did when you were in the 45th Division. Specifically, April 29th, 1945."

A switch turned off. The kindly smile was replaced by an intense glare and his eyes became cold.

"Why do you ask?"

"I saw a picture in a box of his military pictures and stuff one day. It showed him by a train next to a kid in a striped uniform of some kind. He didn't look too happy. He wrote the date on the back."

Paterson leaned back in his chair and groaned. "You found the pictures." He shook his head. "He was told not to keep those."

What the hell did that mean? I wanted to ask but kept my mouth shut. Based on the other photos in the box, that was the only one he kept of whatever this was about. I decided not to tell him that.

"Yes, sir. I have all the pictures and think I deserve an explanation."

"That was a long time ago, Sergeant. All water under the bridge now." He stood up as a signal for me to depart. It was clear I was being dismissed.

"With all due respect, sir, that's bullshit. You need to tell me what the hell that picture is about."

The colonel glared at me. In a low menacing tone he said, "Son, I don't need to tell you a goddamn thing. Now get the hell out of my office."

I didn't budge.

"Get the hell out, Sergeant!"

I stood stock still. "I need to know. Please, sir. He's my father."

I'll never know if it was the shift in my tone or if he decided to unburden himself. But that seemed to do it. He sat down heavily in his chair and stared at me for an eternity before speaking.

"It's classified. If I tell you, I'm breaking regulations. I could be cashiered out of the service." He stared as if challenging me to go on.

"Sir, I have no intention of telling anyone about this. It's for my own benefit. What happened that day? I'd like to bring some closure to my life."

"Closure to your life? As if just talking about it was so easy and could bring one closure." He shook his head at my stupidity, then reached in a side drawer and pulled out a cigar, bit off the end, and spit it into the wastebasket. As he lit up he looked at me with an unblinking stare for an entire minute.

"I know about the pictures because I took them. He asked later if he could keep them. He wanted a record of what happened there and what we all saw. Your dad apparently kept them, despite being told by the I.G. to get rid of the whole lot." The colonel shook his head as if clearing it. "Hell's bells. Take a seat, Sergeant. This is going to take a while." He leaned back in his chair and said, "We were approaching a German concentration camp called Dachau the morning of the twenty-ninth of April..."

***

It was well past noon when Paterson's story ended. He lit a fresh cigar.

"By sheer luck of the draw, I was on the other side of the camp when that took place. I'm not better than your father. I just wasn't there and faced with the choice at the time. I took the pictures with your dad's camera to document what happened."

When he finished I realized maybe I didn't know my dad after all. I thought I did. But really?

My throat was dry. I wished I had a glass of water.

"You said you knew my mom as well."

"I did. I was at their wedding, like I said."

"What can you tell me about her?" I wasn't sure I wanted to know, but I had to ask.

He seemed to chew that over for a while before saying anything.

"Sergeant, your mom Anna was a peach. When I first met her I wasn't so sure. She seemed to feel personally responsible for what happened a few miles from where she lived. The fact she was a civilian didn't seem to salve her conscience. She was desperate to get the hell out of Germany at the time. There were lots of women like her then. I told your dad that. Said if it was true love she'd wait. He did what I advised."

He blew a ring of blue smoke from his cigar before continuing.

"She waited two years before he would commit. Part of it was his fear she was using him to escape. Part was her fear he would hold her responsible as a local for what we found there in the camp. They circled around each other for months to see if each one's motives were clear. Once they decided, they were crazy about each other."

I knew I probably shouldn't but blurted it out anyway.

"Colonel, why are you wearing the Thunderbird patch? You could have one from Korea or from one of your tours here. Why are you wearing the 45th?"

"Son, when I saw the survivors that day, I saw people who had been through hell. As we tried to clean that damn place up I realized something. The German prisoners looked down on the Poles. The Poles looked down on the Jews. The Jews looked down on the Russians. The Russians looked down on the Gypsies. I don't know who the Gypsies looked down on, but there was probably someone." He gave me a painful smile.

"Let me give you an example how bad it was there. A week after we liberated the camp, we almost had a riot. The Poles threatened to burn the place down if the Jews were allowed to hold a public worship service on the main parade ground. It was all so unbelievable."

He shook his head and his jaw tightened.

"The people there were not saints. They were survivors. Many of them did things to live they'll never admit to anyone but God. As human beings, we want our stories to be neat and tidy. Right and wrong, heroes and villains. We had the villains all right—the SS. Sometimes though, there are no heroes, just people."

He paused as if lost in thoughts of that time.

"The men of the 45th fought in Europe for two years and suffered twenty-five thousand battle casualties. It had nine Medal of Honor winners. It was considered one of the top three infantry divisions out of almost four dozen serving in Europe. Two years ago, it was disbanded due to a National Guard reorganization. Now it's history." He looked down at the patch on his right shoulder and said softly, "Combat patches are to remind ourselves of our service. What we found that day in April was something I think no man could be prepared for. It showed just how barbaric war can be on both sides. You want to know why I wear this patch?" He let out a long sigh. "To remind me every day to be a better man and not to forget."

Silence followed. I found myself staring at the floor and thinking hard.

There was a knock on the door.

"Come in," said the colonel.

The door opened and closed. I was still staring at the floor as I heard, "Reporting as ordered, sir."

I looked up and saw the face of Frank Ross.

42

Ross entered the battalion commander's office and saw the colonel behind his desk. About three feet to the right was a young seated sergeant staring at the floor in contemplation. Very young. Probably a Shake and Bake infantry NCO grad.

The colonel returned Frank's salute. "What can I do for you, Sergeant?"

"Sir, I'm the NCOIC of the emergency-run supply convoy from Camp Davis, detailed to Camp Eagle because of the typhoon. We arrived this morning. Division told me to take a section of the convoy and deliver our supplies to the 506th here at Evans."

Ross noticed that the young sergeant was no longer staring at the floor but looking wide-eyed at him.

"Paperwork?" said Paterson, indicating the file held under Ross's left armpit.

Frank gave the manila folder to the colonel, who opened it and perused the contents. He felt the young sergeant still staring at him and glanced over to confirm it. There was no mistake. It was a look of absolute hatred. Why, he didn't know. The sergeant's nametag identified him as Nickels. He'd never met the kid before. He was sure of it. Yet the malevolence was unmistakable.

Returning his eyes back to the colonel, he noticed the 45th Thunderbird patch. He had seen them a few times over his Army career. He'd studiously ignored those men. They weren't on the I.G. list and were no more culpable than he was as an SS man. Honor dictated they be left alone.

He wasn't sure what possessed him to ask—he never would be sure why—but he did. "Sir, were you by chance in the 157th Regiment during the War?"

The colonel kept reading the report, but nodded his head affirmatively.

Frank looked down at the desk nameplate: Lieutenant Colonel Thomas Paterson, with the crossed rifles infantry symbol on the left and a silver maple leaf on the right.

There are times when one sees his life unwind before him. This was one of those times.

"You were at Dachau."

The colonel stopped reading the report and looked up at him.

Frank pointed at the colonel and looked at the young sergeant saying, "Sorry, kid. I have to correct something, and you're going to be collateral damage. You don't deserve this." Reaching into his pants pocket he withdrew a switchblade and flipped it open.

The young sergeant yelled, "You bastard!" and lunged at Frank's knees like a football player making a tackle. They both went down in a heap.

He could hear the colonel saying, "What the hell is going on here?"

Down on the floor he was asking himself the same thing.

The knife was knocked from his hand by the unexpected rush from the kid. He was a big man and stronger than the young sergeant. Ordinarily it would have been no contest. But the kid was on top of him and had him in a headlock. He took facial blows from what seemed like a possessed demon.

Frank saw Paterson coming around the desk. If he got to the knife first it'd be all over. He bunched his fist and rammed it into the Adam's apple of his attacker. That caused an immediate release of the headlock as his attacker's hands grasped at his bruised throat and clawed for air.

The colonel stumbled over Nickels blindly thrashing about on the floor and fell on all fours next to Frank. As he struggled to get up, Frank seized the knife and plunged it into the man's chest. Thomas Paterson, LTC, RA, fell in a heap across Frank's torso, pinning him to the floor. Above him were the approaching sounds of the strangled gurgles from Nickels's attempts to breathe as he crawled toward the colonel's body. Frank threw Paterson off him just as Nickels grabbed the handle of the knife jutting out from the dead man's chest. As he pulled the switchblade out of the colonel's chest, the young sergeant's wild eyes telegraphed that Frank was next.

The office door was flung open by Paterson's clerk. "What the—oh my God!"

"Get the MPs," grunted Frank. He pointed at Nickels, who had managed to get to his knees, still clutching the knife. "This guy murdered the colonel."

43

October 24, 1970
Long Binh Jail (LBJ) Stockade
Long Binh, Vietnam

I was kept overnight in a military police cell at Evans. Clearly I was guilty, having been found with the murder weapon in my hand and getting ready to finish off Ross according to a witness. I couldn't speak because of my bruised throat. I didn't push it. I was too busy trying to figure out what had happened. Why attack the colonel? Why didn't Ross know who I was?

The next morning, handcuffed, I was put on a C-130 and flown to Tan Son Nhut Air Base outside Saigon. A jeep transferred me and two other prisoners to the Long Binh Jail (LBJ) Stockade. The first guy, about nineteen, was glassy-eyed and clearly stoned. His shoulder patch identified him as 1st Air Cavalry, and his nametag said Williams. He was an E-2 private. To be here any length of time and still be an E-2, meant he was either not the sharpest tool in the shed or was previously busted for drugs.

The second was a man in his mid-twenties. A PFC, over six feet tall, a bald bear of a guy who weighed in at probably 250 pounds. All muscle. He had a CIB badge patch and a unit logo from the Americal Division. His nametag said Daniels. All the way to LBJ, he reminded us that he was black and was going to get us white bastards as soon as our backs were turned. Jones was too stoned to be impressed. But Daniels made a definite impression on me. I had no intention of ever being alone with him. I believed every racist threat he uttered, and there were a lot of them.

LBJ turned out to be a series of buildings in a two-square city block area, surrounded with a cyclone fence crowned with concertina wire on the perimeter. Brown canvas was wrapped around the fence. The jeep driver said it kept local pedestrians from talking to inmates or throwing drugs through the fence. Tall pole lights were interspersed along the fence and a guard tower was located on each of the four corners of the prison. A wooden sidewalk outside circled the enclosure.

We were checked in at the guardhouse under a sign with crossed revolutionary war pistols on top. Below, the sign read 71st MP Detachment: Firm but Fair. Beyond the sign the stockade separated into three compounds. Two entry gates were labeled minimum security; the third was maximum. A mess hall, chapel, admin building, and a huge supply building in the middle of the installation sat between compounds two and three.

A guard escorted us to the administration building for in-processing. I was being held in maximum security pretrial confinement. I had heard tales about that place, none of them good. I was about to find out how much was true.

Our handcuffs were removed in a small white shed

where we were stripped naked. A mouth and buttocks cavity search followed. Sticking any foreign objects up there never entered my mind. But Williams's rectum yielded several heroin capsules about the size of a small finger joint.

Showered and with a fresh buzz haircut, we were issued new fatigues without badges, unit patches, or rank. We weren't allowed to salute an officer and when called to attention I was to remove headgear and say, "Prisoner Nickels reports." It was calculated to show you'd screwed up big time and were no longer a regular member of the military. Now you were a prisoner.

We emerged clean, yet less human, with our new shining skinheads and baggy uniforms. Williams, the drug addict, went to the minimum compound. Daniels and I were in adjoining cells in maximum security.

Maximum security at LBJ was called Silver City. The cells were steel shipping conex boxes painted silver and placed in double rows inside a large concrete block building with one door. Each box was six feet by six feet, and had headroom for a six-foot- two-inch man. Originally made for shipping heavy freight, the boxes were converted to cells by cutting open the middle front, and adding iron bars. A small rectangular sliding partition allowed a guard to pass a food tray into the cell. Inside: a cot, netting, and waste bucket. The corners of each box were cut open six inches for air circulation. There were no windows.

People in max were the thugs. Murder, treason, fragging, robbery, black marketing on a large scale were all represented here. The potential for violence required two guards for every six inmates, and the guards always traveled in pairs. Each MP carried both a .45 and a shotgun.

Reveille was at 0500. The guards ensured you were awake and standing in the direction of the American flag even though you couldn't see it. You were allowed a daily thirty-minute break outside your cell for exercise and a cold shower. You weren't allowed to mix with other prisoners while you did so. Break time was especially prized, since your cell was inside the concrete building and there was no sunlight. It was your only chance to feel the sun and breathe untainted air. Afterwards you were tossed back into the container. Lights out for the solitary overhead bulb in your cell was at 2100.

After lights out and the guards' rounds in the compound, there was a prisoner block call. Actually a black block call. That's what the black prisoners called it. They began by calling out a chant, "Black call in the house. Black call in the house." Then they started identifying each other in the building. "Black House A, Cell number one." This would be followed by a name, usually a made-up Black Muslim one, followed by their hometown and state.

Once everyone who was black was identified from their cells, the threats began. They talked about the coming revolution and how they were going to kill the swine and dogs. It didn't take a genius to figure out who they were talking about. I was glad there was a steel box between me and them.

From the next cell the disembodied voice of Daniels announced that when he got back to the World he was going to track me down and kill all my family. I lost my fear then.

With a bruised throat I replied in a croaking voice, "Good luck with that, you dumb bastard. Think you're going to start a revolution here? What a retard."

My reply wasn't what Daniels expected. More curses and threats followed, but I didn't listen. My life wouldn't be worth a plugged nickle if he got hold of me, but right then I was past being intimidated by racist assholes.

The biggest issue in a container cell (besides boredom) was the heat. At 110 degrees most days, it was stifling. The air circulation was beyond poor. Stripped down to your shorts and boots it became like a runaway sauna. If you took off your boots during the day you'd burn your feet on the metal floor.

Over the next several days, as my throat began to heal, I came to realize you could separate the guards into three distinct groups. Some were professional correction officers with a 95C MOS who treated us well enough under the circumstances. Others were conscripted cooks and truck drivers, declared surplus to their units and sent here. Scattered among these were some sadistic pricks volunteering for this kind of work.

It didn't help the atmosphere at LBJ that the prisoner population was seventy percent black and the guards seventy percent white. The black guards were regarded by the black prisoners as Uncle Toms and traitors to their race. With guards pulling 12-hour shifts for two weeks straight before getting a day off, being cursed by prisoners on a daily basis, and having urine or feces thrown at them, many—both black and white—felt they were just as much a prisoner as the inmates. No one, guard or prisoner, wanted to be there. It was a recipe for trouble.

Regardless of the guard, they saw me the same way. I was a murderer. Not an ordinary one. I'd killed a high ranking officer. They were curious and wanted the story. I kept my mouth shut because I didn't trust them squealing details back to the investigators. I saw the awe in the questions, though. Enlisted men might dream of striking back, but I'd actually done it. Coupled with my infantry status and experience, I was a hard-core case. At least they thought so and other prisoners took note. I was left respectfully alone by the guards during our thirty minute outside cold shower and exercise period. Even the black prisoners curtailed their verbal harassment of me, except for Daniels. I was a celebrity of sorts.

All it took was facing a hanging at Fort Leavenworth.

***

After a week at LBJ I hadn't heard my official charges or been provided with a lawyer. That was supposed to happen within seventy-two hours of confinement, according to scuttlebutt from other prisoners discussing their individual cases. Not that it would do any good to complain.

The prison grapevine said under an article of the Uniform Code of Military Justice (UCMJ), the Army could hold you in pretrial confinement for two weeks before bringing charges and providing you with a lawyer.

If they missed the deadline, you were let go and sent back to your unit. I didn't know if it was true but couldn't help crossing my fingers. Realistically though, I knew they weren't going to let the killer of an assistant battalion commander go free.

On the tenth day, all maximum security prisoners were offered a chance to get out of our cells for the day by volunteering to pack sandbags along with men from the minimum security barracks. Most of us jumped at the chance. My throat was healing, but I was going crazy with the forced inactivity. Any opportunity to get outside unrestrained, even under heavy guard, seemed like a good idea.

Volunteers were loaded onto several trucks and driven outside the compound to an area the size of half a football field north of the stockade. A gigantic white sign said Welcome to Sandbag Heaven at the entryway. It should have said Laterite Hell. There was little actual sand at the site. Instead the ground consisted of a hard, red clay called laterite. It had to be broken up into fine dirt with pickaxes and shovels to fill the sandbags.

It was hard work and murder on your hands. We'd done plenty of sandbagging up north, but the dirt here was different. Picture pounding concrete into powder with hand tools. Your quota was to fill fifty sandbags in the morning with a partner holding the bag and another fifty in the afternoon with you holding the bag and him filling it after they served you a brown bag lunch and milk. If you screwed around, you didn't get to go out the next day. If you made their hundred sandbag quota, and finished before 1700, you got to rest under a thicket of nearby trees and feel the breeze from the delta.

One of the guards had a portable radio featuring the number one hit on the country music charts, Lynn Anderson singing "I Never Promised You a Rose Garden." I was being taunted by fate.

The sandbags were picked up by truck and airlifted to units all over South Vietnam. A sign posted by the parked trucks showed the numbers of bags filled to date: 754,241. The goal was one million before the end of the year. It seemed they might not make their objective this year. I didn't give a damn. Yet I found myself taking a perverse pride that, despite being prisoners, we could do something worthwhile.

On day thirteen any hope for an early release due to lack of an appointed lawyer and formal charges faded.

Just before 1700 a jeep drove up to Laterite Hell, parking next to the guards. In it was the driver and a captain in the Judge Advocate General Corps. Something told me the JAG officer was looking for yours truly. Sure enough he was.

I was sitting under the trees trying to catch that elusive delta breeze, having finished my sandbag quota ten minutes earlier. Protocol called for me to stand as he approached, but I found myself thinking "what the hell." Secretly, I had hoped the Army would forget my lawyer and have to free me on some technicality like on TV.

Fat chance.

The captain approaching me was in his late twenties and wore a nametag that listed him as Jones. I remained sitting, but he didn't take offense at my lack of courtesy. Instead, he plopped himself down beside me, took out a handkerchief, and slowly wiped the sweat off his entire head. He refolded it, put it away, and began to speak.

"Hell of a hot day."

I didn't reply. Just closed my eyes and sought a stray breeze.

"If you're Nickels, then I'm your lawyer."

Again I didn't reply.

"For a guy facing a hanging, you're one cool customer."

I gave it up.

"What's there to say? You have a witness. Obviously, I'm guilty. Case closed."

"Actually, we have two. Ross and the colonel's clerk."

That got my attention.

"He didn't see a damn thing...the clerk, I mean. He was outside the room the entire time."

"Really? Well, that is interesting. Because he's going to sign a statement that he did see everything. So do you think he's a liar or a wannabe?"

"What's a wannabe?"

"Someone who wants their fifteen minutes of fame and exaggerates their importance in an event to get it." He finished folding his handkerchief and put in back in his pocket.

"He's a wannabe, all right."

"Hmmm." Jones seemed to roll over in his mind my assessment of the clerk before asking, "So what really did happen, Sergeant?"

"Ross did it," I said.

"Really? Now why would he do that?"

What could I say? I wasn't exactly sure myself. If I told what I did know I'd go to jail for impersonating a soldier, at the very least.

"Ask him," I shrugged.

"Nickels, I want you to understand something. Even though I'm an officer, I'm your defense attorney first and foremost. That means I'm here to fight for you. Right now, there isn't anyone else in this whole world who gives a damn about you. I saw your records and know you've got no relatives. I'm assuming there's no girlfriend out there either, correct?"

I said nothing.

"Which means I'm your only hope of getting out of this mess. Unless you want to be hung. I saw it done once. Grisly sight. The noose didn't break his neck like it was designed. Happens sometimes. So instead of an instant death, he was slowly strangled. Flopped around a lot like a fish caught on a hook. His eyes bulged out, tongue swelled up, face turned a dark purple and he lost control of his bowels. Now that was embarrassing."

I turned and looked at him. Was he making fun of me?

"My point is, you don't want it to happen to you, believe me."

"If I tell you what I know, I'll implicate myself in some other stuff," I said glumly.

He seemed to weigh this carefully before replying.

"Nickels, you need to understand that as your attorney, I am required to hold everything you say to me in confidence. It can't be used against you. The Army doesn't get to know. Think of me as your priest, at least in a legal sense. My lips are sealed."

For the next several minutes I thought hard about what he said. He just sat there waiting as I worked it all out mentally.

I had no other choice. It was time to spill the beans.

***

"Son...of...a...bitch. Son...of...a...bitch."

Captain Jones just kept shaking his head and muttering that drawn out phrase at various points in my story starting from Carlsbad to the present.

I held nothing back. For the first time, I had a receptive ear and I took advantage of it. The guards and sandbaggers had long since returned to LBJ by the time I finished.

Jones stood, dusted himself off, and motioned to his driver who was sitting in the jeep reading *Stars and Stripes*.

"Hendrix, it's time for us to head on back." He turned back to me and stared intently as if he was seeing me for the first time. He shook his head and said, "Son of a bitch."

I might have taken offense except for the fact he was smiling.

"Captain, I heard if I got pre-trial confinement here I needed to have the charges read within seventy-two hours. Other guys said it's two weeks. Can that get me out on a technicality?"

He shook his head ruefully.

"Sorry. The fine print in a war situation means they

can take several weeks bringing charges and wait several months before bringing you to trial." He paused, brows knitted, lost in thought. "Sergeant, I don't know how, but we are not going to let this stand. I'll assure you that. We are going to have an Article 32 pre-trial investigation. The question will be how to fight this without revealing too much about you. Let me mull this over for a while."

We got in the jeep and took the two-minute ride back to the stockade main gate where Jones signed me back into the compound.

"Ross will have to come to LBJ to make a statement for the preliminary hearing. It will be held in one of the buildings on site here. It's going to be interesting to hear his version of events. Very interesting indeed."

"Will I get to be there? I want to know what he's claiming."

Jones clapped me on the back as two MPs arrived to escort me over to my Silver City cell. "I promise to have you there but you will only get to listen, not speak. Understood?"

I nodded. As I was being led away, I yelled, "How soon do you think that will be?"

"Sometime next week. Keep your chin up."

44

November 14, 1970
LBJ, Vietnam

It was another eight days before I saw Ross. That morning I knew something was up. The guards refused to answer any questions as I was taken from sandbag detail and allowed my first hot shower since arriving. Then they gave me a fresh set of prisoner fatigues. I was to look good at the hearing, even if I wasn't allowed to say anything.

It was set to take place in the admin building in the middle of the compound. Nearby was the staff mess hall, a large supply building and a chapel. It was the normal part of an Army outpost surrounded by the abnormal.

Captain Jones was there with a legal stenographer and two guards in a room resembling a small courtroom. A Major Ferguson represented the prosecution. I figured my spot was at the defense table and sat down next to Jones. On the desk was a red book, *Manual for Courts Martial, 1970 Edition*. Things were starting to get more real.

"Okay, here's the deal," said Jones. "Ross is going to appear in a bit to make a sworn statement. I'll get to ask some questions. But this is not the trial, which is why there's no judge present. You're to keep your mouth shut.

Understood? No football tackles or funny business today."

He waited till I nodded.

A minute later, Ross appeared. As he walked by to sit at the prosecution table across the aisle I examined him closely. I'd hoped he would appear worse for wear, that I'd given him a black eye or something from when I'd had him down. No such luck. He looked totally normal.

It ticked me off how he acted like he didn't know who I was. I mean he looked at me in a totally blank way. That really got my goat. My whole body tensed up, and I found myself clenching and unclenching my hands on the desk.

Jones noticed and put his hand on my shoulder. "Easy," he said.

We were about to begin when a guard entered the room, hurried up to the major, and began whispering to him in an urgent manner. Ferguson summoned our two court guards over and ordered them to accompany him and the first guard.

"This hearing will be delayed for a few minutes," was all he would say as they left. An overhead fan swirled the steamy air as the rest of us sat there staring at each other uncomfortably.

Until we heard the first gunshot.

Followed by another.

It was close. Very close. Next was a series of shots followed by a lull. Then through the windows there came the hum of voices. A hum that got louder. Whatever was happening was headed in the direction of our building.

Captain Jones went to the window. He turned and looked at us. "Gentlemen, I believe we've got a riot on our hands."

All three of us—me, Ross, and the stenographer—hurried over to look. A large group of prisoners was pouring out onto the grass lawn, yelling and screaming. Several had guns taken from guards. Many had metal bars or pipes of some kind. Some were entering the motor pool; others were going in and out of the mess hall. Still more were heading toward the maximum security compound.

A group of twenty or so headed for the admin building.

Headed for us.

The shit had hit the fan.

***

We fled toward the back door and flung it open, looking for a place to hide or defend. Before us lay a barracks, a tiny chapel, and a large three-story supply building with a disabled truck on blocks by the front door. No one wanted to head for the barracks and find more inmates. That left us to defend the chapel or try to hide in the supply building.

"What do we do?" asked our bewildered legal clerk.

Ross didn't say a word but ran toward the supply building. I started after him until I noticed Jones and the clerk weren't following. They were running toward the chapel.

I was going to yell for them to come with me but decided silence was probably the best option considering the circumstances. I knew one thing for sure. I couldn't let Jones die here. He was the only one who knew my secret and could help me. I veered left and ran through the front chapel door behind the fleeing duo.

The first thing I noticed inside was how cool it was. The building was made of cinderblock with no windows and only two doors, the front and a back side door facing the supply building. We quickly locked each door and barricaded them with several heavy church pews.

"Where are the windows?" asked the clerk. When he asked that, Captain Jones chuckled. "They weren't put in, so as to keep the air conditioning inside. This is the only building on site to have continually running AC. I was told by the chaplain it was one way to get inmates to show up for services."

Even without windows we could hear screams, yells, and curses as men passed by. Some rattled the chapel doors. A few beat on the front door with some type of heavy instrument. One bullet flew through the door and lodged in a pew. Our legal clerk was fit to be tied and highly indignant.

"Why, those sorry bastards. Just who the hell do they think they are?" he said.

An hour went by but the constant flow of people passing by or yelling didn't let up.

Then the lights went out. It was pitch black inside.

It took us several seconds to realize the air conditioning was off as well.

"The power was probably shut down by the prison command to get the inmates to give up," said Jones. "That's not a good sign for us, though."

The building began to warm up. Since it was only the

size of my old English classroom back home that didn't take long. With air conditioning, our concrete box minus windows kept the inside cool. Without it, the chapel was going to turn into an oven quick.

We lasted three hours before realizing we had to leave. The temperature outside was well over one hundred degrees. Inside it was much higher and difficult to breathe even after stripping off our shirts. It was suffocate here or get out.

Jones proposed we break out toward the west gate. It was the closest exit. The infirmary was there and if we posed as inmates with a hurt prisoner we could get to it and possibly bluff our way out by pretending to seek medical help. The only problem was we didn't have anyone hurt.

"Captain, let me have your Zippo." I went over and illuminated the air conditioner. It was sitting in a cutout in the wall which ordinarily would have a window. Two thirds of it was outside the wall, and part of the remaining third was inside with us, supported by two metal bars bolted into the inner wall.

"I have an idea. But one of you is going to have to give it up for the team." I held up the Zippo so they could see my face. "We need someone who seems really hurt. Best for that would be a scalp wound. It'll bleed like mad and look bad but won't be permanent. So who wants to volunteer?

"I'll do it," said the legal clerk. "I'm smaller and Captain Jones can carry me to make it look even better."

"Okay, then. Come over here." He followed me to the air conditioner. "Take off your t-shirt. Close your eyes and bend over by the first bar extending from the AC."

When he did, I slammed him headfirst into the edge. It split his forehead and scalp nicely—about seven inches—and he began to bleed profusely. I wrapped his t-shirt around his head to complete the effect.

Once he was bundled up, Jones held up the lighter and I stepped back to admire my handiwork.

"You look like a hurt inmate to me," I said. I helped them remove the pews from the back door. "It's time for you guys to go."

"You're not coming?" asked the wounded man.

"No, my future isn't with you two. I wish you the best of luck."

"Nickels, come with us," said Jones.

"Captain, my pain is all I have left of my family. That's going to end now, one way or another."

"Son, you don't have a chance against this guy. I promise to help you legally."

I didn't reply. Just stared back at him in the flickering light until he took a long breath and exhaled. "Have it your way. I'm taking him over to the west gate. I think we'll have a good chance to escape there. We'll get help to you as soon as we can." He handed me his lighter. "Good luck, Sergeant."

"Good luck to you, sir."

With that they were gone.

It was time to survey my situation. Using my newly acquired lighter, I saw a row of pews, some hymnals, and a Bible on a pulpit. On the rough concrete floor were two coffee cans half filled with water, serving as ash trays. A chaplain's ministerial robe was draped over a chair next to a small cardboard box of communion wafers.

What would Prophet do in this situation? Which tip would help? Two minutes later I slipped out of our chapel hothouse and headed unseen to the mounted disabled cargo truck on blocks, next to the front door of the supply building.

I figured, correctly, that I'd find a tire iron inside the truck cab. That would be my main weapon. My backup would have to be my accumulation of fieldcraft from Prophet.

In my heart I'd known this confrontation was unavoidable. I felt like an actor who had rehearsed many times. Now it was time for the live take.

45

With no electricity, it was dark inside, with numerous stacks of wooden boxes on pallets and shadowy aisles. Intermixed were several supply trucks with canvas coverings, left in the process of unloading. Outside, the building looked as if it had three stories, but inside it was a large shell. A dim light from a yellowed skylight showed a catwalk overhead, thirty feet above the concrete floor. It was designed to get you from one side to the other side of the building quickly, without having to negotiate the supplies and truck maze below.

I crept down the aisles one by one. They weren't the same size or neatly stacked, and some had blind turns with spaces big enough for Ross to hide in. I held my tire iron ready and checked my line of sight as I went down each aisle and around the trucks. My heart was pumping hard, but I'd learned that fear is something everyone has. You use your training and experience to overcome it.

"So you came. You've got guts, kid. Not that it's going to do you any good."

I felt the hair rising from my neck and arms. The voice came from overhead. He was on the catwalk, watching me.

In the dark I heard him continue. "It took me a long time to become a killer. Do you think you can do it? Can you survive?"

"I don't know. In your case I'm willing to try." I hoped my voice sounded steady.

Knowing he was watching my every move, I made my way to the left side concrete wall. There was a staircase leading to the catwalk above. I found it, gripped the cold metal handrail, and began my ascent, step by step.

Just as on the main floor I had to maneuver around boxes and machinery along the catwalk. And like below, that meant Ross had plenty of spaces to hide.

I didn't hear him behind me till I felt the knife at my throat.

"Don't move or I'll kill you here and now." I froze. "Drop the tire iron." It clattered on the catwalk with an echoing metallic sound.

I threw my whole body backwards, slamming him against the railing, and heard the air leave his body. I followed with a head butt but it didn't have much effect. I was going to be killed if I didn't do something else quick. It was all happening in slow time as I twirled around and focused on the knife. It flashed and sliced me on the right forearm. Blood flowed. It hurt but his action allowed my left knee to ram him between the legs, resulting in an anguished yell of anger and agony. He dropped the knife, which disappeared through one of the small open squares of the catwalk and fell to the ground below.

My triumph was short lived. Ross grabbed me by the throat and hoisted me a foot off the ground. I'd made the mistake of getting too close and in his reach. I tried to dislodge his hands but they were like a steel vice. He hurled me over the railing. It was a thirty-foot fall.

I was a dead man.

Three seconds later I crashed. Not on concrete, not on a wooden pallet. I crashed on a supply truck's rear canvas covering, barely missing the driver's cab. The collapsing thick covering stopped my fall enough to prevent serious injury, but the impact on the metal floorboard rendered me unconscious.

Coming to, I heard the steady clatter of boots on the metal stairway and the sound of someone whistling. Ross was coming to examine his handiwork. I didn't have much time. A minute earlier I'd thought I was going to die. Now there was some hope. Slight, faint, but hope nevertheless.

Slowly, painfully, I sat up. As Ross approached his whistling grew louder. Scooting butt first to the end of the truck bed, I shoved myself feet first to the floor. I was woozy and grabbed the edge of the truck to steady myself.

Out of a forest of shadows, I saw a blurred movement from the corner of my eye. Once again a pair of powerful hands seized me. This time they threw me against the side of the truck where my head cracked against the metal. For a few seconds I forgot what was happening as I desperately sucked air. Then the shadow came again, and it entered into the beam from the skylight. Its eyes were a cold icy blue looking at me with grim determination.

Ross grabbed my neck. The pain was excruciating and my vision blurred as I clawed at his hand. It was useless. I had only one chance, and the time was now. I reached inside my left pants pocket while throwing a right jab at Ross.

That move ended it.

Ross released his grip and raised his arm to protect himself from my right jab, which was a feint. Instead, there was a blow to the stomach that probably felt like the sledgehammer kick of a mule. It left him gasping before he realized he hadn't been punched after all. He had been slashed. Viciously and cleanly. Trembling, his hand slid toward his stomach and felt the size of the wound. Now he'd feel a wet sliding sensation. It was only then he'd realize he'd been disemboweled.

I stepped back and watched him silently.

Ross tried to keep his intestines inside his body. Once out there would be no hope of survival. Not that there was much of one anyway. I knew that. But he had to try. The pain was minimal because he was in shock. His only hope was to hold himself together until a doctor could arrive. Maybe, just maybe, they could sew him back together and prevent peritonitis.

He stood there, his hands clutching his abdomen, trying desperately not to collapse. It was hopeless. He fell like a tree as he crashed to the pavement. It must have hurt like hell. I could tell he was starting to feel the pain.

"Didn't know you had a knife," he gasped.

"I didn't."

"But..."

"I figured you'd get the tire iron from me unless I got lucky. So I improvised back at the chapel. The floor was made of rough concrete. I took an ashtray coffee can and scrubbed the bottom lid on the floor till it came off. Bent the lid in half, sharpened the end, and put it in my pocket.

Took less than sixty seconds. It was all I had."

"Pretty stupid plan."

I shook my head dismissively. "I learned it from someone a lot better than you. And anything that works isn't stupid." I squatted down next to him. "Why did you kill my family?"

"I don't know what you're talking about."

"My name isn't Nickels. It's Peterson. We met at Carlsbad."

"Not possible. I killed the whole lot."

"No, you didn't. You—" I groaned with the flash of insight. "Wait...I came in late to the amphitheater and sat next to Nickels. He'd entered with my parents and sister." I shook my head. "Cripes, you thought Nickels was me." I shook my head again, this time in disgust. "You were never staring at me. It was always Mom and Dad. Susie and Nickels were just collateral damage. That's why you didn't recognize me at the colonel's office."

He didn't reply.

"Why did you kill the colonel? He didn't do anything to you. You'd only just met."

"No, we met a long time ago."

I gave him a puzzled look.

"It was him. Him all along."

"I don't understand."

He began to laugh. It came out as a low bitter chuckle and built upward. His body, with its exposed glistening purplish-grey, gory entrails, shook.

"When I came to the office and saw the patch and the nameplate, I knew I'd made a mistake. I killed your father thinking he was my brother's killer. But it was Paterson who shot Heinrich at the railway and tried to kill the rest of us at the coal yard wall outside the hospital in Dachau...I copied the name on the list wrong. Peterson instead of Paterson. They were the same age, build, and hair. Had the same first name, the same rank, and were in the same company. When I saw your father, I was convinced he was the one. But it had been twenty-five years. When I went into that damn room, I realized I'd screwed up earlier. But I'd come to far to let him get away when he was sitting right there behind his desk."

He shook his head ruefully. Was it was over the unnecessary deaths or his mistake in copying the name list? I couldn't tell. "A one-letter mistake. One lousy letter in a name." He grimaced. It was clear he was beginning to feel the pain increase. "And now I'm going to die."

"Colonel Paterson told me it was my dad that shot that officer. He claimed he was over on the other side of the camp when it happened."

Ross shook his head again. "He lied. That's where your dad must have been."

"So my dad was innocent and you killed my family?" I kicked him viciously and he screamed. "By mistake?" I kicked him again. "You stupid fucking moron." I let out a long breath and stared directly into his eyes. "How did you know my mother?"

"She was my brother's fiancée. I didn't know she'd married your father until I saw her at Carlsbad. The fact that she would marry Heinrich's killer meant she and her bastard brats had to die as well." He groaned loudly. "One damn letter in a name ..."

I didn't respond. I'd seen enough battle injuries to know it would soon be over.

***

Ross took forty minutes to die.

I watched and listened as he related the whole sordid tale about what happened at Dachau and the years that followed. How he had tracked down and killed other men on his list. How he had saved the worst offender for last, the man who had fired the shot that killed his brother. How he had a private investigator track us down and how Dad's secretary told him about our vacation plans and dates when he posed as a salesman on the phone.

Outside I heard the the MPs advancing and shooting tear gas at the rioters. When Captain Jones showed up with the guards, Ross confessed to the murder of the colonel. After that he began babbling about his being an honorable man and righting past wrongs that others refused to do. He shuddered with labored effort as he finished his rantings.

When he finally breathed his last, I felt nothing. No triumph. No elation. No revenge. But there was justice. That was something. That was what my family deserved and got.

It was enough.

46

I checked out of the stockade the next morning. A white-helmeted MP guard gave me a hard look, and very slowly looked over my departure paperwork. I didn't know if he was trying to intimidate me or if he was a special Category IV enlistee like Project and dumber than dirt. I didn't care. I was getting out of LBJ. There wasn't a damn thing he could do about it. My forearm was stitched up and my old fatigues were returned with unit patches, badges, and rank. I was officially a soldier again and not a prisoner.

He stamped my papers.

Feeling good, I headed for the main gate where a large sign overhead said YOU ARE LEAVING USARV STOCKADE. DO NOT COME BACK.

Captain Jones waited outside with a jeep. He volunteered to drive me to Tan Son Nhut Air Base where a seat had been arranged on a C-130 going to Camp Eagle. As we drove along, he had some last words.

"Nickels, I heard someone once say life is like a long corridor with numerous side doors. The one you choose determines your death. Pick the wrong door and you have to go through it with no turning back. Ross picked his door a long time ago. Remember that."

There was a pause and I could see the wheels turning inside Jones's brain.

"I'm going to offer you a choice. I think I know what you'll choose but you have the right to decide where you go from here. You can choose to reveal the truth and go home free and clear, or you can stay on as Sergeant Travis Nickels and finish up your tour."

"Thanks, but I elect to stay."

"Figured you'd say that. Sometimes the line between adolescence and adulthood is erased early. I think in your case there probably is no going back."

He parked the jeep by the airport terminal. "One thing I can do for you. I'll have some contacts talk to personnel up at your HQ. You'll get one of those five month early outs when your tour is up and go back to the mainland. The Army owes you something, even if they don't know your secret."

We shook hands and I boarded my flight to Camp Eagle. There I bummed a ride on the back of a truck heading to Evans. Turning into the main entrance almost felt like home.

I spent the night on my old cot in my old hooch. My locker had the taped name of someone other than me on it. I tore it off and threw it in a wastebasket.

The next morning Strode picked me up by jeep and drove me out to the chopper where three cherries were awaiting our arrival. I thanked him for the ride, and he shook my hand goodbye. His time was up and he was processing out for home the next day.

I approached the helicopter to return to the field, but

something seemed wrong. I stopped and found myself frozen in place. Strode saw what was happening, came and stood at my side. The chopper was in ready takeoff mode, and they were all waiting on me.

"I can't go back, Sarge. I can't. I don't know why, I just can't."

Strode leaned toward my left ear and said "Yeah, you can. You're a short timer. What you're feeling is normal. You're feeling the fear of coming so far and being taken out at the very end. Fight it. Don't let it rule you now. Trust me on this. I've been there. Once you get on the chopper, it'll all disappear." He put an arm around my shoulders and led me toward the helicopter, while pretending to be talking to me so no one was the wiser.

"Oh, yeah, I forgot to give you this," he shouted over the noise of the helicopter engine. Strode reached into his front pocket and took out a folded tan envelope with a clasped seal.

"Open it after you get there."

I nodded dumbly and boarded my ride without saying anything. Strode stood there and watched us go before heading back to his jeep.

Fifteen minutes later, I was let out with the cherries at our landing zone.

That evening I remembered Strode's envelope and looked inside. It contained a short timer's calendar showing thirty-eight days left in-country. Each day was represented in squares surrounding a color photo of the 1970 Playboy Playmate of the Year, Claudia Jennings. Where he'd gotten it, I had no idea. It wasn't something you could find at the

PX. Made in a print shop in Da Nang would have been my guess. I was touched he'd taken time for such a gift. I needed it. I got a pen from my rucksack and carefully marked an X in the first square. I found myself smiling.

"Okay, what gives? Why the hell are you so happy to be back?" I looked up. Big Red was looking at me quizzically.

"Hey, we're both so short we only speak to midgets. Only thirty-seven more days left for the both of us, after today," I said. Only then did I notice he was wearing E-5 stripes.

"Congratulations, man." I was glad to see he wasn't still a PFC but wondered how he'd pulled it off. Darn if he didn't blush.

"Well, about that..."He hesitated and then plunged onward. "I got my E-4 back the day after your...escapade. Last week Strode had the L-T make me an acting sergeant with the stripes and responsibility, but not the cash to go with it. Promised if I did well he'd see I got a shot at the E-5 promotion board at Evans next month."

"Then next month you will be an actual E-5. Strode is the real deal."

I explained what Strode did for me earlier, and he grew serious.

"Yeah, he turned out to be a good guy, good leader. We needed him here." He drew a deep breath and exhaled. "Speaking of which, I have another surprise for you. At least I think it'll be one." He looked kind of sheepish.

"Try me," I said.

"I'm going to reenlist and extend my tour for a second year."

"Are you shitting me?" Of all the people in the world, he was the last one I would ever have thought of becoming a lifer.

"Well, it's like this. With Dimes dead, you gone, Prophet dead, and—oh, I forgot...Peddler got taken out while leading point two weeks ago. All that, and Strode leaving, gave me a lot to chew on. Look at all the newbies coming in. Who's going to watch out for them? It needs to be someone who knows what the hell is going on."

"That's you?"

"That's me. Not something I expected. But there it is."

I hated to admit it, but even as he was saying it I knew he was right. He'd done well out here. People looked up to him and trusted what he had to say. He would make a good platoon sergeant someday.

"What did Strode have to say about this?"

"He laughed. Told me to think about it and be damn sure. So I did. When he was getting on the chopper to head back to Evans to process out, I told him it was still a go. He shook my hand and said he hoped to serve with me sometime in the future."

I thought of Prophet at that moment. "When we were cherries Prophet was finishing his tour. I wondered why he signed up for a second one but was too intimidated to ask. I think it was because he saw things the way you do. I don't know if either of us would be here without him."

So there it was. When it was time for me to go, Big Red would elect to stay.

The days passed faster than I had any right to expect. We lost a few men—both dead and wounded—but me and Big Red saved a few by sharing our experiences. At least we tried.

Division policy kept you in the field until the last four days of your tour. When that date came, Big Red walked with me to my waiting Huey.

I didn't know how to say goodbye. I hugged him in that way guys do when they want to be close but not too close. As the chopper took off for Evans, I yelled out "Currahee" to him over the engine noise. He waved back and, grinning, shouted out, "Airborne."

My time in the jungle had come to an end.

***

I was processed out at Camp Sally and given the usual manila envelope of my records. At the last station, a nervous PFC caught up to me and asked if I was Sergeant Nickels. Despite seeing my nametag, he made me rattle off my serial number before believing he'd found the right man.

"We forgot to give you one of these." He reached into a small purple cloth bag he was carrying, pulled out a bronze coin the size of a half dollar, and handed it to me. One side had the division logo below an etched Brave Eagle header. The flip side showed an eagle in flight with For Valor as the header.

"What's this?" I asked.

"It's the 101st challenge coin." The clerk seemed upset I didn't know what he had given me.

"Division issues one to departing personnel who've

been on the front lines and won a valor award. Your record shows two Bronze Stars with 'V' Device, Purple Heart, Army Commendation Medal, Air Medal, and Vietnamese Cross of Gallantry. Plus your Combat Infantryman Badge, of course. You definitely qualify. It's division's way of saying you met the challenge of our 'Rendezvous with Destiny' in Vietnam. You acquitted yourself with honor."

I looked at the coin again and thought of Prophet. "You'll face the dragon and win. Believe me," he'd said. As usual he was right.

The REMF guys sitting around me were suitably impressed. I mumbled a thank you and put it in my wallet next to my wedding ring from Baby Doll, in the space where I had kept the note from Rita Human.

We were trucked over to Phu Bai airport, where a yellow archway departure sign was posted for individuals heading back to the States. Five hours later a C-130 flew us to the 90th Repo Depot at Cam Ranh Bay and housed us in a four-building complex for the night. The next morning we exchanged our MPC for good old dollars before being bused to the airport restricted area where our plane home was parked. Yells and shouts of "Short," "Fuck the Army," and other war whoops echoed from our bus.

Our freedom bird featured a Tiger Airlines logo on the side of the DC-8 fuselage. Rain fell and a fog grew, causing some of the men to mutter. Would the weather cooperate or would we be delayed for a day? Everyone got on board in a quiet, almost reverential manner. After an anxious hour, we took off amid more tension—would there be a mechanical problem of some kind? Minutes ticked by before we could feel the grinding of the wheels pulled up into the fuselage as the plane leveled off from an upward tilt toward the clouds. At that point there was a collective sigh in the cabin, and several guys clapped.

We stopped in Guam for refueling and proceeded to the Land of the Big PX, arriving a day later at Travis Air Force Base. A dark blue Air Force bus took us to the Oakland Army Terminal where we separated into two groups: those whose enlistment was over and those who still had time to serve. Thanks to my five month early out, my enlistment was over.

Our discharge group had to listen to a thirty-minute talk from a reenlistment NCO on the advantages of a career in the United States Army. He did so halfheartedly, probably knowing in advance it was a lost cause. It was. No one in our group raised their hand at the end of the presentation to indicate any further interest.

We were taken to supply to swap our old gear for new uniforms. Uncle Sam wanted us to look good for the civilian population on the way home. That—coupled with my wings, ribbons, and a new pair of jump boots—had me looking pretty damn sharp.

At the mess hall, everyone was given a steak dinner with all the trimmings. Some of the men were grateful. Others just poked at it, wanting only to hit the road home.

We came to the last station, the discharge desk, where we were given our DD 214 document. "Be sure you don't lose your 214. It's your official service document for the Veterans Administration benefits if you want to go to college on the G.I. Bill or buy a house with a VA loan."

With that, we were done. A large red arrow painted on the concrete floor led through an exit door into the night. From there you could see the lights of the main gate on the right. On the left I saw the hangar from twelve months earlier, still housing outbound soldiers heading to Vietnam.

As I passed the gate guard shack, I stopped in the darkness just beyond the bright yellow light cast by the lamps. A line of taxicabs sat waiting to take G.I.s to the San Francisco airport, train station, or bus depot to catch their final leg home. It was January 1, the start of a new year.

"Where to, Sergeant?" asked a middle-aged cabbie standing by a beat-up Yellow Cab that had seen better days.

Good question, I thought. Should I go back to Munson Lake and reveal what had happened? Could I handle being back in high school? Living with a foster family? Or did I go explore this land I'd fought for, a country didn't seem to care much one way or another that any of us had been gone. Either way I'd have to take a chance. I thought of Dad saying how things always had a way of working out.

"Well, buddy, what's it going to be?" My cabbie was getting restless. I told him my destination, got in the back seat, and hoped I was making the right choice.

I knew only one thing for sure. I was done with Vietnam.

It would be another four years before I discovered Vietnam was not done with me.

But that's another story.

AFTERWORD

The youngest service member killed in Vietnam was Dan Bullock, a U.S. Marine. He died June 7, 1969, shortly before the middle of his fifteenth year. He'd altered his birth certificate and enlisted nine months earlier. Young as he was, he went through the normal military training available prior to going overseas.

Paul Mahar was another case entirely. At the age of nineteen he met a newly married childhood friend who was on orders to Vietnam. Mahar ended up taking his place as an infantryman, despite an arm injury that had previously rendered him unfit for the draft. Without any military training, he served with the 25th Infantry Division in 1966 and 1967 and was promoted twice. Coming back to the United States, he turned his gear over to his friend and assimilated back into civilian life. Mahar's story would wait until 1981 before he revealed it publicly.

The I.G. report on Dachau and the conduct of the 157th Regiment of the 45th Infantry Division became public only after being found in the National Archives in 1991, long after most of the participants were dead. Dachau concentration camp is now open for tourists.

Carlsbad Caverns still has two entryways for tourists and the Bottomless Pit in the Big Room. If you want to watch the nightly migration of bats, avoid visiting in the winter.

The Oakland embarkation graffiti wall is one of the few structures of the old terminal that still exists and can be seen if you are in the area.

LBJ had major race riots in 1966, 1968, 1970, and 1971. There were also minor riots and sit-down strikes as well. In each case events were sparked by the rage of blacks against whites and persistent racism in American society.

If you were to visit Vietnam today—a favorite for many veterans after all these decades—you would find no trace of Camp Evans or LBJ. They are gone forever.

It was only in the 1990s, after the Gulf War, that the stigma of the Vietnam war started to lift. Veterans began to reclaim their status in American society after decades of being ignored or slighted. The process was further facilitated by the 9/11 tragedy. Military service became honorable to the general public once again.

Every Vietnam veteran is grateful for the change.

A SPECIAL WORD FROM THE AUTHOR

I hope you enjoyed this book. If so, I'd like to ask a favor. Would you consider giving it a review on Amazon? Authors live and die by reviews and typically less than 1% of readers leave one. It takes less than five minutes of your time. Thank you.

CPSIA information can be obtained
at www.ICGtesting.com
Printed in the USA
LVHW041448270119
605404LV00004B/612/P